LYNNE FRANCIS grew up in East Yorkshire. After gaining a degree in English Literature from London University, she worked in non-fiction publishing. She now lives in the unspoilt East Kent countryside – perfect for writing, walking and inspiration.

The Mill Valley Girls series:

Ella's Journey

Lynne Francis

A division of HarperCollins*Publishers*
www.harpercollins.co.uk

Published by AVON
A Division of HarperCollins*Publishers* Ltd
1 London Bridge Street
London SE1 9GF

www.harpercollins.co.uk

This Paperback Edition 2018

First published in Great Britain by HarperCollins*Publishers* 2017

A catalogue copy of this book is available from the British Library.

ISBN: 978-0-00-829065-8

This novel is entirely a work of fiction. The names, characters and incidents portrayed
in it are the work of the author's imagination. Any resemblance to actual persons,
living or dead, events or localities is entirely coincidental.

Typeset in Birka by Palimpsest Book Production Limited, Falkirk, Stirlingshire

Acknowledgements

Special thanks to my grandparents for lending me part of their story, to Stephen Done and Mike Fitton for helping me on railway matters, to Kiran at Keane Kataria Literary Agency for believing in me and to the team at Avon for their work in bringing this book to life.

Dedicated to the memory of Freda Pegden 1924–2017 and
Lucy Westmore 1958–2017

PART ONE

1896–1902

Chapter One

'Ella?'

She thought she heard someone calling her name, but it was hesitant, and the bustle and hubbub of the crowd whipped the words away. She paused and turned but, unable to spot anyone she knew, she continued on her way, shopping list in hand. Parliament Street market was busy so close to Christmas, although at least the crush provided a bit of warmth on such a raw, bitter day. Ella's brown wool coat, on permanent loan from Mrs Sugden, the housekeeper, fitted well enough but it was thin and barely held the cold at bay. She was glad of her red knitted scarf – a bright flash of colour – and another loan, this time from Doris, from one of the maids. When Ella Bancroft had first arrived at Grange House, the two women had been puzzled by what they perceived as her lack of appropriate clothing.

'A shawl will never do!' Mrs Sugden had exclaimed the previous November when Ella, wrapped in the shawls that had seen her through the Yorkshire winters back in Northwaite, was set to leave the house with her shopping list and basket. 'You'll be nithered. And you're in the town now. You need to wear something that's a credit to the household. You'd best borrow this.'

She'd pulled the brown coat from the cupboard in the passageway. 'I won't miss it. I've another I prefer.'

Ella had slipped it on: it fitted her quite well. She thought it was probably some time since Mrs Sugden had worn it as it was putting it kindly to say that the housekeeper was a good deal broader than Ella, who was slender and taller than average. She'd judged it best not to comment, however, and instead expressed her gratitude, although privately she felt that the thin wool wouldn't do the same job of keeping out the cold as her thick woollen shawls. And so it proved but, nevertheless, she felt almost elegant when she ventured out in the coat, which was a feeling quite new to her. Stevens, the butler, had said admiringly, 'That red scarf of Doris's puts the roses in your cheeks,' making Ella blush and thus further increasing her rosiness.

She wished she had a pair of gloves. The wind was biting and her numb fingers struggled to grasp the coins as she made her purchases. Tucking the last paper bag into her basket, she smiled at the stallholder who was stamping his feet and blowing on his fingers in an effort to keep the chill at bay. With her errands completed, it wouldn't be long until she was out of the cold and back in the kitchen at Grange House. Groceries arrived there in a regular weekly delivery, one of the many things that Ella had marvelled at in the York household. The grocery boys carried great boxes of meat and vegetables into the scullery and, if more supplies were needed during the week, one of the delivery boys would be sent round on a bicycle, with his front basket loaded up and his apron flapping as he pedalled. But sometimes Mrs Sugden took it into her head that they needed a nice bit of samphire to go with the fish for that night's dinner, and old Mr Grimshaw's stall in the market was bound to have some, or she'd heard that there were some particularly fine quail's eggs to be had that day. Ella was both entranced and unnerved by her errands, puzzled that a bright-green weed would be deemed suitable to serve at the table, or that such a creature as a quail existed.

'Ella!' This time the call was louder, more forceful, stopping her in her tracks. She turned again, scanning the crowd. As her eyes skimmed over the good citizens of York, intent on last-minute Christmas purchases, they were arrested by an almost-familiar figure.

'Albert?' she said uncertainly. 'Albert Spencer?' He stood before her: out of breath, wiry, dark-haired and little changed in appearance from the young man she'd last seen several years before.

'You know your way around!' he exclaimed. 'I've had a hard job keeping up with you in this crowd. Is it always like this?'

Ella glanced about her and smiled. 'Yes. Always busy with those in search of a bargain or two, particularly so at Christmas. You're not familiar with the market then?' She looked enquiringly at Albert, trying to get over her astonishment at seeing him after so long.

'No, no, I was here by chance.' Albert sounded hurried. 'But I'm glad I was. I wasn't sure it was you at first, but then when I followed you I knew I was right. You move just like Alice!'

Hearing her sister's name gave Ella a jolt and she glanced quickly at Albert.

Oblivious to the effect he'd had on her, he carried on. 'What are you doing here? It's so long since I've seen anyone from home! I'm aching for news. It's too cold to stand around here though. Is there somewhere we can talk?'

Ella hesitated. Mrs Sugden would scold her if she was late back, but she wanted to hear Albert's news, even if she wasn't keen to share hers with him. He had a confident air, which was that of a grown man now, far removed from the mill boy she had walked to work with seven or more years ago. The cut of his clothes marked him out as prosperous; not like her employer Mr Ward, of course, but not dissimilar to some of the tradesmen who came to the house to discuss plans for the houses that her employer was building on the edge of the city. Ella was becoming practised at pinpointing who belonged to which level of society, even though such things had been a complete mystery to her when she first arrived in York. Back in Northwaite where she had grown up there had been those that worked at the mill, those that owned the mill, and the overlookers in between. A few other figures, such as the parson and the doctor, occupied a level above the overlooker and below the mill owner, Mr Weatherall, and his family, but there was little to consider beyond that.

Here in York there were landed gentry right up at the top of the ladder, those who didn't seem to work on a daily basis but whose affairs regularly called them away from home, to Leeds or to London. Then there were those who had a standing and an education, such as doctors and clergy; after that came business people, tradespeople, shopkeepers and a whole layer of workers below who kept the wheels in motion.

The hierarchy 'below stairs' in the grand residences such as Grange House was a little world in itself, from the butler

6

right down to the scullery maid. It had taken Ella a while to sort all this out for herself. She'd only managed it by careful observation and listening to the nuances of conversations: the way in which Mrs Sugden referred to those under her jurisdiction, and those above stairs. Although Ella worked as both a house parlourmaid and a lady's maid these days, her role was relatively clearly defined compared to her previous role in Mr Ottershaw's house back in Nortonstall, just two miles from where she had been born and brought up. Ella shuddered at the memory. As the only maid that he could afford, she had been expected to cover all the household duties of cooking and cleaning, as well as minding the children. The length and hardship of her days had almost made her nostalgic for her time working at the mill.

Albert had noticed her shudder. 'You're cold,' he said and, taking her arm, he guided her through the grand, gilded doors of the tearoom that stood a little way from the edge of the market. Ella hesitated, trying to pull back, but it was too late; they were inside in the warmth and being ushered to a table. She'd passed this place many times whilst on her errands and had gazed through the huge plate-glass windows, wondering what it must feel like to sit at one of the round tables draped with a starched white cloth, having time to sit and chat over coffee served in monogrammed china cups.

Her cheeks flamed, partly from the sudden warmth but more out of embarrassment. Her coat, which she had thought so smart, felt distinctly dowdy and unfashionable in here. She could see some of the ladies at adjacent tables eyeing her up and down, noting her attire, her basket, her lack of a proper hat and gloves, the way her unruly reddish-blonde hair was escaping from the pins holding it in place.

They commented to each other, turning away then glancing back, laughing behind their hands.

Albert was oblivious to this. He ordered coffee for both of them before turning his attention to Ella. 'You've barely said a word,' he said.

Ella tried to overcome her discomfort, and her worry about being scolded by Mrs Sugden over her tardiness. 'I'm sorry. I'm just a bit overwhelmed. I've never been in here before.'

She chanced a look around, trying to imprint her surroundings on her memory. High ceilings, the grey light of winter filtering through the stained glass which edged the windows, the inside lit by gas lamps and filled with the buzz of chatter and laughter, the clink of china and wonderful aromas of coffee, sugar and chocolate. Ella felt her stomach rumble. Breakfast had been a long while ago.

Albert must have read her mind. As the coffee pot was delivered to the table, he murmured something to the waiter, and a plate of tiny pastries swiftly followed. Ella relaxed a little and unwound the scarf from around her neck, trying to sip her coffee and eat her pastry as though she was used to it, although even a cursory glance at her reddened, worn hands would have suggested otherwise.

'So,' Albert said, giving her a probing look. 'How long have you been in York? Do you have news from home?'

Ella started to fill him in on her last few years, her time at Mr Ottershaw's in Nortonstall and the hardships of life there, her chance meeting with Mr Ward and her good fortune in being taken on at Mr Ward's house in York. She managed to intersperse a few questions for Albert, and very soon realised that his apprenticeship and almost immediate employment as a qualified stonemason had kept him fully occupied here in York, and in other cathedral cities. It appeared that he had not returned to Northwaite in all that time. He had sent word home, and frequent amounts of money, but had heard little in return, neither his father nor his mother being 'much of ones for writing' as he said ruefully. Ella knew this to mean that they had never learnt how.

The furrow in Albert's brow had deepened as Ella told her tale, and she feared his next question. Her coffee was drunk and she was very conscious of the passage of time. Mrs Sugden would not be impressed at the idea of a servant meeting up with an old friend and passing the time of day with him in a tearoom. Ella knew she was going to be in trouble.

'I really must go. It was lovely to see you, Albert, but I will be late back.' Ella wound her scarf around her neck as she spoke, and pushed her chair back. Perhaps she could make her escape while he settled the bill? She felt a pang of regret. It had been so lovely to see a familiar face from home, but what use could they be to each other now?

'Wait,' Albert rose at the same time as Ella and handed her basket to her. Ella tried to ignore the contemptuous stares of their neighbours. 'Alice. You haven't mentioned Alice. How is she?'

Ella took a deep breath. She had dreaded this very question. 'She's dead, Albert. I'm really sorry. It happened within three months of you leaving. Alice is dead.'

And with that she hurried to the door, almost pushing the doorman out of her way in her haste to be gone. As she passed the window, she glanced in quickly. Albert still stood by the table, as if rooted to the spot, leaning forward slightly and supported by his rigid arms, fingers splayed and tense on the cloth, all colour drained from his face.

Chapter Two

By the time Ella had reached the Tadcaster Road, a good mile and a half from the tearoom, she was regretting the manner of her departure. It was cruel to Albert, who didn't deserve it. Her own grief over her sister's death seemed to veer between a cold, hard nugget locked away deep inside, to an overwhelming, boiling rage that made her want to run and run, screaming aloud at the injustice of it all. It was partly the latter sensation that had made her want to leave the tearoom so suddenly. Whatever would Albert think? She knew he had been sweet on Alice, but too shy to ever express this to her. Only a little older than him in years, Alice had seemed vastly older than him in wisdom and had always treated Albert more like a younger brother. Ella sensed some sort of unspoken bond between them, which she put down to them having been playmates from a very young age in Northwaite.

Northwaite. It hurt her to think of it even now, high up above Nortonstall on the Yorkshire hills, with views for miles on a clear day, exposed to vicious winds, snow, sleet and hail in the winter. As a child, Ella had believed that the skies went on for ever, something that had only struck her once she was here in a city, where the sky seemed limited by the buildings all around her. Even if she climbed to one of the highest points in the centre, Clifford's Tower, her view was restricted to the silvery stones of the ancient city walls and the trees that shaded the river path. York, sprawling along the river, was set deep within a vale and at times Ella's spirit longed for the soaring open spaces of her childhood home.

The bustle of the city streets, the rattle of the hansom cabs and the calls of the street urchins, the constant passage of people going about their business from dawn until dusk and on into the night, had been both a shock and a source of delight to Ella when she first arrived here. Now she barely noticed it, except when on a hurried errand and she found her way impeded by the sheer number of people out and about. What would her mother make of it all? Ella smiled to herself.

She could hear Sarah's voice as clearly as if she was standing beside her. 'What is so important that they have to be going at such speed?'

Ella's mother's journeys through Northwaite had always involved stopping to talk to everyone she met and enquiring after their family's welfare (even if she had only seen them the day before). It could take her the best part of an hour to travel a few hundred yards. More than anything, her mother would struggle to comprehend that the majority of people passing along these streets were strangers to each other, their houses spread over a wide area of the city or its surrounds, their acquaintance more likely to be a result of their business or family connections rather than neighbourliness.

She would be astonished by the traffic on the streets, too. Ella had seen the occasional motorcar as it passed through

Nortonstall; indeed, that was how she had first met Mr Ward, her current employer. But Sarah would probably have fainted at the sight of a double-decker horse-drawn bus. Ella began to wish that she had thought to ride one of these from the centre of York; although she had walked fast it was so cold that her face felt as though it had been chipped from a block of marble.

The low wall around Grange House – topped with imposing iron railings, spike-pointed and painted black – came into view. Ella paused to catch her breath, puffed out after keeping up a fast pace on her route out of York. More than once she'd had reason to wish that the family still lived in their previous residence in Micklegate, so convenient for the centre of the city, rather than out here on the edge of the city. They'd moved before Ella had arrived in the household just over a year previously, joining the exodus of the newly wealthy who were building themselves the grand houses surrounded with fine gardens that they could never have within the confines of the city walls.

It occurred to Ella that she had no notion of how to contact Albert again, if for no other reason than at least to apologise for her abrupt departure. Seeing someone from her past like that had thrown her completely off balance and it reminded her that the security she was beginning to feel in her new life was easily challenged. Quite apart from that, Albert had been such a dear friend of Alice and indeed of the whole family. Ella had an inkling that his own home life was less than happy and that the Bancroft household, while often chaotic, was very appealing to him. She had a sudden flashback to his visit to the house not long after her niece Elisabeth, known to the family as Beth, had been born, his mixture of shyness

12

and happiness at being included in their happy family gathering. He wasn't to know that the celebration, inspired by his presence, wasn't a regular occurrence, but it had lifted the spirits of the family, mired in bleakness by the chill of the winter and the desperation of their situation. In fact Sarah Bancroft, alone after the death of her husband, with five of her own children to bring up and now a grandchild too, often wondered how food was to be put on the table that night.

Albert had been deeply uncomfortable around Beth that day, being an only child and having no prior experience of babies, but Ella remembered that they had all taken a lot of joy from the evening. She felt sure, though, that his visit had more to do with a wish to see Alice, who was no longer his daily companion at the mill.

He'd changed such a lot in the intervening years, and it gave Ella pain to think of how Alice, too, would have matured if she had only survived her wrongful incarceration in jail. Although Albert had mentioned his work as a stonemason at York Minster, nothing had been said about where he was living now. She had no idea how to go about finding him.

Taking a deep breath, Ella skirted the wall to the servants' gate set into the side, and pushed it open, only too aware of how late she was. As she hurried towards the heavy door that led into the servants' domain she remembered how fearful she had been when she passed this way last year, clutching her worldly possessions in a worn cloth bag. Mrs Sugden, or Mrs S as Ella soon discovered she was known to all the servants, had been kind, almost motherly to her that day, accurately assessing her fright and state of mind. Ella, having seen the sterner side of Mrs S's nature many times since then, feared her reception wouldn't be so welcoming today. She must have spent an hour or so in Albert's company: she really was very late.

And so it proved. Mrs S bore down the corridor towards her as Ella attempted to hang up her coat and slip unnoticed into the kitchen with her purchases.

'Wherever have you been?' Mrs S demanded, her gaze direct and angry. Scarcely waiting for a response, she continued, 'You'd better smarten yourself up at once. Mr Ward wants a word with you. He's in the library. With Mrs Ward.'

Ella was vaguely aware of pale, worried faces peeping around the kitchen door behind Mrs S's back. There was a hush over the whole area, the usual noise and bustle subdued. Ella sensed that the other servants were frightened, but of what she couldn't begin to imagine. She hastened to wash her hands and to tuck stray strands of her reddish-blonde hair under her cap, hurriedly pinned in place so that she looked like a proper parlourmaid as she pushed through the green baize door into the house itself, and into the chill of the hallway.

Her mind was in a whirl. Could she really be in this much trouble just for being late? Or had something happened at home? Surely, if this had been the case, Mrs S would have been the one to break the news? This had a much more serious air altogether. For the second time in less than a quarter of an hour, Ella took a deep breath and steeled herself. Then she knocked on the heavy door of the oak-panelled library, pushing it open when the murmur of voices within stilled and Mr Ward called 'Enter'.

Chapter Three

Mrs S was summoned to conduct Ella from the library to her room. Very little was said as they crossed the threshold through the green baize door and climbed the steep and narrow back stairs to the servants' quarters, tucked away in the attics. Ella looked out of the windows as they crossed the half-landing on each floor to mount the next flight. The sky outside was darkening and, over the fields beyond the garden wall, lights were beginning to twinkle through a greying dusk. The rush to get everything ready for Christmas had resumed down below, but up here it was cold and quiet.

Mrs S broke the silence. 'I've moved Doris out of the room. She can share with Rosa until it is decided what's to be done.'

She pushed open the door to the room and Ella passed through, automatically heading for the window to gaze out.

'You'd be as well to put your things together. I don't think the master will be wanting to keep you after this.' Mrs S sighed and closed the door. Ella, staring unseeing out of the window, heard the key click in the lock.

Her cheeks were hot with shame and indignation, her mind a jumble of words unsaid. The thought that floated to the top of this seething mass was the likelihood of the loss of her job. How would her mother manage without the money that Ella sent home to her? How could she begin to tell her what had happened?

Ella turned away from the window and sank onto the bed. Scenes from just a few minutes earlier began to play out in her head.

Mr Ward had been sitting at his desk, Mrs Ward silhouetted in the window, her back to the light so that Ella had found it difficult to read her expression. There was no mistaking Mr Ward's mood, however. His brows were drawn together in a frown and his mouth pursed into a thin line.

'Ella, we have reason to believe that you may have been involved in an act that has proved injurious to the health of one of our guests.'

Ella was puzzled, her mind racing to make sense of this turn of events. So it was nothing to do with her late return from town, or her family? This was something quite unexpected.

Mr Ward continued, 'I see you do not deny it. You must have been aware of the potentially fatal consequences of your actions when you entered into this ridiculous pact with Grace. I would like you to go away and think very hard about your behaviour. I have already consulted Mrs Sugden about your character and, whilst she assures me that you have conducted yourself in an exemplary fashion whilst in our employment, I am not minded to be lenient in my view of this. You have run the risk of bringing my good name, and that of my family, into disrepute by your actions. You will go to your room, Ella, and think long and hard on this.'

He turned his attention back to papers on his desk, to

signify the interview was at an end. Mrs Ward had not moved throughout Mr Ward's speech but, as Ella turned to leave – stunned by what she had heard and unsure of how she might defend herself – she saw that Mrs Ward was gazing on her husband with an expression that was very hard to read.

On the silent walk to her room, Ella had struggled to piece the jigsaw together. Something had clearly happened that involved Grace, the youngest daughter of the household, and somehow Ella was taking the blame for it. With a sinking heart, she pictured the small bottle she had handed over to Grace earlier in the week. Stoppered by a cork and without benefit of a label, the pearly glass held a dark, mysterious liquid.

'Shake it well,' she'd whispered. 'And mind, no more than two or three drops in his drink. Be sure to keep the bottle well hidden.'

Chapter Four

O ver on the other side of town, Albert could barely remember how he had found his way home from the tearoom after Ella had delivered the terrible news. After she'd gone, he'd been vaguely aware of curious glances, of conversations briefly stilled, of whispering behind hands. Within a minute or two, though, the large room was filled with its previous level of chatter and he had paid quickly and left, the atmosphere deeply at odds with his shocked frame of mind.

Alice was dead. Ella had given him no further details of what had happened to her sister, of how or exactly when it had happened. He couldn't comprehend it. Throughout his apprenticeship, spent living alone in York, he had been sustained by the thought of the woods and valleys that surrounded Northwaite, his true home, and of Alice going about her day-to-day routine there. At first, he had thought more often of Alice than of his family, reliving her companionship on walks to the mill in the morning, his visit to see her at home when her baby Beth was born, the warmth and welcome of her family in such contrast to his own. He'd longed daily to be back in Northwaite, but as time passed in York and the opportunity to return home hadn't arisen, the longing had faded into something held at a distance, in the back of his mind. Alice and Beth, he realised now, had become frozen in time, exactly as he had left them, seven years ago. Seven years! Albert was startled to realise just how much time had passed. No wonder seeing Ella had given him such a shock; she must be almost the same age as Alice had been when he had left Northwaite.

Albert had arrived home without being conscious of how he had done so, his feet treading an automatic path while his thoughts were engaged elsewhere. He needed to find Ella again, to discover exactly what had happened to Alice, and he knew he would have no rest until he had. And if he couldn't find her, then he would return to Northwaite as soon as possible and seek the truth there. It wouldn't be the return he had imagined, the return he had subconsciously been putting off until the moment was right. He had wanted to go back as a success, to show his family what he had made of himself, but above all to impress Alice. For well over a year now, his skills had been sought after both in York and elsewhere as word had spread within the close community of stonemasons. So why hadn't he gone back? Had he feared that the vision he had held in his mind for so long, a fantasy of the part he could play in Alice's life, could never be realised?

Albert thought back over the events of seven years ago. He tried hard to put the shocking news that he had just heard in context to see how it impacted on everything he knew. His career as a stonemason was a direct result of the fire at the mill, which had employed the majority of the working-age population in his home village of Northwaite. Alice had once worked there, Ella worked there and he himself was a nightwatchman there. On that fateful night, he had tried to put out the fire but it was beyond him, and the mill owner's son had died in the blaze, attempting to save books and papers from the office. Williams, the overlooker, who had been the only other person present during the fire, had appeared at Albert's house the very next morning. He had news of a reward given by Mr Weatherall, the mill owner, in recognition of Albert's heroic efforts to stop the spread of the fire. And, seeing that the mill would be closed for the foreseeable future, there was also the offer of an apprenticeship as a stonemason in York, to be taken up immediately.

Albert had been grateful to Williams and had never thought to question his role in all this and the haste with which he had been despatched. He was only too delighted to get the longed-for opportunity. Now that very same opportunity, which he had hoped would raise his standing in the world and make him a suitable prospect as a husband, was cast in quite a new light. Alice had died, seemingly very soon after he had left, but he didn't yet know why. A piece of the jigsaw was missing; he needed to talk to Ella again.

Albert sat at the table, still muffled in his overcoat, and looked around, taking in the sparsely furnished room, his neatly made bed in one corner, the desk positioned by the window to make best use of the light, the one easy chair set by the unlit fire. He buried his head in his hands. What had he done?

Chapter Five

While the family celebrated the festive season, Ella remained confined to her room. She'd spent the night tossing and turning in her narrow bed, dozing fitfully and waking to discover how little time had passed; how the window was still filled with darkness, the sky dotted with twinkling stars. As the stars faded, to be replaced by the grey light of dawn, she felt a sense of relief. Soon she would be able to hear the sounds of the household coming to life; of Doris and Rosa dragging themselves, yawning, down the stairs to start the day. Ella felt a terrible pang of guilt. They would have to take over her duties as well as their own, and all this at Christmastime with so much extra work needing to be done.

Today was Christmas Eve, when the tree would go up in the entrance hall. Last year, Ella had helped to decorate it, her first ever Christmas tree. She'd been entranced by the delicate glass baubles, each one wrapped in tissue paper and carefully boxed. She had never seen anything like it; the tree so tall that the butler, Mr Stevens, had needed to climb a stepladder to hang the decorations from the top branches. He had only managed to place the star on the top by going up to the landing and leaning precariously over, Rosa and Doris hanging on to his coat-tails and squealing while Mrs S stood at the base, alternately telling the maids to shush and gasping in fright herself. When the decorating was finished, and the candles placed in each holder all around the branches, the Wards' youngest son John was called to see the candles lit for the first time.

Ella had felt sure that his saucer-eyed amazement had only been a reflection of her own expression. She could have stared at the tree for hours, drinking in each and every detail, how the flames of the candles sparkled and reflected in the glass baubles as they spun and shifted in the draughts of the hall.

John's governess had gone home for the holidays and although Mr and Mrs Ward were there for the lighting cere-mony, it was Ella that John sought out, reaching for her hand and gripping it hard, wordlessly. She had bent towards him.

'It's beautiful, John. Have you ever seen anything like it?' She so wished that her niece Beth were here. Ella would have taken her around the tree, pointing out the sparkling colours of the spinning baubles, and the little toys and striped sugar canes hanging from the branches.

John found his voice. 'Yes, I have. Last year.'

Ella smiled. 'You can remember it?'

'Of course I can.' John was scornful. 'I'm not a baby. I'm six.' He paused. 'It was in our other house and it wasn't as tall as this one. I think this year's tree is the best of all.'

Mr Stevens, handing out candied fruits, a Christmas treat for the family and staff, heard John's words and bent to offer him a fruit jelly.

'Well, Master John, it's lucky we had enough decorations

to cover such a tall tree. Now, you'll have to let go of Ella. She has work to do and it's time for your bed. Christmas Day is nearly here.'

Ella wasn't sure whether it was she or John who had been the most reluctant to be parted from the spectacle, but the family were moving through to have their drinks and, with extra guests expected, her help would be needed in serving the Christmas Eve dinner. She had bent down to whisper to John, who was exhibiting a mulish expression, bottom lip stuck out and jaw set in preparation for a battle over bedtime.

'John, Father Christmas can't visit unless he knows you are asleep. So off you go to bed now and in the morning you can come downstairs to check. If you are lucky, and if you have been a good boy, perhaps he will have left some presents for you under the tree.'

That had been a year ago. She had been so looking forward to a repetition of the ceremony this year, to experiencing the same magical feel and all the wonderful scents of the house at Christmas. She remembered lingering in the hallway every time she had cause to pass through it, to drink in the scent of the pine needles. Instead, she was locked up here alone in the chill of her room, a world away from the lights, warmth and bustle of the household on Christmas Eve. She heard Doris and Rosa go down the stairs, and huddled back under the covers. There seemed little point in getting up, only to sit fully dressed in the cold, with nothing to do except strain her ears for sounds from below that might give her some sense of belonging to the celebrations.

She must have dozed again, waking with a guilty start to the sound of the key turning in the lock. It was Doris, bringing a tray with breakfast for her: tea, and a hunk of bread and butter. It was poorer fare than Ella could have expected had she been at the breakfast table with the other servants, but she was grateful for it all the same, even though the tea was stewed and all but cold after being carried up the chilly staircase.

'You're to stay up here until Christmas has passed,' Doris said in solemn tones. 'Whatever have you done, Ella? And all the extra work you've given us at this time of year, too. What can you have been thinking of?'

Her words sounded harsh but Ella could see that Doris was torn between scolding and concern. She knew only too well how much Ella needed her job.

'Mr Ward will talk to you again on Boxing Day evening, after the guests have gone, Mrs S said to tell you. She's too busy to come up here herself.'

Doris cast a quick glance around the room and sighed. 'It's little better than a cell, what with all the brightness down below for Christmastime. I must go, I have so many things to do, but I'll try to be back.' And with that she was gone, the key turned firmly in the lock.

Sitting up in bed, covers drawn up under her chin, Ella took a few bites of the bread and butter. She'd thought herself hungry but, although she had gulped down the cold tea, the bread tasted like ashes in her mouth and she struggled to swallow it. Doris's words rang in her ears. 'Little better than a cell.' A cell was where her sister Alice had died, locked up all alone, denied any contact with her mother and with her baby. She couldn't begin to imagine what that must have felt like. Then her thoughts turned to her mother, now living in Nortonstall with Thomas, Annie, Beattie and Beth. She hoped that the money she had been able to send them meant that they could have some sort of proper celebration for Christmas.

Ella wasn't sure how long she had been sitting there, gazing sightlessly at the opposite wall, sighing occasionally and shedding a few tears, before cries from the garden below roused her. Aware of a change in the light, she looked at the window; large fluffy flakes were falling silently against a yellow-grey sky. It was snowing, and snowing hard. Ella swung her legs out of bed, shivering as her feet struck the cold floorboards, and wrapped the shawl from the end of her bed around her shoulders. From the window, she could see that the snow must have been falling for a while. The garden was thick with it and the dark, bare winter branches of the trees were tipped with white frosting. Across the pristine whiteness of the snowy lawn, John was racing up and down, spreading his boot tracks far and wide and uttering little yelps of excitement. He stopped suddenly, spread out his arms and flung his head back, mouth open. It looked to Ella as though he was trying to eat the snow as it fell and she smiled, wanting to bang on the glass and wave. Then she thought better of it and hastily drew back. She didn't want John to spot her and to ask questions, the answers to which might upset him. It pained her to see him out in the snow on his own, with no one to share the fun. If she had been downstairs, she would have begged for a few minutes to spend outside with him. Mrs S would have grumbled but granted it: like all the servants she felt sorry for John, neglected in a household where his older siblings and parents were always preoccupied with their own concerns.

There would be no festivities for Ella this year. She tried to tell herself it was no different to previous years with the Ottershaws, but it was still a cruel blow. She couldn't bear to think about what the future might hold if she were to be sent home. It would mean employment somewhere like the Ottershaws' once again. A life of drudgery for very little reward, slaving for ignorant, boorish people who treated her like the dirt they employed her to clean up.

Ella clenched her fists, driving her nails into her palms. What had actually happened? She couldn't imagine what had gone so wrong, but as the Christmas celebrations rolled inexorably on without her, she had plenty of time to reflect on the events of the past fifteen months, and what had put her in this awful position.

Chapter Six

Ella had first met Mr Ward on a Sunday in August the previous year back in Nortonstall, where she was a live-in servant and where the rest of the family now lived, forced to move away from their Northwaite home after the mill tragedy. On that particular day the sun was beating down with a ferocity the like of which Ella had never experienced before. She'd found it hard to tear herself away from six-year-old Beth, made fractious by the heat but cooled by a game involving a pail of water, set in the shade of the one tree that overhung their tiny yard. Ella, with her niece settled on her lap, had floated leaves as boats on the water's surface, and then splashed her fingers to make waves to rock them, increasing her efforts to whip up a storm.

'Watch out Beth, the waves are going to capsize the boats!' Ella had tilted the pail slightly so that the water sloshed over Beth's toes. Beth had screamed, her shock at the chill swiftly followed by delight.

'Don't get her over-excited, mind,' Sarah, Ella's mother, had warned, folding laundry that had dried almost as soon as it had been spread out to dry in the sun. 'I'll never get her settled after you've gone.'

Of course, when Ella's home-time came, Beth had wailed and tried to tear herself out of Sarah's arms, holding her hands out beseechingly to Ella.

'Don't cry,' Ella begged. 'I'll come back as soon as I can. Be good until I do.'

Now, as she hurried towards the Ottershaws' house, the cries were still ringing in her ears. She'd doubtless be in trouble for being late, even though she rarely had any time off at all. She worked for them all the hours she was awake, and she had the feeling that they would have had her work for them in her sleep too, if it were only possible.

Hurrying down the road, conscious of the sweat trickling down her back and darkening the fabric of her dress under her armpits, she began to wish she had left on time. It really was too hot to be out in this heat, let alone in a hurry.

She rounded the corner then halted, startled at the sight before her. At first, she couldn't quite take it in. It was a motorcar, a rare enough sight in Nortonstall, where horse and trap or horse and cart were still the normal way of getting around, other than on foot. A motorcar was generally viewed with fear, and Ella understood this, being nervous of them herself. On the odd occasion that one had appeared in Nortonstall, it had travelled through at what seemed to Ella to be a terrifying speed and with a great deal of noise, scattering men, women, children, dogs, cats and horses in alarm.

This motorcar, its gleaming paint made dusty by the roads it had traversed was, however, stationary. Moreover, it seemed to be in some sort of trouble. At any rate, a man was standing at the front end of it from which a cloud of steam issued, along with a loud hiss. The man was wafting his hat somewhat ineffectually over the steam. He looked red in the face, whether from the steam or the heat of the sun, or because of the bother, Ella couldn't be sure.

She put her head down, glancing out of the corner of her eye as she passed, but she didn't speak. As a car owner, he was likely to be a gentleman and not someone she would expect to speak to her, either.

She had only gone a few paces before she heard, 'Excuse me!'

She didn't like to look back, but nobody else was around. Was he addressing her?

'Excuse me! Miss?'

This time, she faltered in her step. It looked as though she was, indeed, the object of his attention. Feeling even hotter, with embarrassment this time, she turned to look back.

The man was facing her. 'I wonder, do you know of anywhere I could get water around here?'

Ella took in his appearance. He was short, in early middle age with dark wavy hair and a prosperous air about him. He also looked as hot as Ella herself felt. She wasn't sure if he required the water for himself, or for the car. She looked along the street. Normally it would have been busy, being the high road through town, with the shops open and bustling. But today was Sunday, and the road, shimmering a little in the heat haze, was deserted. The heat had taken everyone away, either to the cool of the river bank or indoors.

She hesitated. 'I live' – she caught herself – 'rather, work, just around the corner from here. I'd be glad to fetch you water, sir, if you can wait?'

The man laughed. 'I can certainly wait. I won't be going anywhere for some time.'

Ella turned to head for the Ottershaws', before turning back again.

'Ah, how much water do you require, sir?' She was still unsure whether he needed it for the car or himself.

'A good question. If you were able to bring a jugful, that should suffice.'

He was either very thirsty or it was, indeed, for his car, Ella thought.

Even more conscious of her tardiness now, she hurried along the street, turning left to climb the steep slope of West Hill towards the Ottershaws' house. It commanded a striking view over the town and appeared to be an imposing house from the outside. That impression was forgotten the minute you stepped through the door. A warren of small rooms led off a dark hallway and from each one, today as on any other day, there came the sound of a child crying.

'So, you've deigned to come back. Do you realise what a burden you have placed on Mrs Ottershaw? How can you expect us to trust you the next time you say you want leave to visit your family?'

Mr Ottershaw had planted himself firmly in the hallway while Mrs Ottershaw, very red in the face and with her hair quite dishevelled, seemed to be grappling with several children at once in the parlour.

'I'm very sorry, sir. I was detained on the way back. I'm afraid I will need to go out again but I promise I will return at once.' Ella attempted to slip past Mr Ottershaw, who was having none of it.

'Go out again! What can you be thinking of? With children to be fed and dinner to be prepared, and you already late? I will not have it!'

Mr Ottershaw stretched a beefy arm across the hallway to block Ella's path. She dodged it with ease, and although he grabbed at her, he caught only air. As Ella headed for the scullery, she called back, 'There's a gentleman in the road. His motorcar has broken down. I promised to fetch water to help him get back on his way.'

When she returned, bearing a large china jug and a glass, Mr Ottershaw was in a more conciliatory mood. 'A gentleman, you say. With a motorcar? Well, I shall accompany you to see whether I can be of assistance.'

Ella doubted whether there was anything Mr Ottershaw could offer that would be of use, his experience of motor vehicles being non-existent, but she said nothing to her employer. She hastened down the steps, Mr Ottershaw pausing only to seize his jacket and a hat as protection against the sun before closing the door firmly on Mrs Ottershaw's protestations. Ella was already at the corner before he caught up with her, puffing and red-faced but determined not to be left behind. The car and the gentleman were as she had left them, although the gentleman had retreated into the small amount of shade cast by the wall of Taylor's carriage works.

'You came back.' There was a hint of surprise in his statement and Ella was stung.

'Why, yes sir, I gave you my word.' She handed him the jug and the glass. 'I thought that you might be thirsty, sir, standing out in this heat all the time.'

There was no ignoring Mr Ottershaw, who was bobbing impatiently at Ella's elbow.

'And this is my employer, sir, Mr Ottershaw.' Ella tried to sound enthusiastic in her introduction.

'Ottershaw at your service,' he said, holding out his hand

to the gentleman who, having no free hand to take it, had to pass the jug and glass back to Ella.

'Mr Ward,' the gentleman replied. 'From York. I was returning there after conducting some business in the area but it seems my car didn't appreciate the hills round here on a day like today. The engine appears to have overheated.'

Mr Ward took the glass of water that Ella had poured for him and gulped it down gratefully.

'Thank you. That was most thoughtful. I hadn't realised quite how thirsty I had become.'

Ella refilled his glass and held it while he turned his attention once more to the car.

'Now, if you will forgive me, I will take up no more of your time. I will top up the radiator and be on my way. Would you mind holding the jug a moment?' He spoke to Ella, as he needed both hands to loosen the radiator cap.

'Oh, but you must come and take some refreshment with us, Mr Ward.' Mr Ottershaw was clearly put out that Ella was getting more than her share of this gentleman's attention.

'I thank you kindly,' said Mr Ward, 'but my family will be concerned at my lateness. And I have been well provided with refreshment thanks to –' Mr Ward hesitated. 'I'm afraid I didn't ask your name?'

'Ella, sir.'

'– thanks to Ella.' Mr Ward took the refilled glass and drained it in one. 'Now my car is suitably refreshed and so am I.'

Mr Ottershaw could feel the situation slipping away from him. 'Mr Ward, my dear wife would never forgive me if I didn't press you to join us. Just to step inside out of the heat, and rest yourself before your journey. We were just about to take tea. Pray, do join us.'

Ella watched the scene unfold with some amusement. Mr Ottershaw may have considered himself a man of some importance in Nortonstall, but he was out of his depth with the likes of Mr Ward. The thought of such a gentleman stepping into the Ottershaws' parlour for tea was in danger of making her break into unseemly laughter and she had to turn away, setting down the empty jug and glass to hide her expression.

Meanwhile, Mr Ward had climbed back into the driver's seat and already had the engine running. Ella stepped back in awe – the vehicle was transformed from a broken beast into a growling, noisy monster. It suddenly seemed much larger and more dangerous than it had before. Mr Ward beckoned her to come closer, so that he didn't have to shout over the noise of the engine.

'Ella, I am most grateful for your help. I feared that I would be stuck in this god-forsaken place for the night. It seems to me that you work for a fool...'

Ella started and glanced nervously at Mr Ottershaw to see if he had heard, but he was too busy mopping his red, perspiring face with a handkerchief to be paying any heed.

'Should you ever wish for a change of employment, I know Mrs Ward would be delighted to have a maid with even a modicum of intelligence in our house in York. Take this, and write to her.'

Mr Ward pressed a pasteboard card into Ella's hand. She glanced at it before secreting it swiftly in her pocket, hoping that Mr Ottershaw hadn't witnessed the action. Ella stepped back again, Mr Ward put the car into gear, nodded to them both and with a roar and a not-inconsiderable amount of dust, the car and the driver went on their way. The road seemed suddenly very quiet and still.

'Well,' said Mr Ottershaw, very put out that he had been side-lined. 'I must say, he was rather a rude man. Why did he wish a private word with you, Ella? Quite improper, I felt.'

'Oh no, Mr Ottershaw, he just wished to thank me again.' Ella was relieved that no mention had been made of the card. She felt very conscious of it, hidden deep in her pocket. Employment in York – could such a thing be possible? Could she go, leaving her mother and Beth behind?

Ella sighed. She didn't have to ask herself the same question about the Ottershaws. She knew they would make her life doubly hard for the rest of the day: Mr Ottershaw resentful of the attention she had received and Mrs Ottershaw furious with both of them for leaving her alone so long with the children. It would be a hard end to a hot day. But an exciting day, nonetheless. Ella had a secret but, she reflected as she trudged back up the hot and dusty road, it was one that she could do little about. She could neither read, nor write. And she certainly wasn't going to be able to ask the Ottershaws to help her with either of those things.

Chapter Seven

Ella hugged her secret to herself. The memory of what Mr Ward had said, and the possession of his card, sustained her through several trying weeks in the Ottershaw household. When the children fell ill one after the other, so that the kitchen was awash with bedclothes hanging to dry and the house filled with the crying or moaning of infants, day and night, Ella stoically carried on. She had some sympathy for the children, even when faced with a succession of permanently running or crusted noses, their seemingly endless capacity for being sick and the often-rude manner, learnt from their parents, in which they summoned and treated her.

Mr and Mrs Ottershaw were another matter. They liked to let it be known that Ella was there on sufferance, out of the goodness of their hearts in employing someone whose sister had, in their view and, it would seem, everyone else's view, committed a hideous crime. It seemed to Ella that their apparent Christian charity was an excuse to misuse her, to pay her even less than the pittance considered a fair wage ('as no one else will have you'), to work her all hours ('you will understand the risk we have borne in taking you in'), and to refuse her the right to visit her family ('the afternoon off? How could you ask this of us after all we have done for you?').

It was only when they refused Ella a visit home after she had had word that Sarah, too, was struggling with a house full of sick children – Ella's siblings Thomas, Annie and Beattie having taken it in turn to succumb, with niece Beth now gravely ill – that she finally snapped. Mr Ottershaw, in his usual pompous manner, had denied the request, citing a concern that she would return bearing yet more illness into the bosom of his family, then buried his head back in the newspaper. Ella had retired quietly to the kitchen. Two pink spots of rage burnt in her cheeks. She stood in the centre of the room, fists clenched, and thought but for a moment or two. Then she undid her apron, folded it and laid it over the kitchen chair, and went into the small room off the kitchen that served as her sleeping quarters. She took her few possessions off the shelf along with the dress that hung behind the door, and wrapped them in a woollen shawl. Then she drew her good shawl around her shoulders and stepped back into the kitchen. After a moment's indecision, she went to the china pot at the back of the dresser shelf, where she knew that Mrs Ottershaw kept coins to pay the small bills of tradesmen, and took what little lay in there. It would have to do in lieu of the money she was owed for the month just worked, for which she reasoned she was unlikely to be paid. She slipped the coins into her pocket, where Mr Ward's card still nestled reassuringly, and set off for the front door. In the hallway, she hesitated before knocking on the parlour door, and entering. Mr Ottershaw, irritated, looked over the top of his newspaper.

'I'll bid you and Mrs Ottershaw a good day, sir. And I hope

you will be more fortunate in the future in finding a servant that suits,' and with a nod Ella left the room, and the house, before Mr Ottershaw could reply.

She was trembling, whether with anger, shock or terror at what she had just done, she could not say.

Sarah listened without comment to her tale when she reached home, then hugged her and sent her to fetch ink and paper. While Ella set to, mopping fevered brows, singing calming songs and bringing cooling drinks of water for the sickly family, Sarah wrote a note to Mrs Ward and took it herself to the post office. When Mr Ottershaw came to the door that evening to demand that Ella should return, having broken the terms of her employment, Sarah informed him that he was putting himself at risk of the fever in coming to their house. Furthermore, she had reason to believe that the Ottershaws themselves had broken the terms of their contract with Ella on many occasions and they should make it their business to look elsewhere for a servant. And with that she shut the door firmly in his face.

Chapter Eight

When word came back that Ella was to present herself as soon as possible at the Ward household in York, she was thrown into a panic. Once she had escaped the drudgery of the Ottershaws' house, the planning of her further escape from Nortonstall had been all consuming. Now that it was going to happen, Ella was seized with doubt. She had never left the confines of her immediate locality before. Although in her younger years she had roamed far and wide across the fields and moors, she had barely travelled a distance greater than five miles from home. Now she was to travel nearer sixty, and the greater part of that journey was to be via the railway, from Nortonstall to Leeds and then on to York. Although the railway had run through the town for a while now, there were still those who viewed it with deep distrust and wouldn't dream of setting foot inside a carriage, let alone allowing it to transport them anywhere. Ella had seen and heard the trains as they passed through the town, but she had never had reason, nor the money, to take one. Nor, if she was honest with herself, did she wish to. The Wards had enclosed her fare for the trip and, although Ella had favoured the idea of begging a ride with a carter leaving Nortonstall for Leeds, Sarah wouldn't hear of it.

'When have you ever been to Leeds?' she demanded. 'You won't have the first idea of how to go about finding yourself a ride from there to York.'

'Yes, I will.' Ella was defiant. 'The carter can help when I alight. He's bound to stop at an inn and it will be easy to ask around there to find someone who's travelling on to York.'

'Well, I won't have it,' Sarah said. 'You'll be lucky to accomplish the journey in a day, so you'd have to find lodgings or journey through the night. All manner of things could go wrong.'

She was working herself into a state and even Ella began to be daunted by the possibilities of unforeseen disaster.

'In any case,' Sarah continued, determined to put a stop to the debate. 'Mrs Ward has sent you the fare and will expect you to arrive in good time, and fresh to start work. The train it must be.'

So Ella found herself standing on the platform at Nortonstall station, watching anxiously down the tracks as the engine approached, a plume of steam trailing through the chill morning air behind it and hanging there, like mist. A great flourish of squealing brakes and belching steam heralded the train's arrival at the platform, quickly followed by a rush of activity as doors swung open, porters were hailed, and the passengers who had been waiting quietly on the platform were now galvanised into action. Ella stood for a moment, bewildered and made nervous by the noises of the train at rest, the creaks and groans of the metal and the chug of the engine.

'Are you taking this train? You'd best make haste, miss.'

One of the porters, wheeling a trolley of mail sacks, paused momentarily beside her. Ella shook herself free of her reverie in time to realise that the doors were closing and the only people left on the platform were passengers leaving the station.

'Third, is it?' the porter said. 'There, the last carriage. Hurry now.'

Tightly clutching her bundle of belongings and pasteboard ticket, Ella all but ran along the short platform to the last carriage. A whistle blew as she put her foot on the carriage running board and hands reached out to take her arms and pull her in as the train started to move, with a squeal of protest and yet another belch of steam. The door was slammed behind her and Ella, suddenly breathless, stood embarrassed among the men pressed up by the door.

They passed her between themselves like a parcel until she found herself at the end of the rows of hard bench seats, which faced each other and were mainly occupied by women clutching baskets and small children.

'Any room for a little 'un?' one of her rescuers asked cheerfully, and a woman at the end of the bench obligingly scooped up a young child and made room for Ella to sit down.

'Nearly miss it, did you?' she asked, looking Ella up and down.

'I... why, yes, I suppose I did,' said Ella. She sat in silence for a minute or two, aware of her fast-beating heart and the high colour on her cheeks.

'I've never travelled on a train before,' she suddenly blurted out to her neighbour.

The woman laughed, while a couple of near neighbours smiled.

'Well, you've discovered the joys of them now, love. No

going back. They're the quickest way to get around. Where are you headed?'

'York,' said Ella. 'Well, Leeds first.'

'Best watch yourself at the station,' her neighbour advised. 'Plenty of people there looking to take advantage of a young girl like you travelling alone. Keep to yourself and keep a tight hold on your things.' She glanced at the bundle, bound up in a shawl, on Ella's lap. 'There's plenty there whose job it is to part you from your possessions.'

Ella spent the rest of the journey taking in her surroundings and getting used to the novelty of seeing the countryside moving fast past the window as she tried to settle herself on the hard, slippery seat. After a while, fields gave way to rows of back-to-back houses and, an hour after she had climbed on board, Ella stepped down from the carriage and onto the platform. She stopped, transfixed. The other alighting passengers bumped and jostled her but she was oblivious. She'd never seen a building quite like it: great metal arches soaring skywards and everywhere noise echoing and the smell of coal fumes hanging in the air.

Light streamed in through the huge curved glass roof as well as from the end of the great building. Here, where the station opened out onto the tracks, Ella could see the comings and goings of even more trains. There weren't just two platforms, as at Nortonstall, she quickly realised as she let herself be carried along with the remaining passengers heading for the gate, but many platforms.

'The train for York?' she enquired tentatively of the man at the gate, who was checking and taking their tickets.

'Not here, love,' he said. 'You need New Station.' Ella was dumbfounded. She hadn't realised she would need to change stations, as well as trains. The ticket collector looked her up and down, taking in her bundle and lost expression, and took pity on her. 'It's just around the corner. Follow Wellington Street, then turn into Bishopgate Street. You can't miss it. Follow the crowd.'

Ella did as he said, tagging along behind a group of people who were striding purposefully along as they left the station. Nonetheless, her heart was beating fast and she was worried that she might get lost. She barely had time to register how big and busy the streets were, and how tall and grimy the buildings, before she found herself turning away from a grand square straight into bustling crowds of people who were coming and going from a vast and forbidding brick-built building, much larger than anything she had ever seen before. Once inside, Ella was quickly overawed by the size of the space and the confident manner in which the other travellers seemed to be going about their business. Enquiring somewhat timidly about the next train to York, she was directed to the ticket office where she joined a queue, feeling anxious as to whether she would have enough money left over to cover the fare then thankful that she did, and that procuring it hadn't been as difficult as she had feared.

With the new ticket safely in her possession, she decided to find the platform straight away. Mindful of the words of her companion on the earlier train, she kept her head down and her bundle clutched tightly to her.

It was only when she reached Platform Two and ascertained that she still had a half hour's wait before the York train that she felt able to relax a little and take a proper look around. It seemed as though trains were arriving every few minutes, the doors flying open to disgorge a rush of passengers from the second- and third-class carriages, all intent on going about their business, while the first-class passengers descended at a more leisurely pace, looking about them for porters to take their luggage, or strolling away, the ladies elegant in long skirts and tailored coats with glossy fur collars, fashionable feathered hats on their heads, arm in arm with gentlemen in smartly cut suits. Ella stared in awe, saved by the distance from appearing rude. She had never seen such fashionable, well-dressed people before. In Nortonstall, people dressed for practicality and hard work, with their best clothes saved for Sundays and funerals. Such an array of colours and fabrics as was now passing before her was unimaginable. Cream wool coats trimmed with dark brown fur, rich russet jackets bound with black, hats in red or maroon velvet, decorated with great swoops of feathers.

Ella shivered in the cold wind that swept through the station concourse and pulled her shawl tighter around herself, suddenly very conscious of her dowdy appearance. She'd peered into the Ladies' Waiting Room as she had passed it, but had been too daunted by the smartness of the occupants to consider entering it. The warmly lit interior of the station café was appealing; she would dearly have loved a cup of tea to warm herself, but was worried both about the expense and feeling out of place.

With a great deal of self-important puffing the train for York finally pulled in, sending clouds of steam billowing up to the roof. Ella hung back as the door opened and the wave of passengers swept by. Those in a hurry were already hovering on the running board with the carriage doors open as the train slowed to a halt; others descended at a more leisurely pace, the ladies pulling on gloves and straightening hats, checking on their travelling companions before heading off to – Ella couldn't imagine what. Shopping? Visiting friends or relatives? A life of leisure activities wasn't something she had ever thought about, nor did she have time now. Instead, it was time to take her seat in the third-class carriage, mercifully less crowded than before, and to contemplate what might await her at the other end.

Chapter Nine

Ella followed the other passengers out of York station then hesitated, unsure of which way to turn. She ignored the line of hansom cabs waiting for fares, looking instead to her left and right for someone who might help her with directions. Tucked away at the far corner of the station façade she spotted a vendor selling flowers and made her way towards him. His face brightened at her approach.

'I wonder, could you help me? I need to get to Knavesmire.'

The man sighed. 'It's always directions. Hardly ever a sale. If I had a farthing... Ah well, never mind, I'm happy to help a pretty lass like you, with manners to match.'

He pointed out the route that Ella would need to take, advising her that it was not much over a mile, before he offered her some anemones. Waving away her protests that she couldn't pay, he pinned a couple of flower heads to her shawl.

'They're out of season and I've barely enough to sell. It will help brighten up a grey day for you. I wish you luck.'

Ella thanked him for his kindness and set out. Before she turned away from the city, out towards Knavesmire and the countryside beyond, she took a moment to gaze at the high grey-stone walls, set atop great green-carpeted mounds of earth, which surrounded the city. Within, she could make out an imposing church tower and a jumble of roofs while up ahead of her a turreted stone arch, the like of which she had never seen before, linked two sections of the wall over a road that led into the city. Lingering, she wondered whether she had time to step through that arch and discover what lay beyond it. Instead, promising herself that she would return to explore further at the first opportunity, she turned her back on the city and set out, facing into the wind. Before long, the streets of small terraced houses that led off from each side of the road gave way to grander houses set in large plots ranging along one side of the road, facing onto a great swathe of green on the other.

As a chill mist drifted across from Knavesmire, Ella found herself standing before Grange House, a house quite unlike anything she had ever seen. Set back behind a low wall, with a sweep of gravel in front, it had an oddly top-heavy appearance. Two storeys high, with additional windows in the attic, it had a prominent gable at one end, half-timbered at the top only, with this feature repeated around some of the windows and the front door. Perhaps most startling to Ella was the redness of the brick. The houses in Northwaite and Nortonstall were all built of grey stone with grey-slate roofs. This one was set beneath a red-tiled roof, and although the windows had pale sandstone surrounds, the predominant effect, Ella felt, was of a house shouting 'look at me!' to anyone who passed by. Her momentary doubt that she had come to the wrong place was quelled by the sight of Mr Ward's motorcar parked on the immaculately raked gravel in front of a separate brick-built building. Ella, sensing instinctively that she would not be expected to approach the grand front door, looked anxiously around for another way in. She spotted a discreet gate tucked into the side of the wall and, biting her lip in a sudden surge of anxiety and shivering hard in the chill mist that rolled in ever more thickly from across the road, she opened the gate and followed the path round the house.

Her first timid knock at the dark-painted solid door remained unanswered. Steeling herself, she seized the knocker and let it fall once, twice against the wood. Ella was filled with a sense of panic – why had she ever thought it a good idea to leave behind the safety of the hills and valleys where she had spent all her life, where she knew every person, every path, bird and flower, for a place as foreign as this? The thickness of the door blotted out any sounds from within and so Ella, poised to flee, was startled when it opened suddenly, revealing a girl little older than herself in a maid's uniform. A warmly lit interior was visible behind her.

'Mrs Sugden, it's the new girl,' the maid called over her shoulder, before seizing Ella's arm and pulling her into the hallway.

'You're frozen,' the girl remarked before an older, larger lady appeared, her dark dress rustling as she moved, grey curls pinned back from a face that appeared stern, but broke into a welcoming smile at the sight of Ella.

'Thank you, Doris. Please go and attend to the bell, then when you come back you can show – Ella, isn't it – to her room. Ella, come this way.'

Ella found herself propelled into a small room off the hallway. Set up as a mixture of office and parlour with heavy ledgers piled on a big desk, it had a welcoming fire burning in the grate.

Mrs Sugden pushed Ella gently towards a chair by the hearth.

'Sit yourself here and get warm. You look done in.'

Ella, gratefully taking the suggested seat, registered the note of concern in the housekeeper's voice.

'Have you eaten? You've missed lunch but I will ask Cook for a cup of tea, then we can discuss your duties here.' And with that Mrs Sugden, bustling in the purposeful manner to which Ella would soon become accustomed, left the room. She returned shortly after, bearing a cup of tea in a plain china cup and saucer, setting it on a table beside Ella who, overwhelmed by the strangeness of this long-anticipated situation and the unexpected kindness of the housekeeper, found herself close to tears.

'Now, when Doris comes back she'll show you to the room that you're to share with her so you can freshen up and put your belongings away.' Mrs Sugden glanced briefly at the bundle Ella clutched on her lap. 'Then you can meet the rest of the staff at tea. We'll need to fit you for your uniform.' Mrs Sugden paused to scrutinise Ella. 'You're taller than I expected and a good deal more slender but I daresay we will find something that will do for now. I know little about your experience other than what was in your mother's letter so I think it best to keep you in the kitchen for the first few days until I've seen what you are capable of, and where you'll best fit. Now, drink up that tea before it goes stone cold.'

The remainder of the day passed in a whirl that left Ella's head spinning by the time she fell thankfully into bed. Doris, who was in possession of a head of auburn curls and a tidy, well-formed figure, had brought her up to their shared room after her interview with Mrs S, as she had called her, and had sat on the bed watching as Ella unwrapped her belongings.

Horribly conscious of how few things she had, and how shabby they might look to someone else, Ella turned her back on Doris as she shook out a couple of dresses and quickly hung them up. She laid her hairbrush on the top of the chest of drawers, folded a few undergarments into one of the drawers and then turned.

'There, done,' she said.

Doris had been watching her without comment. 'You didn't bring much with you,' she remarked.

Ella felt her colour rise. 'No,' she replied, and then hesitated, unsure of what to say.

Doris regarded her shrewdly. 'No matter. You'll be in uniform most of the day. We'd best go and see what we can find to fit.'

In bed later that night, Ella had relived the embarrassment she had felt in front of Doris and, later, Mrs Sugden. It was already late and she had to be up at five, but her head was buzzing with the effort of taking in so much new information. The room was dark but she could make out the shape of Doris in the next bed, already peacefully asleep. She ran through what she could remember of the other staff: apart from Doris, she had met Rosa who was lady's maid to Mrs Ward, Mrs Dawson the cook and Mr Stevens the butler. At the tea table, she had learnt of the Wards' three children: three well-grown daughters, Edith, Ailsa and Grace and a son John, who was only six. She had listened to the gossip as the servants gathered to eat before heading off to fulfil their evening duties. Mrs S had then shepherded Ella to a tall cupboard in the servants' hallway, unlocking it with one of the keys on a chain kept at her waist. She'd pulled out several dresses and held them up against Ella, narrowing her eyes and pursing her lips as she assessed the fit.

'I think these will do. Try them on in my room for size. This one is for the kitchen, but if you make progress and go above stairs, you'll need this,' she said, indicating the darker of the two dresses. 'Mrs Ward will be pleased if we can make do with what we have here rather than having to order up something new. You are tall, which means you could do very well above stairs, but we must be sure that does not cause your dresses to be too short. Too much ankle will never do.'

Mrs S appeared to be talking to herself as much as Ella as she ushered her back into her parlour and shut the door. Ella had no idea what Mrs S meant by her comments about her height but, in any case, Ella soon forgot them, overcome with shyness at having to strip to her underclothes in front of the housekeeper. Although she had made every effort to keep her things as clean as possible at the Ottershaws', Mrs Ottershaw had resented the smallest scrap of soap or hot water used for Ella's personal cleanliness, or for the washing of her clothes. And new garments were out of the question, so everything had to be darned and patched until it was no longer feasible to wear it.

Mrs S tactfully turned her back and busied herself at her desk as Ella slipped hurriedly into the first dress, a rather shapeless affair in heavy cotton, well-worn at the collar and cuffs but clean and serviceable.

Ella cleared her throat and Mrs S turned. She frowned. 'Hmmm, a little on the large side but the apron should pull it in. I think it will do well enough for the kitchen. Now the other, if you please.'

Ella quickly unbuttoned the first dress, stepped out of it

and just as quickly pulled the other one over her head. The fabric was darker in colour but lighter in weight and she immediately felt that the fit was better.

'Ma'am,' she ventured.

The housekeeper turned to her. 'Mrs Sugden,' she corrected, then stopped, taking in Ella's appearance. 'This will do very well,' she murmured, half to herself. 'Wait a moment,' she commanded, then left the room, returning with a white-lace cap, cuffs and apron. She helped Ella with the cuffs, then propelled her to the mirror over the hearth and showed her how to re-pin her hair so that the cap sat well on her head.

Ella, unused to spending any time before a mirror, was quite taken with what she saw. Although there were dark shadows beneath her eyes and the dress was still a little large for her, she had never seen herself looking so smart. To her surprise her eyes filled with tears for the second time in the day.

'Well now,' said Mrs S briskly, 'you'll be wearing this within the month if you do well helping Cook, Mrs Dawson, in the kitchen. The girl who usually fills that role has left and until she is replaced that will be your job. Doris can explain your duties above stairs. At first, you will be cleaning and laying the fires before the family are up and about but, once I have seen how you get on, and whether what was said in your letter holds true, I see no reason why you shouldn't make progress. Now, you've had a long day. Away with you to bed – tomorrow will be here soon enough.'

Ella turned again in her bed, eyeing her dress for the next day, which was dimly visible hanging against the back of the door. She made a conscious effort to stop the merry-go-round of her thoughts, travelling back instead to the family home in Nortonstall, to imagine Beth sleeping soundly in her bed. Was Sarah awake and worrying how her daughter was faring so far away from home? Or had she, too succumbed to slumber, worn out by the demands of her granddaughter Beth, and of Thomas, Annie and Beattie, the rest of the family still at home? In distant contemplation of the tiny room in Nortonstall, that now served as a bedroom to both Sarah and Beth, Ella finally drifted into sleep; alas, not deep and dreamless but restless and disturbed with anxiety about the unknown day ahead.

Chapter Ten

Immersed within a dream in which she was trying to scrub a floor that kept getting bigger and bigger, black-and-white tiles stretching off into the far distance and her bucket of water improbably small for such a task, Ella was aware of someone shaking her. Eyes heavy and gritty, she struggled awake and tried to work out where she was. It took a moment to recognise Doris standing over her in the gloom.

'Come on, up you get. We need to get a move on.'

The chill of the room struck Ella as she swung her feet out of bed and onto the cold floorboards. There was only time to splash her face with the water that Doris had brought up the night before in a china jug: the iciness woke Ella immediately. She gasped and groped blindly for her towel, patting her face with the familiar rough and threadbare fabric. Then she pulled her dress over her head, manoeuvring her nightdress off underneath it, trying to trap as much residual body warmth as possible. Dragging her brush through her hair, she considered herself ready.

Doris looked at her critically. 'You've no need of stays, I

see. That dress is like a sack on you. Did they never feed you at your last job? And Elsie – Cook – will have words to say about your hair. Here, I'll pin it up for you; she'll find you a cap to hide the most of it.'

Ella was suddenly vividly reminded of how her sister Alice, who also suffered from unruly curls, had deftly pinned up her hair for her. A rush of sorrow and homesickness made her sway a little in front of the speckled glass of the mirror and she grasped at the chest of drawers for support.

Doris looked at her with concern. 'You've gone very pale. Are you going to be all right? You've a long day ahead of you, you know?'

Ella nodded, unable to speak.

Doris shook her head and set off down the steep stairs, which led directly from the servants' quarters in the attic to the servants' hallway several flights below. The kitchen, heated by the range overnight, was noticeably warmer. Doris began work at once, showing Ella how to stoke up the range for the morning, before filling great pans with water and setting them to heat.

'We'll be needing water for the whole family for washing, when they get up.' She pointed to the big china jugs, lined up ready for the different family members, plain and severe for Mr Ward, decorated with flowers and bows for the women in the family.

'They've got a bathroom up there, you know,' Doris confided while Ella nodded, uncomprehending. Whatever was a bathroom? 'But the water's never hot enough in the morning so hardly anyone uses it. Mr Ward sometimes does, just to prove it was worth all the expense of putting it in. Never on a winter's morning, though.' Doris chuckled to herself, before showing Ella what she needed to lay out for Mrs Dawson who would be coming down shortly to get the family's breakfast underway.

'Right, upstairs next.' Doris seized the cinder pail, brushes and pans from the scullery. 'There are fires to do in the breakfast room, parlour and library, then while the family are breakfasting you'll need to be up the back stairs to sort out the bedroom fires and the beds.'

Ella's stomach growled with hunger but she knew only too well there'd be nothing to be had for a while yet, until the house was ready for the family to start their day. A glass of water would have to tide her over for now.

Doris laid a warning finger to her lips as she pushed open the heavy door that separated the servants' domain from the main house. Holding the metal pails carefully to avoid any clanking that might wake the family prematurely, Doris led the way. Ella followed then stopped, transfixed. She was standing in what must be the hallway. Wood panelling lined the walls, and those of the main staircase that swept upwards to a vast window, the width of the half-landing and the height of what appeared to be the whole house – Ella couldn't say for sure because it vanished upwards, out of her range of vision. Although it was still early and the gloom had barely lifted outside, she could tell that light would flood in and fill this space once the sun was up. It reminded her of a church window but it was certainly larger than anything she had seen in the Northwaite village church.

Doris was holding open the door on the other side of the hall, making impatient jerking motions with her head.

'You need to get on,' she hissed, as Ella came closer. 'Clean the fireplace in here while I do the one in the parlour. Then

I'll show you the library one while I go down to fetch the water jugs.'

Ella had to stop and stare again when Doris drew back the heavy curtains in the breakfast room. She couldn't help herself. The window looked over the gardens at the back, bleak and stark on a November morning but, again, what a window! It ran nearly the full length of one wall. Ella revolved slowly, taking in the vases of flowers on the tables, the fine polished furniture, and the paintings on the wall. Doris was over by the fireplace, hand on hips, her peaches-and-cream complexion flushed, tapping her foot impatiently.

'Ella, we really haven't got all day.'

Obediently, Ella spread out the cloth that Doris handed her, to protect the fine rug before the hearth, before she set to raking out the ashes and piling them into the pail.

'Not too rough, mind,' Doris warned. 'Here, put the lid over the pail to stop the dust rising. I'll be in the hall when you're done,' and with that she hastened out.

Ella concentrated hard on cleaning out the grate, leaving just a fine sprinkling of ash as she had been taught to do as a base for lighting the new fire. The kindling, paper spills and coal scuttle, filled the night before, were already in place and Ella had prepared and lit the fire in no time. The chimney had a good draw on it, she noticed, as the flames took hold and the wood began to crackle. Adding the coal a little at a time, she sat back on her heels to observe her handiwork. Glancing briefly around the room again, she was hardly able to comprehend the contrast between the cottages she was used to and such a grand room. The ceiling of this one room must be as high as the roof of the cottage she grew up in, she thought to herself as she gathered together the brushes and the pail and folded up the cloth. She arrived in the hallway at the same time as Doris, who stuck her head back into the breakfast room to check on Ella's efforts.

'Well done,' she murmured. 'But you'll need to be quick in the library upstairs. The household will be up and about before long and it wouldn't do for them to see you abroad. We can risk using these stairs just this once, but Mrs S would be furious if she caught us. We're supposed to always use the back stairs.'

Ella followed Doris up the broad polished steps of the main staircase, barely having time to register the view revealed through the great window as dawn broke. A formal garden was spread out below, while beyond the garden wall fields stretched off into the distance. A glimpse, then they were in the dark, panelled corridor and Doris was opening the heavy door of the library, which this time overlooked the front of the house. Doris folded back the panelled shutters from a pair of huge windows to admit the daylight, which revealed several floor-to-ceiling bookcases, with leather-bound volumes on every shelf. Ella, standing in the middle of the room, had the feeling that today was going to be a day of marvels unfolding but, as Doris reminded her, 'there was no time to waste.'

The library fireplace suited the grandeur of the room. Rather than the wooden mantel and decorative tiles of the breakfast room, this fireplace had a more masculine stone hearth and surround. There was still faint warmth in the embers, suggesting to Ella that Mr Ward probably sat up late in here, after the rest of the family were abed. She dealt swiftly with the cleaning and re-laying of the fire and, although she longed to loiter and take a proper look around, she dared not. She was on her way down the main staircase when she met

Doris and Rosa coming up, bearing a china jug of steaming water in each hand as they headed for the bedrooms.

'Hurry,' Doris hissed, whilst Rosa frowned at Ella. 'They'll be getting up any moment now. No one must see you here.'

Back in the kitchen, all was a hive of activity. Ella barely had time to sort out the ashes (some for the roses, the rest of the cinders to be kept for the cinder man), before she was washing her hands in the scullery and helping Cook to prepare the eggs, cold cuts, toast, coffee and tea.

'We need more help,' Doris muttered as she loaded up the trays for Mr Stevens. She had swiftly laid the breakfast table upstairs in a spare five minutes after delivering the hot water. Rosa, as Mrs Ward's lady's maid, remained upstairs a little while longer to help her to dress. Now it was Ella's turn to lay the table downstairs. There was just chance to take tea and bread and jam, perhaps an egg or two if they were lucky, while the family breakfasted – hopefully without summoning them to provide more tea, coffee or toast. Ella found the routine little different so far to a typical morning at the Ottershaws', although without all the young children, but the scale of the house and the formalities to be observed added to the workload.

When she had first arrived, Ella had been sceptical that such a number of servants could be required to run a house of so few people. Now she could see what Doris meant by her heartfelt plea for more help and, as the day progressed with the washing of the breakfast dishes and the immediate commencement of preparations for lunch, Ella felt she had a clearer insight into the workings of the house. Every servant had to know and perform their role like clockwork for the house to function at all. Orchestrated by Mrs S, the household moved through its day. Dirty laundry was sent out, clean laundry counted back in. Food for the evening was ordered by Cook once Mrs Ward had made her decision about the menu. The grocer's boy came to collect the list as, although there was a telephone, another innovation for Ella to marvel at, it was in Mr Ward's study and for his personal use only.

Lunchtime came and went in a blur and Ella was glad to be able to sit down in the afternoon for the hour that Mrs S insisted on to allow her staff a chance to rest, provided there were no visitors and the family didn't need them. It was a chance to talk with Mrs Dawson while she baked, or to do some sewing for the household, but not to do any of the heavy work or cleaning or any other of the myriad duties likely to arise during the course of an average day at Grange House.

Ella was used to long days of hard work. At the Ottershaws' she never stopped from five in the morning until she fell into bed around ten or eleven at night. She supposed the difference was that there she had fulfilled all the roles – cook, maid and nursery maid. As if reading her mind, Mrs Dawson, stirring egg yolks into a custard for the evening dinner, commented 'You'll be finding this very different from your previous employment? I heard you were a maid-of-all-work over near Leeds?'

'Not so close to Leeds,' Ella replied, sewing steadily as she took up the hem of a nightgown, back from the laundry and in need of repair. 'Out in the country, in Nortonstall. Yes, I worked for a family with four small children and you're right, it was hard work. But I'm not sure this isn't harder...'

'You'll get used to it,' Mrs Dawson said. 'It's your first day and there's a lot to learn in a big house like this. And we're short-handed at present. We need a new kitchen or scullery maid then you'll be above stairs, I'll be bound. Doris and Rosa are run off their feet up there. So much for this being a labour-saving house. Mrs Ward was convinced we could manage here with fewer servants, not like the last place in Micklegate.' Mrs Dawson paused and looked at her critically. 'It looks as though a breath of wind could blow you away. Here, have another piece of cake; you need feeding up a bit if you're to have enough strength for the work upstairs.'

She pushed a plate of sponge cake towards Ella and patted her own hips ruefully. 'The curse of the cook – too much sampling of our own food. Who would trust a thin cook, though?' and she chuckled to herself as she strained the custard into a large bowl, the rim patterned with a trellis of roses.

That night, as Ella fell into bed, she barely had a moment to reflect on all the tasks she had accomplished during the day, and all the amazing sights she had seen, before her eyes closed and she was seized by sleep.

Chapter Eleven

It took very little time before Ella stopped feeling like the awkward new girl. Familiar with most of the duties expected from her, after her years spent at the Ottershaws', she was also quick to master anything new. As Mrs Sugden had foretold, she soon found herself drafted in as an upstairs maid in the afternoons, initially to help out when the family had visitors for afternoon tea. She wore the smarter dress, with apron, cap and cuffs, for these occasions. Mrs Ward had nodded approvingly the first time she appeared in it. A glamorous woman, taller than her husband, she kept herself at a distance from her staff. Ella had been introduced to her formally, shortly after arrival, when Mrs Ward had looked her up and down and asked Mrs Sugden whether she was the one whose mother had written. Answered in the affirmative, she had thanked Ella for coming to her husband's aid when his car broke down, then had turned and walked away to signify that their conversation was over.

'I hear from Mrs Sugden that you are doing well,' she said now, as Ella paused with the tea tray to let her precede her into the sitting room. 'I expect we will find plenty of employment for you above stairs.'

So it was to prove. Ella frequently helped out on lunch service, which, taking place as it did under the fierce gaze of Mr Stevens, she initially found terrifying. An affable man at the servants' table, he adopted a very different persona in his role of butler above stairs, where he had status as the key servant in the household. His manner and demeanour, the result of years of experience, led Ella to believe that he was much older than she was, although it became apparent in time that there was barely a ten-year age difference. Aware of his sharp scrutiny, Ella found her hands shaking so much that the serving spoon rattled against the tureen as she went around the table with the vegetables. Some of the serving dishes were so heavy that she longed to rest them just for an instant on the table while a guest deliberated over-long as to whether or not they would take the soup, or dithered over which vegetables to have. Whenever she glanced up, though, she would find Mr Stevens's eyes upon her and she would straighten up and try to remain composed while her shoulders and arms burned with the effort.

One of her favourite roles in the household was spending time with John, the Wards' youngest son, who was a frequent visitor to the kitchen. Only that morning he had appeared, a large book clutched to his chest, and settled himself at the kitchen table.

He was silent for a little while, deeply absorbed as he turned the pages, before he said: 'What sort of bird is this? Where can I see one?'

Ella had paused, broom in hand. 'What do you mean, Master John?'

John stabbed his finger at the page of his book. 'This one. Look.'

Ella peered over John's shoulder at the illustration of a small black-and-white bird, with a preposterous brightly striped beak. It looked ridiculous, quite unlike anything she'd ever seen in the Yorkshire woods and fields of her childhood, or in the back gardens of these houses in York for that matter. She was thankful for the illustration though; the words beneath were a meaningless jumble to her.

'You'd best ask your governess,' Ella said. 'I've no book learning. Miss Gilbert is the one to help you.' She was brisk, sweeping the crumbs from beneath his feet as they dangled from the kitchen chair, but she felt very sorry for him. She ruffled John's hair, poured more milk into his glass and cut him another piece of cake. She knew Mrs Dawson wouldn't begrudge it. 'Such a shame,' she'd confided in Ella, her arms dusted with flour almost up to the elbows as she set about rolling the pastry for an apple tart, 'barely seven years old, and small for his age, and they're talking about sending him to boarding school. Why have the child if you can't be bothered with him, I ask you?' She'd sniffed and wielded the rolling pin more vehemently.

'Now, don't go letting all this cake spoil your appetite for your tea or I'll be in no end of trouble,' Ella warned. 'Why don't you put your books away now and run around outside for a bit? Look – the sun's shining and you could put your coat and scarf on and take your ball?'

Ella knew it was unlikely. John was a solitary boy, an after-thought, his sisters older than him and too pre-occupied with their own affairs to spare the time to entertain him. He spent more time with the servants than with anyone else in the house.

63

John sought out Ella whenever he could. She became used to the door of the kitchen creaking slowly open in the afternoon and John poking his head shyly around it. If he couldn't see Ella, usually to be found sewing or folding laundry, he would ask Doris or Mrs Dawson where 'Lella' was. He seemed determined to use this baby name for her, no matter how many times he was corrected, so eventually everyone let him be. Nor did he pay much heed to his governess, who would appear in the kitchen within five minutes of his arrival, looking cross and requesting that 'Master John should leave the women to their work and come back upstairs at once.'

Each time, Mrs Dawson would say comfortably, 'He's not bothering us, Miss. Why don't you let him be, sit yourself down and have a cup of tea?' Each time, Miss Gilbert would demur and haul John, protesting bitterly, up the stairs. Ella found it upsetting to watch and felt a sense of guilt, as if she had somehow encouraged his presence in the kitchen. Finally, when he appeared for the fourth time within a week, she had the wit to speak before the cook. She poured tea from the big brown pot into one of the fine china cups, pressing the cup and saucer into Miss Gilbert's hands.

'Why don't you take this upstairs and enjoy some peace and quiet in your room?' Ella suggested. 'I can bring John up to you in half an hour or so. We'll use the back stairs. It can be our little secret.' She turned to John. 'Does that sound all right?'

Miss Gilbert needed little further persuasion. The dignity of her position as governess, a cut above the serving staff, was maintained and she was happy enough to hand John over to the care of someone else for a while. Although she was an excellent governess, she was less successful in keeping a small boy, who longed for a playmate, entertained at this stage of the day.

So it became an established routine that John would be found in the kitchen, gravely folding sheets with Ella or, when the weather was fine, out in the garden collecting vegetables for dinner. Ella made a point of keeping him out of sight of the house windows as much as possible, unsure of whether Mr and Mrs Ward would approve of him fraternising with the servants. If Ella was called away to answer a call from the youngest daughter, Grace, or to deliver a tea tray, John would talk politely to Mrs Dawson, his eyes always on the door, waiting for Ella to return.

'I don't know what it is, Ella,' Mrs Dawson marvelled. 'You're more like his mother than –' '– his mother is.' Rosa helpfully filled in, when the cook became stuck for words.

Ella blushed. 'Don't say that. I looked after children in my last employment. I expect I'm just used to being around them. Maybe John recognises this somehow.'

She couldn't bring herself to mention her niece Beth, whom she missed so badly and who was growing up without her being there to see any of it. Every time she thought of her family back in Nortonstall it gave her a pang. She wondered how Beth was getting on, and how her mother was coping with a small and lively grandchild to care for. Reading between the lines of her last letter, which Mr Stevens had kindly read out to her, her mother wasn't as well as she would have Ella believe. Although they were well into springtime now, spending winter in a cold, dank cottage was cruel when you were hale and hearty, and nothing but a feat of endurance if you were ailing. It would be a long while before she had earned enough leave to give her time to travel home to stay the night, and see the true state of things.

She loved spending time with John, but it was also bittersweet – or at least at first. After a month or two, she appreciated it for what it meant to him – a respite from the loneliness of being in a big house with siblings so much older – and for the pleasure it brought to her amidst the routine of her working day.

Miss Gilbert's employment as governess only covered week-days and Saturday mornings, and for the rest of the weekend a young girl, Betsy, from outside the city was engaged to come in and keep John company. However, it soon became apparent that he was devoting his energies to giving her the slip so that he could roam the house and grounds in search of his 'Lella'. As he sat and watched the work going on around him in the kitchen, or trailed around after Ella as she returned laundry to bedrooms, he chattered constantly. They would hear plaintive cries of 'John!' echoing around the house and garden as Betsy, the poor child, as Ella thought of her, searched high and low for her missing charge.

Mr and Mrs Ward seemed to have lost the inclination to involve themselves in John's upbringing. It was as though their older children had exhausted all their parental feelings, leaving none for John at all. As Mr Ward's business had grown, their weekends revolved around entertaining, attending dinners or leaving York to spend the weekends at house parties around the country. When they came across John as they drifted down for a late breakfast or returned after a weekend away, their luggage piled in the hall as they divested themselves of the coats, hats, scarves and gloves that their car journey demanded, and Mrs Ward's perfume wafting around her with her every movement, Mr Ward would bend slightly to ruffle John's hair, murmuring 'All right, son?' as if he had forgotten his name, before heading upstairs to his library and shutting the door. Mrs Ward would crouch down to John's level and look him in the eyes, saying 'Darling! Have you had a lovely weekend? What have you been up to?' before standing up to adjust her hair in the mirror or look through the post, while making absent-minded, although encouraging, noises as though she were listening to his responses.

It upset Ella to see the hurt on his face as his efforts to engage with his parents were ignored, and she would hover as discreetly as possible in the background, waiting to bustle him down to the kitchen for cake, or out into the garden to see the hens that their gardener had introduced into a pen tucked away at the bottom of the kitchen garden, out of earshot of the house. The servants' duties were lighter at the weekends when the Wards went away, so Ella was free to spend more time with John, by common consent. Eventually the older Ward girls, who generally remained at home during their parents' absences, chaperoned by an aunt on the maternal side, remarked that the 'little miss from Tadcaster' was a rather pointless addition to the staff given that John preferred to spend his time with Ella – and so it was that Betsy was quietly let go. Ella took over her role, in addition to her other duties and at no extra pay. She didn't mind though. John had become a substitute for her own family whom she missed so very much.

Chapter Twelve

'Ella, didn't you mention that you were from a village somewhere near Halifax?'

Busy with her own thoughts, Ella was startled to realise that she was being addressed. She had carried the tea tray into the parlour and, as always, was admiring the delicacy of the cups as she poured. The porcelain was so fine, you could almost see your fingers through it. Boughs of painted cherry blossom wreathed each cup, with stripes as blue as a summer sky edging the saucers. Ella paused as she prepared to set the tea cups in front of the visitors.

'Why, yes miss, thereabouts.'

'I have forgotten the name of it. Where was it again?' Grace persisted.

'It was a town, miss, not a village. Nortonstall.' Ella answered cautiously, economical with the truth, not sure that she had divulged these details to Grace previously. She had a sudden premonition of danger. Mr Stevens had told her that Grace had a visitor and that they would both require tea in the parlour, but she had had no inkling as to who the visitor might be. She stole a glance at Grace's friend as she set her cup in front of her. A little older than both Ella and Grace, she was neatly dressed in a restrained, rather than fashionable, manner. She was unmarried, Ella gathered, as she wore no ring on her wedding finger, but Ella could glean nothing else from her appearance.

'Esther, didn't your family live somewhere around there?' Grace turned to her friend, whom Ella was surprised to see looking a little uncomfortable, too, at the line the questioning was taking.

'Very close, in fact. Northwaite.' Esther's tone discouraged further questions but Grace pressed on, as Ella offered milk and sugar, trying to prevent her hands from shaking.

'What a coincidence! Perhaps your paths have crossed in the past? Esther's family, the Weatheralls, owned one of the mills in the area. Where was it that you were working, Ella?'

'At the Ottershaws' in Nortonstall, miss. I think it is very unlikely we would have met.' Ella had no intention of revealing her brief period of employment at Hobbs' Mill in Northwaite, which belonged to the Weatheralls, let alone the fact that she was originally from Northwaite rather than Nortonstall. Her heart was thumping so loudly in her chest she was sure that the two young ladies would hear it, as she edged towards the door. She kept her head down, but even so she was aware of Grace looking at her curiously and it was all she could do not to turn and run. She prayed that Grace wouldn't mention her full name to Esther – if she even knew it – for then Esther would be in no doubt that Ella was the sister of Alice Bancroft, dead nearly seven years and blamed for the fire that had destroyed the Weatherall's mill and caused the death of their eldest son Richard, Esther's brother.

'Thank you, Ella. Actually, would you mind seeing whether

Mrs Dawson has any of her sponge cake left? It's Esther's favourite, isn't it?' said Grace, waving away her friend's protests that the seed cake already served to them was perfect.

Ella was trembling as she pushed through the door into the kitchen. If her background was discovered, her job would be lost and with it the income that her mother and the family so relied upon. Her mind raced, trying to work out the connection between the Weatherall and Ward families. Mr Ward had mentioned some business in the area when she had first encountered him in Nortonstall, with his broken-down motorcar. Was it business on behalf of Mr Weatherall that had brought him to Nortonstall?

'Whatever is the matter with you?' Mrs Dawson asked, as Ella passed on the request for sponge cake. 'You look as though you've seen a ghost. You're as white as a sheet. Sponge cake, indeed: and what's wrong with that nice seed cake, baked just this morning, I might ask? Here, take this up for them. It's yesterday's and not as fresh as what they already have, and I was putting it by for Master John.'

The cook, put in a bad humour by Grace's request, didn't question Ella further but it was with dread that she knocked again at the parlour door. To her great relief, when she entered Mrs Ward was in the room and the conversation had turned from the earlier topic, but Ella was aware of Grace watching her keenly as she set down the sponge cake, offered Mrs Dawson's apologies for it, and asked Mrs Ward whether she, too, would take tea. She was saved from the possibility of further interaction with Grace and Esther by Mrs Ward's refusal, and she was able to take refuge in sorting the returned laundry into piles for the rest of the afternoon, leaving Doris with the job of clearing away the tea things.

Later in the afternoon, Ella was putting neatly folded linen into the chest of drawers in Grace's room, marvelling yet again at the large number of items it was deemed necessary for a young lady of wealth to have. Absorbed in her task, she didn't hear Grace's footsteps until she was almost upon her. The youngest daughter of the house was the only one to bear a resemblance to her mother: tall, with glossy brown hair that always behaved perfectly. She carried herself with a confident air borne out of having been, at least until John was born, the cosseted baby of the family.

Ella whirled round, startled, instantly feeling guilty as though she had been caught out in an act more suspicious than putting away the laundry. Grace was regarding her with an expression that Ella found hard to read; with hindsight, she would have said that it was akin to a cat stalking its prey.

'I had an interesting conversation with Esther this afternoon.' Grace paused and Ella turned back to her task with a sinking heart.

'Yes, I couldn't remember why they had left their mill to come and live in York. I knew it had something to do with the tragic death of Esther's brother Richard. Esther reminded me that he had died in a fire that destroyed the mill. A fire started by one of their ex-employees.' Grace paused for dramatic effect. 'She was called Alice Bancroft. Isn't that your name, Ella? Ella Bancroft? Are there many Bancrofts in the area that you come from? Was she a relative of yours?'

Ella felt as though iced water was being poured slowly through her veins. She started to shiver, before slowly pushing the full linen drawer closed and turning back to face Grace.

'She was my sister...' Ella spoke barely above a whisper.

There was a long pause. Ella raised her gaze to meet Grace's. The room was very quiet; she was conscious of the crackle of the fire in the bedroom grate, the slow tick of the bedroom clock, the faint 'clip-clop' of a horse's hooves passing along the road outside. Grace's dark-brown eyes held Ella's gaze; was there the faintest hint of triumph in her expression?

'I see...' Grace said slowly. She turned away from Ella and went to look out of the window. 'You realise what this will mean if I tell Father?'

Ella nodded, mutely. She had seized on the word 'if' rather than 'when', and a small flicker of hope was born. Did Grace mean that she would be prepared to protect her secret?

Grace pressed on, either unaware of Ella's acquiescence, or unconcerned by it.

'It is clear to everyone how fond John is of you. Mother is always commenting on it. I would be sad to see you go and I know John would be, too. But Father would be furious to know that we were harbouring the sister of a common criminal under our roof. Not just a –' Grace searched for the right words, '– a run-of-the-mill crime, either. But murder, and the murder of the son of a family friend.'

She swung round suddenly to look at Ella. 'What did you hope to gain by your employment here?'

'It wasn't like that, miss.' Ella, stung by her words, could contain herself no longer. 'And I would never have sought employment here if I had known of any connection with Northwaite.'

Ella subsided, defeated by the enormity of what was happening. She would have to return to Nortonstall and tell her mother that she had now failed twice in her employment and had left without references from either of them. Grace, however, hadn't finished. She turned back to look out of the window.

'Perhaps we can be of use to each other? If I keep your secret from Father, perhaps you might be of service to me in due course? I think I will ask whether I may have you as my lady's maid. You will need to remember, of course, that I bear a risk in not revealing your history.' A thought seemed to strike Grace and she turned sharply from the window. 'Heavens, could it be possible that you might murder us all in our beds?'

Ella opened her mouth to speak, but no words came out. She sensed Grace's critical regard upon her.

'No, I think we are quite safe. You do not seem to have a violent nature.' Grace paused. 'Let no more be said. It is as if Esther had never spoken. She has no inkling of the situation, and let it be so with everyone else. Only you and I know the truth. It will be our secret.'

As Grace spoke she gave Ella an encouraging pat on the shoulder. Ella shrank away from her touch, then hoped that Grace hadn't noticed her reaction. She couldn't afford to antagonise her. As Grace turned and left the room, Ella's thoughts raced. Whatever assumptions Grace may have made, she didn't know the truth. She only knew who had been blamed for the fire, which wasn't the same thing at all. It was quite possible that the only people who were in possession of the truth were dead. In the midst of her distress Ella felt a flash of sympathy for Esther. She, too, was still living with the sadness of the death of a sibling. She, too, had been horribly reminded of it today, by Grace.

Chapter Thirteen

'So, you will do it for me?' Grace's voice was hushed and urgent.

Dressed in her high-necked white nightgown, she was gazing at Ella's reflection in the mirror while she brushed out her hair before bed. Ella was bemused. Grace's proposal had taken her by surprise.

Edith, Grace's eldest sister, was engaged to be married, and as a result she'd moved up a notch in the world, her visits to fashion houses and jewellers having taken on an air of even greater importance now that she was preparing for her wedding and her future. Grace was envious of the status her sister had acquired and had taken it into her head that she had to be next. She considered Ailsa, her older sister, currently visiting relatives in Edinburgh, to be no great beauty and thought she was unlikely to captivate a suitor anytime soon. Grace, however, had her sights very firmly set on Edgar Broughton, the son of a baronet, handsome and debonair. Despite her best efforts, Grace had as yet failed to do more than engage him in light and polite conversation at the various social events of the season. To her chagrin, she had been unable to even elicit the promise of a dance from him at the recent ball at her aunt's house in London's Manchester Square.

However, Edgar Broughton and his father were due to visit the Ward household, staying overnight in York on the way to their family seat in Northumberland for Christmas. Grace had decided that this was her best chance of winning Edgar Broughton's heart, and she wanted Ella's help to do so.

Ella regretted that, early in her first year of employment at Grange House, before she had learnt the importance of keeping her distance, she had mentioned something of her background to Grace. Mistaking their similarity in age as a possible affinity, she had told Grace about her mother Sarah's prowess as a herbalist, and how her custom had dwindled over recent years. She hadn't chosen to elaborate on why, but she had let slip that the family were reliant on what little money Ella could send them to survive. Grace's attention had been caught.

'A herbalist? She made potions?'

'Medicines, really.' Ella corrected her. 'I suppose you might call them potions because of the way they were made. We grew the herbs in our garden, or Alice would collect them from special places in the woods.'

Ella bit her lip, regretting mentioning her sister Alice in front of Grace. Grace, however, had other things on her mind.

'Which herbs? Which potions were the most popular?'

Ella tried hard to explain that the medicines were individually tailored to people's needs, and that the constituent herbs would differ.

'Did you learn how to do this?' Grace demanded.

Ella hesitated again, torn between the truth and embellishing her abilities. She had, after all, watched Sarah at work many times.

'Yes, I know some of the basic methods,' Ella had replied and had thought very little more about it until that very evening, several months later, when out of the blue Grace had proposed, nay demanded, that Ella should make her a love potion. Her plan was to slip a few drops into Edgar Broughton's drink so that he would be helpless, captivated by her charms.

Ella, unfamiliar with the popular novels of the day, much loved by Grace and girls of her generation with time on their hands, couldn't imagine where she could have come by such an idea.

'These medicines are designed to cure illness, Miss Grace,' she said, gathering up the stockings and petticoats that her mistress had discarded on the floor. 'They are not meant to be employed to bend someone to your will.'

'Oh Ella, it's just a bit of fun. And anyway, some would say that love *is* a sickness. True, Edgar doesn't suffer from it as yet, so maybe you can make me something that will *create* a sickness, rather than cure it?'

Grace was pressing her with some urgency. Edgar Broughton was due to arrive within a few days, and Grace was prepared to exert some leverage to get her way.

'Ella, I wouldn't like to have to tell Father about the actions of your sister, and about the disrepute that she brought your family into. I hesitate to remind you about my charity towards you over Esther Weatherall. But it would reflect very badly on me if it became known that I had preserved your reputation and risked that of our own family.'

Ella was confused by Grace's reasoning. Surely if her father knew that his daughter was hiding things from him, she would be in deep trouble? There could be no mistaking the threat implicit in her words, however, and Ella had not put the earlier request out of her mind entirely. She had resolved that, if it became unavoidable, she could, with the aid of a mixture of liquorice water and a few drops of harmless oils, produce a potion that would satisfy Grace: one suitably dark and mysterious in appearance to convince her that it was capable of a type of sorcery.

Ella realised that Grace was watching her, reflected in the mirror, and waiting for an answer. Although the two girls were of a similar age, there the resemblance ended. Grace had a healthy sheen about her, the result of years of a good diet, plenty of rest and loving attention paid to her skin and hair. Ella, although she had filled out a little over the last few months, looked pale and not a little tired; she had been on her feet since dawn and despite her best efforts to maintain her appearance, she noticed that her hair was beginning to tumble loose from her cap, her collar was awry and her cuffs were no longer pristine.

Resisting the urge to adjust these things in a mirror that wasn't her own she said, 'I will do my best to help you,' and laid the hairbrush down on the dark wood of the dressing table. The hairs caught in the bristles gave her an idea.

'I'll need to take a few of these,' she said, 'something that is a part of you, to blend into the mixture.' She was beginning to warm to the idea of herself as some kind of sorceress and she pushed out of her mind the thought of what her own mother would say to such nonsense. Sarah need never know, and if it would satisfy Grace, and above all keep her own job safe, then there was no harm in it, was there?

Chapter Fourteen

So it was that she'd given in to Grace's demands, and made her the love potion she so desperately desired. Ella had risen very early the next morning, long before she had needed to set about her usual duties, clearing the fireplaces and laying the fires to warm the rooms for the still-sleeping household. Creeping down the stairs, she'd prayed fervently that her hurried dressing hadn't roused Doris sufficiently to wake her. Doris had murmured in her sleep and flung her arm back, then turned on her side and seemed to settle as Ella silently opened the door.

She tiptoed in stockinged feet down the stairs, only pausing to lace on her boots when she reached the chilly flagstones of the kitchen. It had been bitterly cold overnight, frost sprinkling the whole of the garden so that it looked as though it had been lightly dusted with snow. It would look magical as the sun rose, but Ella couldn't afford to wait for that moment. Instead, she moved swiftly around the kitchen, setting water to boil on the stove before extracting a couple of twiggy sticks of liquorice root from her pocket and crushing them with the heavy pestle and mortar that sat permanently in the back kitchen. She poured a little water over the crushed root, added a couple of drops of vanilla extract from the big brown bottle in the larder, stirred in some sugar and cast around for anything else that might be suitable to add. She counted out four drops of oil of cloves, before taking a teaspoon and tasting the hot liquid. Grimacing, she'd added more sugar.

The sun's rays were creeping up over the chill blue of the horizon as Ella strained the liquid over the stone sink. She poured it into a jug, then into a couple of small bottles, purchased with this in mind from the apothecary in the market on one of her forays into town. She tucked the bottles into the pocket of her apron before she set about erasing all traces of her early morning activity. Only too aware that the kitchen was probably filled with the aroma of her brew, she opened the heavy kitchen door into the garden, gasping at the shock of the cold air as it rushed in.

Ella set more hot water to boil, so that no one would have cause to comment on the heat of the pot, then bent down to stroke the kitchen cat as it wound around her legs. Hearing the heavy bolts of the kitchen door drawn back it had hurried across the garden, desperate to be inside away from the bitter cold and eager at the prospect of a little milk.

'What are you doing?'

Ella straightened up guiltily, cheeks instantly aflame and heart pounding.

'You know I don't like that cat in here.' It was Mrs Dawson. Ella knew her words to be untrue; she had seen the cook sneaking a fish head or leftovers from the dinner table to the cat on more than one occasion.

'It was so frosty out there, I felt sorry for her,' Ella said, glad to keep the focus on the cat and away from her exploits in the kitchen.

Mrs Dawson glanced out of the window. 'I knew when the berries followed on so close to the harvest that we were in for a hard winter,' she said. 'Now, for heaven's sake, were you born in a barn? Close that door and get on with those fires upstairs. We need to get them going early today, with the rooms so cold.'

Ella, arming herself with a shovel, a brush and the cinder pail for the ashes, was grateful to slip away, taking care as she did so not to let the bottles chink against each other in her pocket. As she turned to close the door into the passageway behind her, she saw the cook stoop to stroke the cat.

'A little milk for madam?' Ella heard her say, as she pulled the door softly closed.

So this was Grace's love potion: the bottles were unstoppered and left to cool on the windowsill after Doris had risen, when Ella had returned upstairs to remove the apron she wore for household duties before she went to help Grace with her morning toilette.

She had handed one of the bottles over to Grace that evening, reminding her in a whisper to add only two or three drops to a drink. Ella saved the other in case she was asked to provide further supplies. Edgar Broughton was due to visit the following night and Ella anticipated that it was by no means certain that her love potion would have any guarantee of working.

These actions, just a few short days ago, must be the cause of her incarceration now, Ella reasoned. If only she could turn back the clock. If only she hadn't felt pressured to submit to Grace's request. Something that she had told herself was just a bit of girlish fun on Grace's part was already proving to have far-reaching consequences.

Chapter Fifteen

When Mr Ward finally summoned Ella from her room again, it was Boxing Day evening. The fire had burnt low in the library where he was sitting alone, a half-empty decanter and glass set in front of him as witness to many hours spent in deliberation.

'I will get straight to the point, Ella. You are in very serious trouble.' He paused.

Ella's heart was beating fast. What exactly was she going to be accused of?

He continued. 'I have tried hard to comprehend how this could be, as I consider myself a good judge of character, but I have to accept that the trust I had in you was misplaced. I can only believe that your character must have been tainted by the wickedness of your sister.'

Ella was stunned. Surely Mr Ward had no knowledge of her sister? Whatever it was that he was referring to could only have been divulged by Grace.

Mr Ward continued, 'Edgar Broughton, whilst a guest under our roof, has suffered a serious misfortune; one so grave that he may not recover. My understanding is that this is entirely due to poison that you have chosen to administer to him, for reasons that remain unclear to me.'

Ella's legs felt as though they might buckle, her hands were shaking and she couldn't seem to get her thoughts straight.

'Well, what do you have to say for yourself?' Mr Ward was short-tempered, his Christmas spoilt by this unpleasantness, which he had been bracing himself to deal with.

Ella took a deep breath, but even so there was still a quiver in her voice. Would he read it as a sign of guilt?

'I admit I prepared a draught, but it was harmless, sir. Just a mixture of liquorice water, herbs and oil of cloves. There was no poison.'

Grace had clearly played down her own role in the affair. Would it do Ella any good to try to convince Mr Ward of the truth? She thought rapidly, then realised with a sinking heart that the odds were stacked against her. The testimony of a servant – a girl from a 'bad' family at that – could never outweigh the word of the daughter of the house. Her family's experience when Alice had been so wrongly accused – thrown into jail no less – had taught her the futility of trying.

There was a pause. 'I wish I could believe you but the evidence is plain enough. I will have to refer this to the magistrate and I think, Ella, that you must expect a custodial sentence of several years, despite your previous good character.'

Ella drove her fingernails into the palms of her clenched fists and willed herself to stay standing, even though she felt on the verge of collapse. She would not show herself weak, give him the satisfaction of seeing tears, and beg his forgiveness.

'You have made a mistake, sir,' she said, trying to sound calm and not defiant.

'Then that is for others to decide.'

This was a double injustice and one she could see no way of resolving. The only consolation, if one was to be found in this sorry affair, was that Mr Ward looked unutterably sad as he spoke. He sighed, turned away from Ella and gazed into the fire as he spoke again.

'Go back to your room. You will wait there until I have summoned the constable, but you should pack your things. And do not speak to any of the other servants. Nor to anyone else in the household,' he added, as an afterthought.

PART TWO

1903–1904

Chapter Sixteen

The carriage rolled away, leaving York on the Tadcaster Road – and thus Ella was spared a last agonising view of the city that had so enthralled her when she arrived. She was huddled in her seat, exhausted, her belongings on her lap, wrapped once again in a shawl. This time, she wore Mrs Sugden's coat for her journey, pressed on her when she had tried to return it early that morning.

'My dear, you only have to take one look at me to know that it will never fit me again. I hope it brings you more luck than your stay in this house has done.' Mrs S had sighed and Ella, startled at being addressed as 'my dear' was sure that she caught the glimmer of tears in the housekeeper's eyes.

Mrs Sugden hadn't sought to lower her voice in front of the other servants and Ella's own eyes welled up as she remembered how they had each come forward in turn, pressed her hands and offered comforting words. Doris and Rosa were crying, and Doris had pressed a package bound up with string into Ella's hands.

'It's just a dress of mine. I've no use for it: I've rather

outgrown it, to be honest, and now you've filled out a bit I hope it will fit. Oh, Ella, you sent all of your money home and never thought to spend it on yourself. You can't go home taking only the clothes you arrived with. You deserve better than that, no matter what is supposed to have passed.'

Mr Stevens was the last to speak to her and Ella feared a scolding, or a frosty farewell. Instead, he grasped her hand in both of his and squeezed it.

'Go home with your head held high,' he said. 'You have worked hard for this family and this household. I hope time will show what has happened here to be naught but a misunderstanding.'

Then word came that the carriage was waiting. None of the family was to be seen as Ella, escorted by Mr Stevens, left by the side gate.

The leaden sky was heavy with further snow yet to fall and there were few people out and about in the streets. Those that were hastened about their business, shoulders hunched against the bitter wind as it spread its chill across Knavesmire.

All Ella could see as she thought back to her departure was the startling sight of Albert's face, glimpsed as he had passed through the gate of Grange House at the very same moment that she was being handed into the waiting carriage by Mr Stevens.

She had been too stunned at seeing him there to react. For Albert's part, his expression of astonishment at seeing Ella had turned into one of bewilderment when she didn't speak to him; in fact, she had turned her head away from him and cast her eyes down. It was over in an instant and she was in her seat, thankful that there were no other passengers as yet, and no need to make polite conversation. She could sink back into her thoughts, uninterrupted. Yet, as the coach driver clicked his tongue at the horses to 'walk on', she couldn't forego one last glance back. Her gaze swept the scene, from the snowy drive up to the front windows where, she was sure, she glimpsed John. Was that a ghostly face, and a swirl of Miss Gilbert's dress, as he vanished from the window of the nursery? Was that Grace, too, a shadowy presence at the window of the parlour, dark hair framing a drawn, pale face? Then her gaze rested on Albert, deep in conversation with Mr Stevens, who appeared to be trying to shepherd him towards the front door. Albert resisted, turning back towards the carriage, a view framed through the narrow back window as it pulled away.

Hours passed in the carriage, inhospitable on this winter's day with just a blanket supplied by the coachman to keep her warm. It became apparent very early on that there would be no more passengers. The luxury of such privacy was lost on Ella; nor did she reflect on why Mr Ward might have gone to such an expense, nor why the carriage was conveying her home rather than to prison. Her thoughts were bound to another treadmill, one which took her ceaselessly over the events of the past few days and stopped at the prospect of what lay ahead, without her being able to form any resolution as to the future or reach any understanding about the past. Her thoughts reached the end of their path, the projected arrival at her mother's front door in Nortonstall, and then returned her right back to the start of the process, which saw her reliving Mr Ward's accusation in the library. No matter how many times her thoughts undertook the journey, she was neither more nor less angry, or upset, or embarrassed. She was numb, as impervious to the relentless repetition of her thoughts as she was to the cold of the coach, and the increasingly inclement weather outside. As the landscape grew bleaker in the fading light, thoughts as to whether or not she would be prevented from reaching her destination by the falling snow or, indeed, the snow banked high on either side of the roadway, didn't trouble Ella. When they stopped, she had to be urged from the coach by the driver, eager himself for the warmth of the inn and a plate of food beside a warm fire before the journey recommenced. Ella sat as silent in the corner of the inn as she had in the carriage, and it was only the repeated anxious enquiries as to her wellbeing by the landlady that persuaded her to take some soup and bread, if only to prevent further attention being drawn to herself.

Finally, when the horses clattered into the familiar streets of Nortonstall, Ella roused herself from her reverie. She was stiff from the time spent sitting in the same spot as the coach jolted over rough roads and the heavy blanket hadn't prevented her teeth from starting to chatter from the cold. Yet on reaching Nortonstall it was as if she was finally galvanised into action. With some difficulty, she caught the driver's attention, requesting to be set down near the bridge in the centre of town. He was doubtful.

'I have orders to see you to your door, miss.'

'The road from here is steep, and no doubt icy. Your horses are tired and may not get through.' She was amazed to hear the strength of her own voice after what seemed like hours, if not days, of mostly solitary company. How easily the lie rolled off her tongue! She doubted there would be any difficulty in reaching the house, but she did not want her mother disturbed by her arrival, the unusual sound of horses after dark no doubt bringing neighbours to windows and setting tongues wagging. Ella wanted to slink home like a cat in the night, to lick her wounds in the privacy of home before she could face venturing out with a story at the ready to satisfy the curious.

The coach driver, more than happy to avoid undertaking a journey that might in any way prove challenging, and eager to be on his way before the weather took a turn for the worse, needed little persuasion.

Ella stood for a moment in the dark street, watching the lamp at the back of the coach until it was just a faint glimmer in the darkness. She sniffed the air, the clean bitter chill of it striking her nostrils along with the scent of wood smoke and the tang of the green dampness of the river. On top of it was a familiar smell that seemed to roll in from the distant, invisible moors high on the surrounding hills no doubt freshly overlaid with snow. For the first time in days, Ella smiled. She felt the tension in her shoulders relax. Suddenly, being home with her family seemed like a much better prospect than it had done throughout the journey, and the preceding days.

As Ella stood on the doorstep and knocked at the door, before pushing it open and startling Sarah, who had been deep in thought by the fire, it felt like she had been away for far too long.

'Ella!' It had taken Sarah a few moments to gather her wits and work out who was standing in her sitting room. 'You're home for a visit! You should have let me know you were coming! I would have...' Sarah tailed off, not quite sure what she would have done but overcome with happiness all the same. Beth, who had been napping, peeped out wide-eyed from behind her skirts.

'Yes, home for a visit.' Ella felt her smile, so newly formed, develop into a beam. There would be no need for explanations beyond that for this evening. And there was so much catching up to be done.

Chapter Seventeen

By the time that Thomas, Annie and Beattie came through the door, heavily muffled against the cold, the room was filled with the aroma of the stew that was gently bubbling on the range which seemed to take up most of the tiny kitchen. The small scale of the house had unsettled Ella at first. Without realising it, she had grown accustomed to the grand rooms of Grange House. The high ceilings, fireplaces and windows now seemed vast in comparison to this tiny space. Ella found herself wondering how they were all going to fit in the house overnight; Thomas and Annie in particular had grown so tall since she had last seen them. Now aged eighteen, Thomas had become a man while sixteen-year-old Annie had blossomed into a young woman. The thought was but a fleeting one, for the excitement her appearance had caused was infectious and soon everyone was talking nineteen-to-the-dozen, questions and answers flying between Ella and her siblings.

'Why are you here?' 'How long can you stay?' 'Will you listen to me sing?' 'How big you have grown!' No one seemed to pause long enough to take in the answer they had been given and eventually Sarah could bear the cacophony no longer. She clapped her hands over her ears.

'Stop!' The chatter died. 'Let's eat. And let's try to talk to each other nicely while we do. No, you sit down, Ella. Thomas and Annie, set up the table. Beattie, fetch the spoons and a knife for the bread. Beth, you sit over by the fire with Ella until we're ready.'

And with that the table was set up, almost filling the tiny sitting room, leaving just enough space around it for chairs and stools. Beth, who had shown no sign of wanting to be parted from Ella since she had arrived, sat on Ella's knee, leaning her head back to rest it under Ella's chin, and observed the proceedings solemnly, sucking her thumb. Ella could tell she was tired, and thought she must be falling asleep in the warmth of the fire until she removed her thumb and tipped her head back to look up at Ella's face.

'Are you my mummy's sister too?'

Sarah heard, and glanced apologetically at Ella.

'She's been asking a good deal about Alice. Trying to understand where her mummy is and where she fits into the family. Because you've been away, I've been trying to talk about you as well as about Alice. I think she links the two of you together.'

Ella suddenly felt an acute sense of Alice's loss. How different might the evening's gathering have been if Alice were still alive? If she hadn't died in prison before she could even be tried, languishing sick and alone and denied all access to her family, her baby. If the clock could be turned back, maybe the mill would still be open and maybe Alice would be working there too, with Ella. They would still have been living in Northwaite, at Lane End Cottage, with their garden and fields all around, not squeezed into this tiny house in

94

Nortonstall with nothing but a yard to speak of. And there would have been two lots of full-time wages, not just the one... Ella drew in her breath. Not even just the one now...

Sarah glanced sharply at her.

'Come and eat. I expect you've had nothing since morning. If I'd known you'd be here I would have made something special. Instead, it's just our usual weekday stew.'

Once Ella was wedged in amongst the others around the table, the talk turned to the New Year. Ella felt a pang. She was sure there would be celebrations at Grange House. A party perhaps? She'd never felt less like celebrating in her life, although spending this evening with her much-missed family was going some way to making up for the loss of her Christmas to incarceration.

The evening sped by in a whirl of chatter and catching up on news. Bedtime was long past when Sarah finally lifted a sleeping Beth off the armchair and carried her up the steep staircase, hidden behind a door next to the fireplace.

'The rest of you can be getting yourselves ready, too,' Sarah warned. 'Ella, you can take my bed and I'll make up a bed down here.'

But Ella wouldn't hear of it. She could see how worn Sarah looked, and she herself was more than ready for sleep. The events of the last few days had taken it out of her.

As she gazed into the glow of the fire's embers, eyelids drooping, feeling very cosy under the quilt that her mother had insisted she should have from the bed, she reflected that it was perhaps no bad thing she was home for a bit. Sarah looked in need of a break, and the one good thing about Ella's enforced return was that she was going to be able to provide that respite.

Chapter Eighteen

Several days passed before Sarah brought herself to broach a subject that had been bothering her.

'Ella, it's lovely to have you here and I know that Beth, for one, won't want to see you go. But aren't you needed back in York by now?'

Ella stalled, playing for time. 'No, I'm not expected back yet.'

Sarah, hands deep in flour as she prepared pastry for the pie intended to eke out their few remaining vegetables, persisted.

'There's something wrong, isn't there? You would never be allowed so much time off.'

Ella had blocked out all thoughts as to how she would explain her dismissal to Sarah. Now there seemed to be no option but to tell the truth.

'I've been dismissed.'

'Ella!' Sarah pulled her hands from the mixing bowl and wiped them on her apron. 'Why didn't you tell me? What happened? It wasn't... the master?' She sat down suddenly on the kitchen chair.

Ella was uncomprehending for a moment. 'You mean Mr Ward? No.' She gave a wry smile. 'No, not that.' She sighed. 'I was foolish. I helped his daughter with an... enterprise. It went wrong somehow. I got the blame.'

'Oh, Ella. What enterprise do you mean? Whatever happened?'

Ella took a deep breath and explained: how she thought she might make a friend of Grace at first, then the unforeseen coincidence of Grace's friendship with Esther Weatherall, the sister of Richard. How Grace had made the connection between Ella, her family, the tragedy at the mill and the Weatheralls, and used her knowledge as leverage to persuade Ella to make her a love potion.

'Love potion!' Sarah interrupted. 'Whatever do you know of the making of love potions?'

'It was an idle boast.' Ella was penitent. 'I pretended to know more of herbalism than I do. Grace seized on the idea of making this potion and wouldn't be dissuaded.'

Sarah was angry now. 'It goes against everything that the practice of herbalism represents. Whatever were you thinking of, Ella?' Pink in the face, her mother was pacing the floor, shaking her head every so often as Ella spoke.

'I know. I'm sorry. It was foolish of me. But truly, it was harmless. Just water, crushed liquorice root for colour, vanilla extract, a bit of sugar, some oil of cloves...' Ella tailed off. 'Yet, somehow it made the object of Grace's affections very ill. I don't know why.'

Sarah looked grave. 'Do you know the nature of his illness?'

'He was poisoned by it – near death, I believe. He was only a young man.' Ella looked stricken. She'd had plenty of time to consider the consequences of her actions, and she found them truly horrifying.

'Ella, remedies are not to be trifled with by someone with no knowledge of them. They have powerful properties. Liquorice root can cause a rapid heartbeat in those who are over-susceptible to it. It sounds as though your mistress may have overdone the dosage. But I don't know whether it could cause someone to die…'

Ella had only half taken this in. Her thoughts raced on. 'The worst of it is, it means… no wages. How are we to support ourselves? I know that Thomas and Annie are apprenticed but they barely bring in a wage between them. Now that you know the truth, I will try to find other work. I fear, though, that with two jobs lost and no reference to be had, I will not be a good prospect as an employee.'

Sarah and Ella considered the situation for a few minutes in silence, then Sarah returned to her pastry preparation, changing the subject to give her time to think.

'Will you chop the vegetables for me?' she asked. 'We will need to add more, though. If you take Beth and go up Pinfold Lane until you reach the field, I think you might find there are turnips to be had there.'

Ella was glad to escape out into the winter sunshine and Beth, too, was delighted. She clutched Ella's hand and chattered all the way along the lane, past the row of cottages where a couple of women were sweeping their front steps. They stopped to smile at Beth, and wish Ella a 'good morning' as they passed by. Ella knew that if she looked back, they would be leaning on their brooms, watching her curiously, questioning each other.

'Isn't that Sarah's youngest? Who's that with her?'

'Looks like Ella. The eldest now, isn't she? Thought she had gone to York to work. Wonder what she's doing back here?'

Any unpleasant thoughts were banished on reaching the field. Despite the stripped brown earth and bare hedgerows, Ella could picture it exactly as it would be in spring, the hedges clothed in green and the ground sprouting the first crops. She had roamed these fields once and had a sudden wish to do so again, to lose herself in the folds of the valleys and forget all about York and what had happened there.

'What are we looking for?' Beth looked expectantly up at Ella, who realised she had been standing at the gate, lost in thought, while the pale winter sun had slipped behind gathering clouds. Beth was shivering.

'Vegetables. Maybe the farmer left some behind when they ploughed the field. We're going to search the field edges. Here, I'll help you climb over.'

Ella was over the gate in a flash, then turned to lift Beth as she teetered near the top. The hunt for food soon turned into a game, and Beth warmed up again from running backwards and forwards. After half an hour, the sky threatened rain so Ella announced it was time to go home. The basket held but three turnips, wizened and blackened from their time overwintering at the edge of the field.

They trudged back, heads down against the wind, which had a bitter edge to it.

'More snow on the way, I think,' said Sarah as Ella, with numb fingers, peeled and chopped their finds to add to the pie. And nothing more was said that day about York, money or finding work for Ella.

Chapter Nineteen

'We're moving.' Sarah announced it flatly over their evening meal, one night at the end of January.

'Moving?' Ella was startled. The others said nothing.

'The rent here is too high. I've found somewhere that costs less but has more space, including a garden. I can grow plants to start making remedies again. People have been asking me for them.' Sarah looked more animated than Ella had seen her all the time she had been at home.

'But where?' Ella felt guilty. She should have found work, no matter how menial, so that Sarah hadn't been forced into this position.

'It's over Luddenden way. I know it's further out, but I'll be able to come to market and sell my remedies there. And there's others travel to school and work in Nortonstall from there.' Sarah turned to Thomas, Annie and Beattie. 'So you'll have company on the walk.'

Their despondent faces said it all, but the privations of the last few years had taught them well. Ella's sense of guilt only increased. She had let them all down.

Within the week, their meagre belongings were loaded onto

a cart for the journey of just a few miles. Ella was thankful that the weather was kind: cold, but bright. The family's mood was low enough without the added cruelty of their possessions being soaked. Only Sarah's mood was buoyant. She chatted cheerfully to neighbours who came out, full of curiosity, to wish them well. Ella kept her head down, conscious of a sense of shame shared by all the children except for Beth, who was too young to fully understand what was going on.

'I'll be in the market within the month,' Ella heard Sarah say. 'I'll see you then.' And they were away, not one of them looking back as the cart took the road out of town, travelling straight for two or three miles before climbing up into the hills.

'There's a track over the top, back to Nortonstall.' Sarah pointed it out to her family. 'You'll be able to take that as a short cut rather than use the road. And here we are.'

The cart stopped outside a cottage fronting one of the only two roads in the village. Sarah had the heavy door key in her pocket and Annie, Beattie and Beth, suddenly excited, ran in to explore while Thomas, befitting his greater age, strolled in after them.

Ella lingered outside. There was a stream rushing below in a deep cutting that divided the village and a squat, strongly built church sat where the bank levelled out. It was peaceful, surrounded by hillsides and woods waiting to cast off their winter shroud. She felt her shoulders release. Perhaps this would be a good move? They could all make a fresh start here, even if it was but five miles from Nortonstall. Her reverie was disturbed as all the children burst back out through the door.

'Come and see! We have a garden!' This from Beattie.

'I have a room! And so do you!' from Thomas.

'There are hens next door,' from Annie.

'There's a hedge!' cried Beth, not to be outdone. The others stared at her, then started to laugh. Ella gave them a warning look.

'A hedge? Then we shall have nests to watch in the spring. Come and show me.' And she slipped her hand into Beth's and ushered everyone back inside to share their discoveries, leaving the carter to unload their boxes unhindered.

Chapter Twenty

The nest was low in the hedge. It was perfectly formed, woven from dried grasses and lined with downy feathers, which cushioned five of the palest blue eggs, spotted with brown. Ella held her fingers to her lips to hush Beth, then lifted her up to see, parting the foliage so they could peep in when she was sure the linnets were away. She'd spotted the male first, his throat flushed crimson, trilling from the top of the hawthorn bush nearby. It wasn't long before she'd realised there was a pair, the streaky brown female already nest-building, even though the weather bore only the faintest hint of spring. She'd delayed telling Beth of what she had seen, fearful that she wouldn't be able to contain her curiosity and would end up scaring the birds away. Once the eggs were laid, though, she felt sure they would stay.

Ella found it hard to believe it was April already. Time had flown by since the move. The first days had been taken up with cleaning and setting the place to rights, unpacking their boxes and making the unfamiliar rooms feel like a home. The weather had been kind and Thomas and Annie had got used to the walk over the moor back to Nortonstall, with Beattie tagging along in the mornings to go to school. Then Sarah had turned her attention to making some simple remedies that she could take to the Saturday market to sell; treatments that didn't rely on a diagnosis. Soothing skin creams, rinses for the hair, potions that could be easily made from the dried herbs that she still had stored away. She planned to plant up herb beds in the meantime so that by summer she would have fresh supplies growing in the garden and could go back to prescribing remedies.

At first, Ella felt useless. She didn't have the knowledge to help Sarah make the creams and although she did her best to work in the garden, it wasn't long before Sarah said kindly, 'Why don't you keep an eye on Beth for me? And then maybe you could make a start on preparing the vegetables for dinner?' Ella knew that Alice would have been far more useful to her mother. And that come the spring, she would have been out searching for the plants that they needed. Ella had no idea how to go about recognising them, let alone where to look. She had no work, no money and she was of no practical use.

Sarah sensed her distress and went to great lengths to reassure her.

'Ella, I couldn't do any of this without your help. Who would mind Beth when I go to market? Who would be there to make sure Beattie is doing her schoolwork? Who would be giving me a hand around the house every day so that I have enough free time to make all the things to take to market?'

Ella had tried hard to be cheered, but as Sarah layered shawls over her clothes in preparation for a Saturday in the spring chill of the market, taking a less-than-willing Thomas with her to carry the goods, she could only feel a sense of failure at her inability to provide for the family. Now everyone apart from Beattie and Beth were making some sort of a contribution to the family purse.

Each week Sarah returned with only a few things sold, her enthusiasm seemingly undimmed. 'It will pick up. It takes time to establish an enterprise. People will try something out and come back when they see that it works,' she said.

One Saturday evening, as Ella pondered the unsold bottles and jars set out on the kitchen table, she was seized by a thought.

'Is there anything here that sets you apart?' she asked.

Sarah looked puzzled. 'I'm not sure what you mean. I'm the only person in the market selling such things.'

Ella turned a bottle between her fingers. 'Even so, there's nothing here to remind them of who you are, of what it is that they should come back for. You need labels: not just with the names but something to catch the eye, something that has your name on it.'

'Oh, I don't think we need to go to such trouble.' Sarah was dismissive. 'It's what's inside the bottle that counts.'

'I have an idea though. Would you let me try something? If it makes no difference, then there's nothing lost.'

Sarah shrugged, suddenly weary from being on her feet all day in the market. 'Whatever you think. I'm happy to be guided by you.'

Ella sensed that her mother was a little put out that she had questioned whether the potions would sell on the strength of their benefits alone, but she decided to press on regardless. She worked late into the evenings, long after the others had gone to bed, painting trailing stems and scrolling leaves around the edge of the labels that were tied to each bottle's neck. She asked Sarah to describe the plants that went to make up each potion and chose the ones with the most attractive flowers to add to each tag, copying their names from a list that her mother wrote out for her.

For the pots, which had previously had their contents scrawled in chalk on their lids, she created wrap-around labels that tied on with rough garden twine. She laboured away in secret, refusing to let anyone have sight of her work, then on the Friday night she shooed the family from the kitchen, closing the door firmly on them and denying them entry until summonsed.

When they all trooped back in, after twenty minutes spent fiercely debating what could be afoot, they faced a curiously shaped mound on the table, hidden under a sheet. Ella carefully lifted the sheet to reveal Sarah's wares. They were neatly grouped with jars stacked, bottles in rows, and all dressed with instantly eye-catching labels.

Sarah gasped. 'Ella! They're beautiful.' She bit her lip and was unable to speak after that. Beattie picked up the nearest jar and turned it in her hands. 'I didn't know you could paint,' she said in wonder. Thomas was too busy preventing Beth from pulling over the whole display to add any comments, but he caught Ella's eye and smiled.

'You're so clever, Ella,' Annie said. 'Everyone will want to buy these now.'

Ella laughed. 'I don't think so. But people might stop and look, and they will remember where to come in the future.' She looked wistful. 'I wish I could come with you to help.'

'I can look after Beth,' Annie and Beattie said at the same time.

'Maybe in the summer,' Sarah conceded. 'When the market is busier. For now, I'm best placed to answer questions and we have but a small corner in the market. It doesn't need the two of us.'

The next day, the last Saturday in April, brought a fleeting glimpse of summer. The sunshine lifted the spirits and brought more customers than usual to the market. When Sarah came home her cheeks were flushed pink from the sun and the excitement of having sold more than she had ever sold before.

'Everyone stopped to admire your labels, Ella. They all wanted to ask questions about the plants I use. Some people bought just because the things looked so pretty, not because they needed them. Two ladies who were visiting for the day bought gifts to take back to friends in Leeds. Can you imagine!'

She added, 'Do you know, it came back to me that my great-grandmother was an artist. We had a picture of hers hanging on the wall when I was growing up. I do believe you must have inherited her talent.'

Sarah's excitement was infectious. Ella couldn't believe how successful her plan had been. She was very taken with the notion that she might have an inherited talent and with the idea that someone might consider these items to be suitable as gifts. Her mind raced: what else might people want?

Chapter Twenty-One

The day in early May when the fledgling linnets left the nest was momentous in more ways than one. Ella had walked with Beth through the churchyard and out of the gate, taking the path along the stream that climbed up the hill overlooking the village. It was a clear, sunny day and Ella was regretting the warmth of her clothing as they made their way up the steepest part of the incline, until they reached the top. Here they were met by a stiff breeze which cooled Ella's hot cheeks and reminded her that summer was still a little way off. From the top slope they overlooked Luddenden and Beth was fascinated, trying to work out which of the slate roofs belonged to their cottage. Ella spun her round to face west towards Northwaite, high up on another hill, then turned her again, to see the moor stretching before them away into the distance towards Haworth.

'Where did you work, Ella?' Beth asked. 'Where is York? Can we see it?'

Ella laughed. 'Not from here. It's a very, very long way. It must be, oh, more than fifty miles. In that direction.' She flung her arm vaguely towards the road to Halifax.

'Is it a big place? Bigger than Northwaite? Can we go one day?'

'Yes, yes and I don't know.' Ella was laughing, but Beth's questions had brought back painful memories. Over the last few weeks she had almost managed to forget about York and the shame of her leaving. Creating the labels for Sarah's remedies had made her feel she was doing something useful at last for the family and Sarah had promised that if business was good again this Saturday, they would find a way to make things work so that Ella could join her the following week in the market.

'Shall we go back?' Ella asked. 'You must be getting hungry. And if we are quiet and don't disturb the birds we can go and see how the herb and vegetable patches are growing.'

'Can I water them?' Beth was hopeful. She'd recently been entrusted with this job and took it very seriously, struggling from the pump down the garden with a watering can almost as big as herself.

'Of course you can. And I can sit and enjoy the sunshine and watch,' Ella teased. 'Race you to the churchyard gate. But take care on the path!'

The last words fell on deaf ears, as Beth was already running off ahead of her. Ella, suddenly aware of the steepness of the descent, followed her as fast as she could, heart in mouth, wishing she hadn't set the challenge. However, Beth, being small, slight and sure-footed, was at the gate long before Ella and was sitting on the grass, absorbed in making a daisy chain.

'Sit down,' she commanded. 'It's going to be for you. I'm going to crown you queen of the daisies.'

Ella, looking at the length of chain made so far, realised

that this could take some time. So she stretched out on the grass beside Beth and closed her eyes. Out of the wind, the sun was lovely. The glow through her eyelids was echoed in the warmth creeping through her limbs and Ella relaxed, letting her body mould itself into the ground. She must have drifted into a doze for she was startled to feel small, warm hands around her face.

'John?' she murmured sleepily.

'John?' Beth's voice brought her to consciousness. 'Were you asleep? Who is John?'

Ella opened her eyes to find Beth peering right into them.

'Too close!' she protested, gently pushing Beth away so that she could sit up.

'It's not straight,' Beth said, clambering into her lap to adjust the daisy circlet on Ella's head. Ella hugged her tight, feeling the small body vibrating with energy.

'John was the little boy in the house where I worked, in York. I don't know why I mentioned him. You're right, I must have been dreaming. I hadn't thought of him in a while.'

'How old is he? Can I meet him?'

'Questions, questions!' exclaimed Ella, giving Beth another squeeze before setting her down on the grass. She got to her feet and took Beth's hand, relishing the grip of her small fingers.

'I'll tell you about him as we walk home.' As Ella told Beth about John, she was painfully aware of the things she couldn't say. How guilty she had felt about having to leave without saying goodbye, how lonely John was in a house full of people and full of toys, how she'd blocked all these things from her mind when describing her time in York to her own family.

'Well, I hope I can meet him one day.' Beth, skipping ahead

up the path to their front door, didn't see Ella's face as she reflected ruefully how unlikely that was to happen. A few minutes later, aunt and niece were back out in the sunshine, sitting on the back doorstep, sharing a plate of bread and cheese.

'Listen.' Ella was suddenly aware of high-pitched insistent bird-calls around them in the garden. 'Do you know, I think the linnets might have left the nest!'

'Where? Can I go and see?' Beth was on her feet and ready to race down the garden but Ella held her back.

'No, sit quietly and finish your lunch and let's see if we can spot where the babies are. They must be in the trees and bushes. They can't have gone far.'

Before too long, Ella and Beth had pinpointed the location of five baby birds in the garden, through a combination of their noisy and persistent demands to be fed, and by the harried parent birds flying back and forth. The babies were tucked away out of sight for the most part, but every now and then one of the bolder ones broke cover and they caught sight of a small ball of fluffy brown feathers, dominated by a wide, gaping beak.

'Why are they so hungry?' Beth asked after they'd watched them for at least fifteen minutes, during which their demands to be fed showed no signs of abating.

'I think it must be because they are growing so fast. The poor parents! They seem to be getting thinner by the minute. I don't think we are going to be able to water the garden just yet. We'd better wait until later. Maybe the little ones will get sleepy and we can do it without disturbing them.'

So Ella set aside her feelings of guilt about not getting anything done around the house and, with Beth nestled in beside her, settled down for another stretch of baby-bird watching. This was the scene that greeted Sarah when she struggled through the door half-an-hour later.

'I'm back. It was another good day at the market. And look who I've brought to see you!'

Ella and Beth both turned and Ella tried to rise, a little stiff from so long spent sitting on the step. Her eyes took a moment or two to adjust to the darkness of the interior after the brightness of the garden. At first, she could barely make out Sarah's companion, other than to discern that it was a man. Then as her vision adjusted she had a moment of puzzlement before gasping 'Albert! Whatever are you doing here?'

Chapter Twenty-Two

'So who can this be?' Albert had demanded, after his surprising appearance in the kitchen in Luddenden, crouching down to bring himself to the same level as Beth. 'Why, I do believe it is Miss Elisabeth –' he hesitated, before adding with a note of enquiry, '– Bancroft?'

'Yes, Elisabeth Bancroft,' replied Sarah firmly, at the same moment as Beth, taking refuge behind Sarah's skirts, peeped out and said 'Beth' very emphatically.

'Beth Bancroft,' said Albert. 'That has a very pleasing ring to it.'

'Albert, you haven't answered my question. Whatever are you doing here?' Ella repeated, having finally recovered from her astonishment.

'Ella!' admonished Sarah. 'At least make Albert a cup of tea before plying him with questions. And me too – I'm quite exhausted after such a busy day.'

Ella busied herself at the stove, stealing covert glances at Albert as if she might be able to deduce the reason for his arrival just by observing him. Meanwhile, he worked his way into Beth's confidence, conjuring a feather from behind one ear and a pencil from behind the other, until her nervous solemnity gave way to laughter.

'Albert has quite a tale to tell,' Sarah said, as Ella dispensed tea from the big brown pot and hunted in the larder to see whether there was a piece of cake to be found for their visitor.

'Sit down, Ella,' Albert said, as Ella sliced the precious remnants of a fruit loaf and spread it with butter. 'You've been a difficult person to find. I was beginning to think you had vanished without trace.'

Ella settled herself at the kitchen table, facing Albert and Sarah, and Beth clambered onto her lap, hopeful of cake to share.

'But I don't understand why you have been looking for me? Nor why I was so difficult to find.'

Albert stirred his tea, thinking back. 'Well, I could scarcely believe my eyes when I saw you in that carriage, being driven away from the Wards' house.'

'What were you doing there?' Ella interjected. 'Were you looking for me?'

'Yes and no,' Albert replied. 'I was looking for you, but not at the Wards' house. I had no expectation of finding you there. After seeing you in the market I cursed myself for allowing you to leave without at least discovering where you worked, and how I could meet you again. I was so shocked by your news of Alice –' here Albert broke off. Visibly pulling himself together, he continued, '– and I had left myself in a position where I had no way of learning more. I had been asked to call at Grange House to discuss a business matter with Mr Ward, some stone carvings that he wished to have designed for the gates of a house that he was building. It was pure chance that I arrived just as you were leaving. I could scarcely believe it when the butler – what was his name?' Albert broke off again.

'Mr Stevens,' supplied Ella.

'Yes, Stevens. When he told me that you had gone for good. He was very circumspect, didn't want to tell me what was going on. Just that you were in some sort of trouble. He was so guarded that I feared the worst, that something had happened back here, to Sarah or to Beth.' Albert paused again, to smile at Beth who had looked up from playing with the crumbs on Ella's plate on hearing her name.

'So when I was shown in to see Mr Ward, instead of settling down to have the expected discussion about the feasibility of his carved-stone gatehouse he found himself faced with an apparent madman, demanding to know the whereabouts of one of his servants.' Albert chuckled at the memory, while Ella allowed the picture he had drawn to sink in. 'It was lucky that he was so keen to use my services, otherwise I would surely have found myself thrown out on my ear. When he told me what you were accused of, then followed up with some story about how you were from the family of a bad lot, that your sister was a murderer...' here Albert broke off as Sarah glanced anxiously at Beth, luckily now bored by the discussion and in the process of slipping from Ella's knee to return to her bird-watching from the doorstep.

'Well,' Albert resumed. 'It was my turn to be speechless. I had no idea that this was the story that had been put about. I almost lost my mind. I was still reeling from the news that you had given me about Alice – that she had died.' Albert swallowed hard and then continued. 'I could barely comprehend what Mr Ward was saying, or how any of this was tied to you, Ella. He attempted to brush it aside and continue our business discussion but I could have none of it. I demanded he tell me what he knew, which turned out to be little of substance, then I set out what I knew of your family, how many years I had known you all, the nature of the Alice that I knew and of her good character. And, all the while, my hatred of Williams grew. In the re-telling it became clearer to me how he must have created all this in revenge for Alice's refusal to marry him. He must have been instrumental in getting me out of the way so swiftly to take up my apprenticeship in York, knowing that my evidence as nightwatchman would have shown him to be a liar about the fire that destroyed the mill.'

Albert paused, stricken all over again by the ramifications of the actions of Williams, the much-hated overlooker at the factory where he and Alice had worked. He sipped his tea before continuing.

'Mr Ward appeared shaken by hearing another side to the story, and when I heard the tale of the so-called poisoning of an Edgar someone-or-other I explained that Sarah here is a herbalist and that you had no doubt learnt a little of the art' – Sarah snorted at this idea. – 'And would surely have had no malicious intent. He said nothing further, beyond suggesting that we meet in a few days' time to discuss the business matter properly as I had clearly had a most grievous shock. When I next attended the house he produced a letter, already addressed, that he said he wished to send to you, Ella. Having made further enquiries he now realised that there had been errors of deduction and that he might have acted hastily. It seemed that this Edgar person was now fully recovered, having not had a heart attack at all, and Mr Ward at least had the grace to look embarrassed. He wanted you to return to discuss

116

the matter further. But when I saw him again, within the month, he looked troubled and said that his letter to you had been returned unopened, with 'gone away' on the envelope. He was at a loss as to how you might be contacted, so I said that once our work was at an end, I would have the time for a long-overdue visit home and I would try to find you.'

Albert paused again to draw breath and to finish his tea.

'I thought it would be easy. Foolishly, I imagined I would walk down the street in Northwaite and find you there. But nobody was prepared to admit to having seen you.' Albert looked troubled. 'The mill fire is strong in people's memories there. They still hold blame. I don't know how easy it will be to change their minds. But when I enquired in Nortonstall, I heard that Sarah had been in regular attendance at the market. I knew then that I would be able to find you. And here I am. And here is the letter.'

Albert withdrew a rather creased, but nonetheless impressive, envelope of good-quality cream paper from his inside top pocket. Ella played for time. She could read but a single word of the writing on the front of the envelope, in a firm, bold script, and that was her name.

'What's in it?' she asked, picking up the envelope gingerly. 'What does Mr Ward want with me?'

'Why not open it and find out?' Albert urged.

'I...' Ella hesitated, embarrassed by her lack of learning, even in front of Albert who had known her so long.

Tactfully, Albert rose to his feet. 'I'll go and find Beth in the garden,' he said. 'That will give you a chance to look at it in peace.'

Ella half-rose to her feet. 'Beth! I'd forgotten all about her! She has probably disturbed the baby birds by now.'

'No, no you misjudge her,' Albert protested. 'I've been watching her, and she's hard at work with a watering can. It looks as though she could do with some help.' And with that he stepped out into the garden.

Ella pushed the letter across the table to Sarah. 'We might as well find out what he has to say,' she sighed, wondering whether, despite what Albert had said, some new accusation had been dreamt up against her.

Chapter Twenty-Three

Sarah skimmed over the letter while Ella waited expectantly, hoping for a clue to the nature of its contents in her mother's expression. The room was very still and Ella was conscious of the sounds from outside, the noisy, unceasing calls of the baby birds and of the indistinct conversation of Albert and Beth, punctuated by Albert's laughter.

'Well?' Ella asked, nervously, as Sarah laid the letter down on the table.

'It's all rather surprising,' Sarah said slowly.

'Surprising?' echoed Ella.

'Yes, I don't know quite what to make of it. I'll read it to you,' Sarah said. She paused, then began:

'Dear Ella,

I have tried to reach you but my letter was returned unopened, forwarding address unknown. I trust that this second letter, which Albert has so kindly promised to carry with him in his efforts to locate you, will have more success in finding you.

Ella, I fear we have misjudged you and I owe you an

apology. A little while after your departure, once Sir Edgar Broughton had fully recovered his health, Grace had the good sense to confess her part in the whole sorry misadventure. I now believe your protestations as to the nature of your 'potion' and fear the fault must lie with Grace in administering nearly the whole bottle —' here Sarah paused and raised her eyebrows as Ella gasped, *'— rather than the much smaller dosage that you advised. It was this overdose, to which Sir Edgar unfortunately proved susceptible, that resulted in his ill health. Much as I would have liked to overlook the whole matter as a piece of girlish nonsense, Sir Edgar's illness has made this impossible and Grace has been dealt with appropriately.*

I would very much like to speak with you in person, Ella, and hope that you might agree to return to Grange House. John misses you very much.

Regards,
Robert Ward'

Sarah laid the letter down for a second time, while Ella struggled to make sense of what she had heard. She wasn't sure what was causing her the most surprise. Was it that Grace had confessed, or that Mr Ward seemed to want to make amends? Ella had just been a servant, and a lowly one at that. Why should he care about the injustice? Why did he wish to speak to her in person? The only thing that did make sense, and that cut her to her heart, was that John was missing her.

Ella frowned, then her expression cleared. There was someone who might be able to clear up some of the confusion, someone close to hand who might be able to rule out the necessity of a trip to York and the need to have a potentially difficult conversation.

On cue, Albert came back into the kitchen, hand in hand with Beth.

'Shall we tell them what we found?' he asked Beth.

Ella couldn't help smiling as she looked at Beth. Her cheeks were pink with excitement and her eyes were shining.

'We've found a fairy tree,' Beth exclaimed, almost dancing on the spot.

'A fairy tree,' Ella repeated, raising her eyes to Albert.

'Yes,' he said firmly. 'Down the garden near the vegetable plot. Do you want to show them what was there, Beth?'

Beth's eyes were as large as saucers as she reached into the pocket of her pinafore and pulled out a silver threepenny bit.

'A thruppence! Let me see.' Ella bent down and Beth handed it over, although rather reluctantly.

Ella turned the small coin between her fingers and traced the outlines on front and back.

'Look Beth,' she said, 'that's the queen's head. Queen Victoria. And here, on the other side, there's a crown and... do you know what number that is?'

'Three,' said Beth, proudly.

'I didn't know we had a fairy tree,' Ella said. 'Do you think the fairies left the gift for you a long time ago and we just never noticed it?'

'No,' Beth said, taking the coin from Ella's palm and quickly returning it to her pocket. 'Albert said that the fairies told him it was a gift for watching over the baby birds.'

'Albert, I didn't know you could talk to fairies,' Ella said solemnly. 'That must be very... useful.'

Albert blushed. 'Ah, they only ever speak to me when there

are little people around. Very special little people,' he added, ruffling Beth's hair.

'Well, we will have to keep an eye on the fairy tree,' Sarah said, getting to her feet. 'But you mustn't expect the fairies to leave you gifts every day,' she warned Beth.

'It's all right,' Albert said hastily. 'Beth knows that they only leave gifts on very special occasions. Like birthdays, or when you've done something particularly good.'

'Or when you have special visitors,' Ella said, smiling and pushing Sarah gently back into her chair. 'Don't you go getting up, Ma. You've been on your feet all day, and had two long walks to market and back. I'll make us all something for supper and I want to hear all Albert's news.'

So while Ella peeled potatoes and carrots and chopped greens, hoping all the while Albert wouldn't notice how frugal the fare was, she quizzed him as to what might be the meaning of Mr Ward's comments about Grace in the letter, and why he would want her to return to talk to him.

To Ella's disappointment, Albert was unable to furnish her with too many details about the goings-on at Grange House after she had left. He had caught a glimpse or two of John at the window, or setting out on walks with his governess. His contact with Stevens had been limited to greetings at the door on arrival, and farewells as he was ushered out. Of Grace, he had seen no sign. He was only party to what Mr Ward had told him, mainly pertaining to his quest to find Ella, and could give her no further insight into what the servants or anyone else might be thinking.

Ella sighed as she chopped and added vegetables to the pot on the stove. Many a time she had had cause to regret her lack of learning. If she had only learnt to write properly, she could have replied to Mr Ward's letter, or written to Mr Stevens or to some other member of the household to find out what had happened. She recognised that it was her own fault; she had taken every opportunity to slip away from school and take to the fields, roaming far and wide and frequently only returning home just in time to prevent Sarah's suspicions from being aroused. Then, at the age of thirteen, she had started work at the mill and, although schooling was compulsory there, the older she was the harder it was to admit to her poor reading and writing skills, so she would skulk at the back or volunteer to run errands rather than play any part in the lesson.

Before the food was ready, Albert pushed back his chair and stood up.

'You're not going so soon, are you?' Ella asked.

'I'm sorry,' Albert said, a little flustered. 'I hadn't realised how late it was.' He glanced outside, where the gathering gloom after the brightness of the day showed that the lengthy days of summer were yet to arrive. 'I must get back home. I've barely been back a week and my company will be expected.'

'But you haven't seen Thomas, Annie and Beattie yet. You'll be so surprised to see how they have grown.' Ella could hear the pleading note in her voice. Albert's visit had initially taken her aback and now she was doubly unsettled by the realisation of how much she was enjoying his company.

'Then all the more reason for me to return.' Albert was firm. 'Sarah and I had a good talk on the way here and I would like to attend to matters relating to our conversation in Northwaite in the next day or so. But after that I will be back.'

Ella was puzzled as to what this business in Northwaite might be, but had no chance to ask. Albert hugged Sarah and kissed both her cheeks, then bent down to give Beth a hug and a squeeze. When it was Ella's turn, she felt her heart constrict, and then thump painfully in her chest. She feared that he would notice, but he seized both her arms and held them at her side while looking her up and down appraisingly.

'Being back here suits you, Ella. I'm so pleased that I found you, and delivered Mr Ward's letter, but don't go rushing back to York just yet.'

And with that Albert picked up his cap and went on his way, leaving a little flurry of excitement in the kitchen, albeit for different reasons. Ella hid her agitation behind vigorous stirring of the food and organisation of spoons and bowls in preparation for the rest of the family's return. Beth, over-excited by the novelty of having a visitor, was jumping up and down and demonstrating how the baby birds were trying to fly, while Sarah also had a lot on her mind, trying to take in what she and Albert had discussed on the journey home from Nortonstall. Was it possible that Albert could succeed in his intentions to clear Alice's name, and somehow put right the wrongs that the family had suffered over the years? Or were the people of Northwaite still too bitterly entrenched in their need to find a scapegoat for the fire that had destroyed their livelihoods and taken the heart out of their village?

Chapter Twenty-Four

True to his word, Albert reappeared at their door a few days later. The weather had reneged on its promise of an early summer and dawn had found the valley thick with mist. This had given way to a steady grey rain that sapped the spirits and put Ella in a pensive mood. She wondered whether she should return to York; whether she should perhaps say as much to Albert so that he could pass the information to Mr Ward on his return. As he had been at home in Northwaite for at least a week now, she imagined his return would not be long delayed.

Mid-afternoon found her creating more labels for Sarah, who was ladling lotions into jars in preparation for the Saturday market. Beth, given some paint and paper, was being kept busy dreaming up her own designs. There was a brief rap at the door and Ella looked enquiringly at Sarah before hastening to open it. Albert stood there, soaked through by the continuous rain that had marked his journey, his boots muddied by the track he had taken across the moor.

'Albert! Come in. Here, let me take your coat. Sit near the

hearth and dry yourself and let me make tea. You must be thirsty from your walk.'

Ella found herself bustling him into a chair and fussing to hide the strange agitation she felt at his reappearance. She noticed Sarah throw her a quizzical glance but luckily Beth, delighted at Albert's visit, created a diversion.

'Come and see my painting,' she said proudly, pulling at his hand.

'Oh, I fear I am interrupting you at work,' Albert said, eyeing the paints and Ella's labels, spread out to dry.

Ella, suddenly mindful of his artistry for his own designs in stone, was mortified. She couldn't gather the labels together without smudging them, so she had to resign herself to his scrutiny.

'Why Ella, they're beautiful.' Albert looked up at her and smiled and Ella experienced a jolt as she looked into his blue eyes, bright beneath his dark brows. 'I didn't know you were an artist.'

Ella, her face hot with embarrassment, stuttered a denial but Sarah was quick to speak.

'She is indeed,' she said firmly. 'Without her labels my lotions and potions would scarcely sell a fraction of what they do. It was Ella's idea to make the labels, and she must have full credit.'

Quite scarlet, Ella gave her full attention to making tea, thankful that Beth's insistence on showing off her own art was now taking the attention away from her. Albert seated himself beside her and began to draw, creating a row of baby birds on a branch, to Beth's delight.

'I wanted to call in again before I return to York,' Albert said, sitting back to let Beth begin to colour the birds with paint.

'York, so soon?' Ella blurted out, even though she had expected it. She turned away from him with the pretence of hunting for the sugar bowl, to conceal how the unwelcome news had unsettled her.

'Yes, I have work I must finish,' Albert said. 'I will be back though, within the month.' He addressed his last comment to Sarah, giving her a meaningful glance, to Ella's puzzlement, then turned his attention back to her. 'I wondered, now that you have had time to think, whether you have a message for Mr Ward?'

'I have.' Ella surprised herself with her sudden resolve. 'I thank him for his letter and I am grateful that he has seen that there is, indeed, another side to the story. I am not ready as yet to return to York –' she hesitated, '– but please let him know that I miss John too, and I would hope to be allowed to see him sometime in the future.'

Neither Albert nor Sarah commented on what Ella had to say and the remainder of the afternoon went by in happy conversation, with Albert filling them in on the latest news, and gossip, from Northwaite.

Ella wasn't sure whether it was an aversion to getting soaked once more, or delight in their company, that made Albert reluctant to depart, but he seemed to find it a struggle to leave. He put on his jacket, now warm and dry from being set near the hearth, then picked up his cap – but paused to add some eyes and beaks to Beth's baby birds. Then he stood awhile before the fire, musing, before sighing, visibly squaring his shoulders and turning to Ella and Sarah.

'I must go. But I will be back within the month, as I said, and I hope to stay a little while longer next time.' He glanced at Ella as he said this and she failed to prevent her colour rising once more, while her heart gave a start within her breast before settling to a regular, if quickened, beat. He set his cap on his head, said his goodbyes and then he was off into the mist and murk of an afternoon that looked and felt more like November than May.

Chapter Twenty-Five

Albert was a man of his word. Three weeks passed and Sarah came back from the market on the Saturday, flushed by the sudden warmth of a sunny June day, excited that sales had been good and steady, and with news that Albert had returned.

'He stopped at the stall and bought something for his mother and then asked whether we could all walk over to Northwaite tomorrow afternoon, if the weather is fine. He wondered whether we might meet in the churchyard.'

'In the churchyard?' Ella queried. She was playing for time, having spent much of the last three weeks going over and over all her brief encounters with Albert since their unexpected meeting in York. Both of them had changed a good deal since he was the mill hand and nightwatchman at Hobbs' Mill, and she was just a young mill worker who had kept him company on the path to work. Now, she realised, he had awakened thoughts and feelings within her that went far beyond those of friendship, and she had spent a good deal of time daydreaming about his return. Sarah had had cause to speak sharply to her on more than one occasion, when the potatoes were boiling dry on the stove or the pie burning in the oven while she stood at the window, gazing unseeingly into the garden.

Yet there was a cloud overshadowing these daydreams of Ella's. Alice, her older sister, had been a great friend of Albert's and it had been apparent to all that knew them that Albert was sweet on Alice. Ella had never been sure whether Alice knew this and chose not to acknowledge it or if she simply didn't see Albert in the same way, thinking of him more like a younger brother. Albert had protected Alice more than once from the attentions of Williams, their cold and domineering overlooker at the mill. Albert must have been hurt when she fell pregnant, and by her refusal to reveal the name of the father of the baby, yet he seemed to delight in Beth and to seek out the company of her family. Ella was only too well aware of the resemblance she now bore to Alice, but whether this was good or bad in Albert's eyes she couldn't say.

Now Albert was back, and they were to meet again, the following day. Ella had spent a long time envisaging how their meeting might go, but her imaginings hadn't encompassed the presence of the whole family. She was very inexperienced in matters of the heart: Alice's untimely death had been so shocking that normal life had seemed suspended for a very long time. Ella had gone about making sure that she found work so that bread was put on the table; work that was not easy for her to find after Alice's death. The blame attached to the circumstances of her death had tainted the whole family.

Ella's drudgery at the Ottershaws' had left her no time for idle fantasy, and by the time she moved to York she had put all thought of meeting a young man from her mind. In any case, there were no suitable candidates in the household, Mr

Stevens being the only man amongst the live-in servants and some years older than she was. Ella, at first shocked upon seeing Albert at the market, then ashamed when he was witness to her disgrace on being sent away from Grange House, had discovered that a dormant seed of longing had been awakened, taken root and started to grow, leaving her excited, discomfited and nervous all at once in anticipation of seeing Albert again.

She wasn't to know that Albert had been similarly afflicted, enjoying his visits to the Bancroft household, their informality and hospitality standing in stark contrast to the cold and strained behaviour of his own small family. Far from welcoming him home after his long absence in York, his mother railed at him for neglecting them. He recognised that his father's dour nature, and bitterness at being more-or-less housebound after being disabled following an accident at work made him unhappy company for his mother. Yet, despite his best intentions, Albert found himself unable to stay at home for longer than an hour or so at a time. At first, he'd been able to cite an errand he needed to perform for Mr Ward as the reason for his absence, asking around the area for the whereabouts of Ella and her family. Then, once they were found, he took pleasure in being with the Bancrofts once more, a pleasure only further enhanced by his mother's fury once she had discovered the nature of his errand, and its outcome.

'That *family*...' she had all but spat out the word. 'That family has brought shame and disgrace on themselves and destroyed the whole livelihood of this village, if not the whole area. If it hadn't been for the actions of that – harlot – Alice Bancroft, why, you would still be living here with us, the mill would still be operating and your father and I wouldn't be struggling as we do.' She went on to list all the people in the area who had been made destitute or had to leave due to the loss of the mill, their only source of employment, but Albert was too enraged to listen further, or to even try to reason with her.

The mill's closure had indeed been a disaster for the area but Alice had been too easily turned into a scapegoat, an easy target for someone else's hatred, and she had been blamed without being able to defend herself. Albert knew the truth and he was determined to see justice done somehow. As for his parents' struggles, well, he had been sending them money regularly from York yet, as he looked around the cottage, he could see scant evidence of how it had been spent. He would ask his mother one day, suspecting that it was stashed beneath their mattress rather than being used to bring comfort to their daily life. He felt sure that his mother had come to prefer being unhappy. Perhaps, in fact, she had always been like that. He couldn't remember a time when things were any different, even when he was a child.

So he had taken pleasure in his visits to the Bancroft family and his heart had turned over, too, at the sight of Ella. But, after his first successful visit, as he made his way back to York by train bearing the news that Ella had been found, he was forced to reflect that his feelings were skewed by Ella's strong resemblance to Alice, as he had last seen her. It was like a stab in the heart each time he beheld her. Then, as he spent more time in her company, he grew uneasy that she wasn't Alice, that she was quite clearly her own person, with her own character and mannerisms. At other times, it was as if Ella really was the Alice he had once known. He returned to York feeling confused, torn between a wish to fall in love with Ella and to marry her, and a fear that if he did so it would be the wrong thing to do, for her, for him and for the memory of Alice. Although this latter conviction, that any involvement with Ella would be a mistake, grew stronger as time passed in York, the family was still in the forefront of his mind. He had formulated a plan that he hoped would clear Alice's name and bring stability back to the lives of her family. He had worked on it during his second visit and now they were all about to discover the nature of his scheme.

Chapter Twenty-Six

'Nearly there.' Even Sarah was beginning to sound discouraged. The heat, unusual for early June, was making the journey over the top to Northwaite a harder trek than usual. Although the elevated path allowed for a cooler breeze, a welcome relief to their over-heated faces, the sun beat down from a cloudless sky. Ella found herself longing to reach the shady churchyard, overhung as it was with trees. As they walked, she resisted looking at the distant church tower, gazing at the path instead, glancing up only occasionally to check that their destination was drawing closer.

It was with a concerted sigh of relief that the family pushed through the gate, having managed to slip through the village apparently unseen. The villagers were resting after lunch, or at work in their gardens, and the hot streets were deserted.

Beth, Annie and Beattie flopped down on the steps of the church in silence. Ella turned to Thomas. 'Let them rest awhile, then you can take them to the pump in the High Street. They'll feel better after a drink of water.' She paused. 'Mind you come straight back here.'

It was unlikely that anyone in the village would recognise

Beth, or any of the younger members of the Bancroft family, for that matter, since it was over seven years since they had left, but she didn't want anyone asking awkward questions. She herself was suddenly very conscious of her resemblance to Alice and found herself wishing that the heat of the day hadn't prevented her from wearing a shawl that she could have drawn across her face if necessary.

Sarah, about to follow the path around the base of the church tower, turned back and beckoned to Ella to follow. Conscious of just how hot and sticky she felt now that they had stopped walking, and wishing she could have followed Thomas and the girls to the pump instead, Ella quickened her pace to catch up with Sarah.

She rounded the corner to find her mother standing in the shade of a yew tree, already deep in conversation with Albert. Ella's heart gave its now-familiar jolt at the sight of him and she smiled as she reached them, her eyes seeking his and looking for a hint that her feelings were reciprocated. Yet it seemed to her as though his eyes skated across her face, and his smile was just a brief glimmer. Disappointed, she put it down to the fact that she was interrupting their conversation, and turned her attention to what they were saying.

'I've spoken to the vicar,' Albert was saying. 'He's new to the parish and has only been here a year. He has no objection to my plans.' He paused. 'I'm not sure that the villagers will feel the same but –' he shrugged, then he reached into his breast pocket. 'Here – I've sketched what I would like to do.'

Ella was puzzled. 'What are you talking about?'

Sarah turned to Ella. 'Albert would like to raise a gravestone in Alice's memory.'

Ella stared at her. 'You mean this is where Alice is...' she swallowed, unable to continue. She looked around her, then she spied a wooden cross, all but hidden amongst the tangle of wildflowers. This part of the graveyard was barely occupied and had been allowed to become overgrown.

'Yes,' Sarah said quietly. 'Alice is buried here. I've only been able to visit the once, before we had to leave Northwaite. It's a sorry mess, with no one here to care for it over the years.' She brightened. 'But it's a lovely spot, a peaceful one. And Albert is going to raise a stone, carved in memory of Alice.'

'Look, I've sketched what I would like to do.' Albert held the paper out to them.

Ella and Sarah gazed at Albert's drawing: the curve of the stone's edge echoed by the entwined plant tendrils and seed heads, bursting with life.

'And you can do this in stone?' Ella marvelled. She glanced at Sarah and saw that tears were spilling down her cheeks. 'Albert, it's beautiful,' she said firmly. 'I don't know how we can ever thank you.'

She stopped, overwhelmed too by the combination of the sudden discovery of her sister's final resting place, by the realisation of how her grave had lain untended all these years, and by Albert's unexpected thoughtfulness and kindness.

Albert looked a little uncomfortable. 'I'm not to be allowed to carve anything beyond her name and the dates of her life. The vicar felt a dedication of any sort might be inflammatory, so I wanted to make her grave stand out for other reasons.'

He looked deeply upset at having to deliver this news, but was saved from further comment by the arrival of Thomas and the younger family members. Revitalised by their trip to get water from the pump, they were chattering away.

Ella and Albert both registered Sarah's stricken look, as she glanced down at Alice's grave and then at Beth.

'What are you doing?' Annie asked, gazing around, at the same moment as Albert said, 'I have something else to show you.'

'Something else?' Annie queried, but her question was ignored as Albert led the family out through the narrow gate in the side of the wall surrounding the churchyard, and along the cobbled path in front of a row of cottages.

'This way,' and he led them out onto the High Street, turning in the direction that led through the village and beyond. Ella paused for a moment, looking back, struck by the peace and beauty of the location before turning and hurrying to catch up with the family.

Albert led them through the village, still thankfully quiet in the afternoon sun, until they reached the last house along the road. Ella had grown increasingly uncomfortable and the chatter of the family had died away. She hadn't been back to Northwaite for over seven years but this street was one she had walked along daily before that. And the house that they were now standing in front of was the one she had lived in from her earliest memory.

Chapter Twenty-Seven

Fifteen minutes later they were all in the garden of Lane End Cottage, Albert looking discomfited as he scuffed at the ground with the toe of his boot, while Ella and Sarah sat in the shade of an apple tree and watched Annie and Beattie play tag around the overgrown vegetable patch with Beth. Thomas was lying on his back in the grass a little distance away, seemingly dozing in the sun.

'It's just a shock,' Sarah was saying. 'You'd told me about your plan for Alice's gravestone, Albert, and that was such a kind and generous thing to do. But this –' she gestured around her, '– I don't know what to say. It's too much. Whatever would your parents say? You can't buy a house for us, Albert. You must buy one for them.'

Albert had a stubborn, mulish expression on his face that Ella had never seen before. 'They don't need a house,' he said. 'They have one. And I have sent money to them every month that I have been able, so they have nothing to complain of. I have had very little need of money while I have been in York; I've lived frugally and worked long hours, and found I had a lot put by. I suppose, in the back of my mind, I had a plan, but now that can never be.' He hesitated. 'I feel so guilty about what happened to Alice. If I had been here, I could have told the constable that they were making an error when they arrested her, that Alice was not at the mill when the fire started. The only person who was there apart from me, was Williams. When Master Richard arrived, the fire had already taken hold. The rest of that evening is a blur, as we tried to beat back the flames until help arrived. My guess is that Alice arrived as the others did, drawn by the sight of the smoke from afar, then coming to see whether they could help.'

Sarah and Ella listened to Albert's account in silence. They had never been able to understand why Alice would have been at the mill at that time, nor why she would have wanted to set fire to it.

'But why...?' Ella stopped, unable to formulate what she wanted to say. Why did Williams blame Alice for the fire? Why didn't Albert say something? Why did Richard Weatherall die? And who did set the fire at the mill, or was it an accident: a smouldering ember in the office fireplace; a piece of machinery that had malfunctioned unnoticed while the mill was on Sunday shutdown?

Albert's thoughts must have been following the same path. 'I'd patrolled the whole building but a short while before the fire started. Williams came by and said he needed something from the office, some paperwork that he needed at home to work on some figures for old Mr Weatherall for the morning. I thought he must have been and gone and I was preparing to patrol again on the hour when I saw a glow from the other end of the mill, which housed the offices. My immediate thought was that Williams might be trapped, but I saw him standing outside, just staring up at the building. And then

Master Richard was there, and they seemed to be arguing. Williams was trying to hold him back, but Master Richard ran into the building. I ran to get water from the river, and others came, but it was too late, the fire had taken hold...' Albert tailed off and stared at the ground, deep in thought. Ella had an urge to go and put her arm around his shoulders – he looked so alone and tormented – but she feared his reaction.

Sarah spoke, her voice gentle. 'What happened afterwards, Albert?'

Albert started at being drawn back to the present.

'After the fire, I stayed at the mill as long as I could. It was dreadful. Old Mr Weatherall arrived and he broke down, sobbing. Someone took him away home again, I'm not sure who. I tried to help, dampening down, making sure that the fire was properly out. It was nearly dawn when I left and it was obvious that nothing could be saved. The mill had gone. I went home and of course my parents were mad with worry. They feared the worst because I hadn't come back. At first, they shouted, but I was so covered in grime and soot, and so exhausted that I think they could see...' Albert tailed off. 'Anyway, I fell into bed and slept and when I woke up they said that Williams had been by, and that I had been awarded ten guineas by Mr Weatherall for my bravery. And with the mill gone, Mr Weatherall had sent word to a friend of his in York and they would have me as an apprentice: a stonemason's apprentice. I was to start at once, so by the next day I had been packed off. I had no idea that Alice had been imprisoned.'

Albert paused for a long time, but neither Ella nor Sarah spoke. They could tell he had yet more to say and what he had already said was a lot for them to take in. As the calls of

Beth and the girls echoed around the garden, Ella viewed the scene with detachment. It was a beautiful afternoon in an idyllic spot, yet it was apparent that Albert's anguish made it invisible to him.

Pulling himself together with an effort, he finished in a rush. 'I did well and set money aside. I hoped to come back and make Alice proud of me. I had no word from home so I knew nothing of what had happened until I saw you at the market, Ella. Then, after I saw you again, as you left Grange House, and heard Mr Ward's tale, it gave me the chance to make contact with you. When I came across Sarah at the market, and talked with her on the way to Luddenden, I saw a way that I could do something in Alice's memory. I didn't hit upon the plan to buy this cottage until after that, when I discovered by chance it was for sale.' He looked downcast. 'I didn't think of the memories it might bring you all and that it might be upsetting for you. I just wanted to honour Alice's memory, to help. I can see now I was foolish.'

Ella and Sarah both started to speak at once but Albert held up his hand. 'No, no, you mustn't mind me. The cottage is a good investment for me. I can rent it out; perhaps use it if I return to live here.' He ceased speaking, looking exhausted.

Sarah spoke again. 'Albert, we haven't been back to the village since... since Alice died. I'm not sure how welcome we will be here. But –' she glanced around and spread her arms wide. 'I've always loved this place, and I feel Alice's presence here so strongly. I was taken aback by your proposal and your kindness. We haven't known much kindness in the last few years. But if you would let us rent the cottage from you, then I think we would all be delighted to live here once more.' She looked questioningly at Ella as she spoke.

'You can see how happy the girls are here, and I can establish my herb garden again. Thomas and Annie's walk to work will be so much shorter and Ella –' she paused.

What would Ella do? Ella was wondering that herself. Hearing how Albert had hoped to come back to Northwaite, once he had achieved enough to make Alice proud of him, had given her an unpleasant reminder that he believed he belonged to Alice, and probably always would. His shocking discovery of her death so many years after it had happened had simply served to reinforce that belief. Ella realised that her anxiety over her developing feelings for Albert wasn't misplaced at all. She sought Albert's eyes, but although he had raised them hopefully when Sarah started to speak, he refused to meet Ella's gaze.

'Why, I can help you all get settled here and then I can return to York.' The idea came to Ella in a flash. Did she mean it, she wondered, or was she hoping to provoke some sort of response from Albert? If so, she was disappointed for, at that moment, Beth broke free from her game and hurled herself at Albert's legs.

'Come and play with us,' she demanded. 'We can play hide-and-seek. It's lovely here. Thank you for bringing us.' And she tugged at his hand and pulled him up the garden.

Ella went over to the hedge and looked out over the gate and across the field. The woods at the far side dipped down into the valley, leading down to where the ruins of the mill stood. Beyond, in the distance, the higher reaches of Nortonstall were visible, grey brick and slate shimmering in the afternoon heat. Had Alice ever stood looking over this gate, she wondered? She herself had used it many a time in her younger years, slipping away over the fields to avoid the chores.

She turned back to find her mother sobbing quietly under the tree. 'Why, whatever is wrong?' she asked, hurrying over to sit beside her and placing an arm around her shoulders.

She was relieved when Sarah shook her head and smiled. 'I'm not sad. Well, I suppose I am. But I'm happy too. Is it possible that things could be about to be made right? After such a long time? It's just that it is a lot to take in. Don't mind me. Leave me be. Go and talk to Albert.' Sarah suddenly looked worried again and Ella felt as though she had divined her thoughts and anxieties about his sudden change in demeanour towards her.

'It looks as though Albert is happy in Beth's company. Let's go into the house and have a look around. Albert's offer is such a generous one, but we need to be sure. We are quite settled in Luddenden, after all.'

So Ella and Sarah went arm in arm into the house, and soon the others drifted in too and although some of the memories that the house brought back were painful ones, there were happy ones too. Ella told Beth how Albert had come to see her when she was a baby, and how shy he was of her, and how he was in awe of her tiny fingers and toes. Then Beth laughed at him and he teased her and told her she was even more frightening now. Amidst all the good humour, Sarah went quietly into the kitchen and moved around it, running her fingers over the dusty surfaces, before sitting down heavily at the kitchen table.

'It's barely changed at all since we were last here, even though others have lived in it.' She sighed and looked around. 'But it's a nice feeling. It's still home. What do you think, Ella?'

Ella was prevented from replying by the noisy arrival of

Annie, Beattie and Beth, who had been having a look around upstairs. They clattered down the staircase and burst into the kitchen.

'Can we go now? We're hungry. And it's such a long walk home.' Beth looked disheartened at the thought. 'But can we come again? I like it here.'

Albert had followed them through. 'One last surprise,' he said, bending to open a cupboard of the dresser. He pulled out a basket, laden with bread and cheese, some cold cuts and a bottle or two of ale. Ella rinsed the dust off the plates and glasses at the pump outside, then they all sat down in the garden and ate the picnic, making the most of the last vestiges of warmth as the sun dipped lower in the sky.

'It's getting cooler,' Sarah said, struggling to her feet aided by Thomas, once there was nothing left of the picnic but crumbs. 'Time to head home I think.'

They were all reluctant to leave: Ella because of Albert; the girls because of the garden; Sarah because of her memories; and Thomas because he couldn't face the walk home. As they passed the churchyard once more, Ella turned back and saw Albert watching them. And, for a fleeting second, she thought there was someone else standing at his side, someone whose height and stature was very like her own.

'A trick of the light,' she told herself, shivering slightly. When she turned to look again, there was nobody there.

Chapter Twenty-Eight

The move was accomplished with very little fuss. Sarah had discussed it with everyone on the walk home, highlighting the advantages in the same way that she had when they had moved to Luddenden so recently. The same carter who had transported them less than six months before was hired to drive them over to Northwaite. They had few extra possessions, other than a box or two of Sarah's wares for market. The hill from Nortonstall up to Northwaite was so steep, though, that they had to climb down from the cart and walk behind it to ease its load.

Sarah's face was aflame with more than the effort of walking as the procession made its way over the cobbled main street of Northwaite. This time, in the middle of a weekday morning, there was no escaping the stares and comments. Women stopped sweeping their steps to lean on their brooms and watch them pass and Ella was nervous in case someone should call out or make comments bolder than the muttered ones she could barely make out.

A figure stepped out of the side road to join the little procession as it passed the village shop and Ella's heart leapt, for it was Albert, come to show solidarity. He walked at the front, by the horse's head, and cheerfully greeted anyone he recognised, not a whit abashed by the stir they were causing.

Sarah had sent Beattie to school and Annie and Thomas to their apprenticeships, with instructions to join them at home time. Ella was glad they were spared the embarrassment. Even Beth, initially excited, had sensed the atmosphere and shrank back to hide amongst Sarah's skirts as she walked. As the edge of the village drew near and Lane End Cottage came into view, Ella breathed a sigh of relief. They hastened up the path and Ella, who had promised herself that she wouldn't, stole a glance back towards the village. With the exception of two or three people gathered, gossiping, she was relieved to see the street returning to normality.

Albert reached into his pocket and presented the big iron front-door key to Sarah with a flourish.

'All yours, for as long as you wish,' he said. 'I will come over on Saturday afternoon to see how you have settled in, and Thomas can give me a hand to sort out the garden. Once the weeds are cut back you'll be able to see how much still survives of your original planting. Not much, I fear, but I'm sure it won't take you long to establish your herb beds again.'

Albert was as good as his word. Sarah had taken the Saturday off from the market, preferring to use the time to set the house to rights. Thomas made his way home from the printworks where he was apprenticed and Albert allowed him enough time to eat a quick lunch before giving him a spade and bidding him join him in the garden. Albert scythed the long grass while Thomas turned over the herb and vegetable beds, pausing now and then as Sarah exclaimed at the discovery of a plant that she could use for her remedies. By dusk, order was restored to the garden and both Thomas and Albert were sprawled full length on the shorn grass, alternately laughing and groaning at their aching muscles. Ella paused to watch them from the kitchen window, musing on their easy relationship. Once again, her thoughts turned to how different things might have been were it not for the mill fire and if Alice still lived. Then, reluctant to pursue that line of thinking, she took glasses of ale and a jug of water out on a tray for the two workers, and promised them supper within the half hour.

As Albert looked up to take a glass from her, smiling his thanks, she momentarily glimpsed the look of longing she had read in his eyes before, but then the shutters came down and he was polite and withdrawn once again. Ella, fulsome in her praise for the work that they had done, did her best to remain unmoved, but she withdrew to the kitchen with a heavy heart. All had changed between her and Albert and she was at a loss as to explain how it was so. Perhaps it was for the best; her planned return to York would hopefully keep her too busy to brood on it further.

Days passed, and to Ella and Sarah's surprise, their return occasioned little comment in the village. It seemed as though the passage of time had helped; either that or those most vociferous in their original condemnation of the family had moved elsewhere in search of work. Indeed, on their first Tuesday in the cottage one of the villagers knocked at their door, enquiring as to whether Sarah would be at the market the following Saturday. Only, she said, she had missed her the previous Saturday and had need of one of Sarah's ointments. Sarah invited her into the kitchen, found the jar she required and then talked to her in greater detail, promising to make up a remedy for her, specially tailored to her needs. It was the start of a trickle of similar visitors, whose numbers swelled to a steady flow within the month. Sarah started talking about having specific evenings for consultations as she found the visitors, although welcome, disruptive to the family routine. Albert, overhearing her discussing this during one of his evening visits, fashioned a stone niche beside the kitchen door over the course of several subsequent visits. It was designed so that Sarah could set a lit candle in a jar there to signify when patients were welcome of an evening. Ella had stood silently by and watched him at work, patiently chipping away and smoothing the stone. Under his practised fingers, contours and a simple swirl of foliage emerged from the pale stone that formed such a contrast to the grey exterior walls.

Albert seemed to neither mind nor enjoy her silent observation. Ella had learnt over the weeks to expect little from him. Even so, it came as a shock one evening when Annie related that she had heard that Albert was walking out with Violet Lockwood. Sarah looked sharply at Ella and scolded Annie for spreading tittle-tattle, then quickly changed the subject. The unwelcome news kept Ella awake throughout the night, tossing and turning in her bed. She knew Violet, remembering her well from her mill days. A little older than Ella, she was the daughter of Walter Lockwood the Northwaite butcher and, unless she had changed, quite a forceful character. But walking out already? Why, it was less than a month ago that Ella believed she had cause to think that there was something between herself and Albert.

Chapter Twenty-Nine

Barely two months had passed since the carter had brought them from Luddenden to Northwaite and here he was again, waiting outside Lane End Cottage in the sunshine of a late August morning that promised a hot day ahead. The letter that Ella had persuaded Sarah to write had received a swift reply from York and, as Ella picked up her bags to take them out to the waiting carter, she reflected that this time she both knew, and did not know, what to expect. Life in a big city would be strange no longer, and she knew both the house and its occupants. Yet she did not know who she would find there or how they would receive her. The letter that Sarah had read out to her from Mr Ward had made mysterious reference to 'some changes in the household' since she was there last. If anything, Ella felt more nervous than when she had been setting out into the unknown. Was returning to York going to prove to be a misjudgement? Weighed against this was her certainty that she couldn't stay in Northwaite and endure the sight of Albert, who had settled back in the village, on an almost daily basis. Nor could she continue to feel so hopeless about her lack of contribution to the household. Sarah had been adamant that her presence was invaluable to her, but even though patients had returned for the remedies that she had been supplying to them seven years previously, and her market stall was still popular, Ella knew that the weekly expenses for a family were high. The peppercorn rent charged by Albert was invaluable; Thomas and Annie would both be bringing in small wage packets once their apprenticeships were at an end, but until then Ella felt it her duty to find a way to provide. On top of that, Beth would be starting at Northwaite school in the autumn. Ella felt her choice was clear. She had to go back to Grange House.

Thomas, Annie and Beattie had said their goodbyes earlier that morning. There had been tears then and Ella did not relish further distress from Sarah and Beth. But she found Sarah on the front path with a furrowed brow.

'I can't find Beth anywhere,' she said. 'I've searched the house from top to bottom and even looked under the beds.'

'Do you think she could have run off?' Ella was immediately alarmed.

'She was upset at the thought of your leaving, but would she have missed the chance to say goodbye?' Sarah was troubled.

'We need to look sharp, miss, if you're to make the train.' The carter had turned in his seat and was viewing the unfolding scene dispassionately.

It was with mounting agitation that Ella loaded her bag into the back of the cart, disturbing a small cloud of dust from the empty flour sacks piled there as she did so.

With a heavy heart, she prepared to mount the step to sit herself next to the driver when she heard a volley of muffled sneezes.

'Beth?' she said, questioningly.

There was a moment's silence, followed by more sneezes. Ella drew back the folded sacks to reveal Beth, her face and hair white with a dusting of flour, tear streaks making runnels down her cheeks.

'Oh, Beth,' Ella said, quickly lifting her out and hugging her, with no regard for the mess it would make of her travelling clothes. 'Did you think to come with me? I'm so sorry to leave you but I promise I will come back soon. You must be good for Ma. And for Albert,' she added as an afterthought.

'Miss —' the carter said by way of warning, as the horse shifted its feet uneasily and tossed its head, sensing his growing impatience.

Ella gathered both Sarah and Beth to her. 'I love you both,' she whispered, then turned and rapidly mounted the step to seat herself beside the carter. Needing no further encouragement, he shook the reins and they were off. Ella turned and gazed at the scene behind her, trying to lodge it in her memory – Sarah clutching Beth's hand and waving; both of them crying; Sarah bending to give Beth her handkerchief; the sun bright behind them; the hills blue in the distance.

The carter stayed silent as Ella's shoulders heaved and shook while they trotted at a brisk pace through the village and down the hill to the station. As he handed her down from the cart in the station yard, the train just coming into view as it chugged around the bend in the valley, he said gruffly, 'Don't take on now. The young 'un will be busy enough on summat else by now, I'll be bound. Aye, and when she's but a few years grown she'll be after joining you in yon big city!'

And with that he shook the reins and headed off without a backward glance while Ella, struggling to compose herself, hastened with her bag to the station platform, just in time to climb into a carriage before the doors slammed shut.

Chapter Thirty

The train was, as before, too crowded to afford Ella any private space, either physical or mental. Although she appeared to be looking out of the small portion of window available to her, her gaze was unseeing. However, she managed to smile politely at her near neighbours and even exchange a few pleasantries, even though her mind was in a whirl and she felt that her heart might break.

Once again, she was leaving behind the family and home she loved so much, to return to a life she had once enjoyed but that now filled her with trepidation. She had no idea of the welcome she would face on her return, if any, nor whether it would be possible to feel secure in her position. John's presence would be the one saving grace, but it was difficult to know how he might feel about her after her sudden, unexplained departure. Would he trust her again? He would feel that she had abandoned him. Perhaps he had a new governess, one he felt closer to, or maybe he had already been sent away to school?

It wasn't until she was sitting on the station platform at Leeds, waiting for the York train, that she allowed her thoughts to stray to the subject that was most upsetting to her. This time, she had no interest in watching the passengers spill from the trains, or wondering about the nature of them, their journeys or their errands for the day. Her thoughts were turned wholly inwards as she mourned the loss of something that she wasn't even sure was real. Perhaps it had been solely her imagination that Albert had feelings for her. Yet she was convinced she had felt some connection between them, a connection that seemed to have vanished as soon as the family left Luddenden for Northwaite. Or did it date back even earlier? Had something happened when he had returned to York with news of Ella's whereabouts? She turned the events over in her mind, trying to put her finger on when she had noticed a change. And now her feelings threatened to overwhelm her.

As a child in Northwaite she had felt happy and secure, wrapped up in her own thoughts as she roamed the fields and woods around their house. Although, or perhaps because, she was the second child in a family of five children, she had a solitary nature and was content in her own company. It was Alice who had borne the burden of both helping her mother and working at the mill. With a sense of guilt, Ella recognised that she had slipped away from the house, and her duties, whenever possible.

Once Alice had given birth to Beth, things had changed. Ella found herself thrust into Alice's role, at least to the extent of taking up employment at the mill. The busy, noisy environment and the need to fit in had come as a shock to Ella but she had soon reverted to her usual dreamy demeanour, which seemed to act as a protective bubble around her. It wasn't until she had gone to work for the Ottershaws, after Alice's death, that she had finally lost this. There was no place for such a disposition in an employment that filled her every waking hour, where it seemed she had full responsibility but not the recognition for running the household. Grange House had been a shock of a different nature. Here she had learnt how to work as part of a team, as she had at the mill, in a position that gave her some status, however lowly. Although she respected her fellow employees at Grange House, and they had been kind to her, in her adult years she had lacked the experience of someone caring for her, of wanting to do things for her. Albert had given her a glimpse of what such a feeling could be like. When he had taken her to the tearoom in York she had been flustered not only by her surroundings but also by his solicitude, even though it was just simple concern for her wellbeing on such a cold day. Until such a concern was exhibited, and by someone of the opposite sex, she had had no idea that she had been starved of such attention. Albert's subsequent visits to the family in Luddenden had opened the floodgates. Ella was terrified of showing anyone how it made her feel, terrified of exposing her vulnerability. And now she could see she had been right to safeguard her emotions. It felt as though, for whatever reason, she didn't deserve happiness and she was foolish to have even allowed herself a glimpse of it; to have indulged in a fantasy of a life that might have been hers. If it wasn't clear that Sarah and the family were now on the road to a better future, thanks to Albert, she would have been forced to conclude that Alice's death had somehow blighted them all.

Ella wiped her eyes. There was no point in indulging in self-pity. Her choice was made and she was fortunate to have been given a second chance in York. There was no point in thinking about Albert any more; she had clearly read something into their relationship that wasn't there. She shuddered as she thought about his involvement with Violet Lockwood; it cast him in quite a different light. She would have to learn to put Albert, and the life she had allowed herself to imagine, out of her mind forever.

Chapter Thirty-One

Back in Northwaite, it wasn't long before Albert was wondering how he had allowed himself to become involved with Violet. In fact, how had he allowed so many things to happen? He knew he would never be able to make Violet happy. His heart belonged to one person only, the person for whom he had worked so hard in York, hoping to return to claim her, to give her a better life, only to discover that she was long dead. He had thought to try to make things right for Alice's family, feeling somehow a responsibility for her death, and he hoped that the course he had finally settled on was the right one. They had the security of a house, at a rent that allowed Sarah to feel her dignity was retained, and he had been able to pour some of his feelings into the carved adornments around the cottage doors and gatepost. He had raised a gravestone in honour of Alice, as he had wanted, and as the vicar had advised firmly against the wording he had wished to carve into the stone, he had settled for a plain inscription with his feelings bound up once more in the flowers and foliage. The headstone stood out from all the others in the churchyard, and for that he was proud.

He was less proud of what had happened with regard to Ella. He had been truly shocked by her revelation of Alice's death on their first brief meeting in York on that miserable day before Christmas. And shocked again to find Ella and lose her in the space of a few seconds as he saw her being driven away from Grange House just a few days later. He had risen to the challenge of seeking her out and his feelings when he did were not only the joy of success, but something more. Ella had changed from the young girl he had once kept company with on the way to the mill, their only link then being her relationship to Alice. Now she had grown into a young woman with a confusing resemblance to her sister and yet a compelling character all of her own. He was both attracted to her, yet terrified by this attraction. Was he drawn to her because of her resemblance to Alice, or in spite of it? If he pursued the attraction, if he married her, would he end up causing further harm to the family, and to Ella? What if it should turn out that the only motivation was her similarity to her sister, something that might easily vanish with time, leaving each of them frustrated by a hopelessly unfulfilling marriage?

Moreover, he knew that his family would never approve. They had a deep-seated dislike of the Bancroft family, blaming Alice for the fire at the mill and the subsequent loss of livelihoods in the area. It made no difference that neither of Albert's parents were employed at the mill – their feelings were based on local prejudice and gossip and had hardened over time into an implacable dislike. They disapproved of Albert having anything to do with the Bancroft family and were furious with him over his involvement in the carvings of Alice's headstone and at Lane End Cottage. He had managed to keep his purchase of the cottage and subsequent rental of it to Sarah from them, and he was deeply grateful that word of it didn't seem to have been spread by the village gossip grapevine.

They would never have accepted Ella into the family, and while this did not worry Albert unduly – for he felt little affection for his parents – he saw it as yet another reason to avoid any entanglement with Ella. So he hardened his heart and turned away from her, although he didn't like to see the puzzlement in her eyes, eyes that sought his at every opportunity, eyes that had gone from sparkling and joyous to sad. When he heard that she was to return to York, however, it gave him time to pause and think. He realised that he regretted his decision and his actions. He had believed Ella to be tied to Northwaite for good, but suddenly he saw that the pair of them might have made a life for themselves in York, away from parental disapproval on his part, and also away from the landscape and surroundings that seemed to be filled with Alice's presence. In a new environment, perhaps love could have flourished, untainted. But by then, it was too late.

By then he had taken up with Violet, already a cause for regret. She had worked for a brief period at the mill, although he had not been aware of her then. She had considered the work beneath her and so her father Walter, the village butcher, had found her employment as a companion to one of his customers, a Mrs Booth who lived in a grand, but run-down house on the Haworth road. When she told him about her place of work, Albert had feigned ignorance although he was perfectly well aware of the decrepit state the house had been in seven years previously, before he left for York. It amused him to hear Violet tell of the grandness of the rooms and the prestigious nature of her employment. A glance at her reddened hands had told him that her work was more manual than cerebral.

He had come across Violet when running an errand for his mother, paying off their monthly account at the butcher's. Violet had been behind the counter, 'just helping out while Father visits a supplier' as she was at pains to point out. She clearly knew who Albert was, although he had only the haziest recollection of her in the village. He had noted her good looks, though, in an almost forensic way. Violet had pale skin in contrast to her very dark hair and the full red lips which had first caught his attention. She was quite short, but full figured with a trim waist: she could hardly have been more different in appearance to Alice, or Ella. Perhaps it was this that gave her some mysterious allure, or was it his determination to shut out Ella from his life? He found himself walking out in the late afternoon at a time that he knew would coincide with Violet's walk home from her work. The exchange of polite greetings moved on to a chivalrous offer to see her to her gate. Albert was initially perturbed to find that what drew him to Violet wasn't the pleasure of her conversation but instead the admiration of her physical form. He found himself wondering what it would feel like to kiss those full lips and that white neck, to feel her shudder with pleasure under his caress. Albert's time in York had not been without its diversions, even though in his mind he had remained completely true to Alice. He spotted in Violet something as yet untapped, something that reminded him of his adventures in York. He became focused on finding a way of unleashing it.

Walter Lockwood must have had a sixth sense for Albert's motivations, however. He asked him straight out, early on and quite bluntly, what his intentions were with regard to his daughter. Albert, taken unawares, could only blush and mumble words that he hoped would satisfy the older man. It seemed they did, for Albert's attentions were encouraged by both Violet and her family. Her four sisters and her parents found cause to leave the couple alone more often than polite society would have allowed. Perhaps Violet's father, recognising that the young man had a skilled profession and the potential for a good future, was shrewder than Albert gave him credit for. At any rate, it took Albert little time to discover what it felt like to kiss Violet's rosy lips while they were left alone in the front parlour. The risk of someone returning unexpectedly to catch them only added to the excitement for Albert. He left after this first visit flushed by more than his proximity to a heartier fire than the evening demanded, and was quick to return to pay his respects to the family again.

Albert's parents, for their part, were keen to encourage the relationship once they heard of it, and encouraged him to walk over to see Violet as soon as their evening meal was done. Albert's mother allowed herself to imagine how sensible such a marriage would be, binding Albert to the village, without considering that his earning power lay elsewhere. Albert, always keen to escape the stultifying atmosphere of his parents' home, and wary of being too regular a visitor to the Bancroft household, found himself increasingly looking forward to his visits to Violet. It wasn't entirely the pleasure of her company that he sought, however, and he failed to see the web into which he was being drawn. Once he had established that creaking floorboards in the hallway would warn of the imminent arrival of a family member, he felt emboldened to move from merely kissing Violet to more intimate

161

caresses that, after initial protestations, she seemed to welcome, moaning softly so that he found it difficult to restrain his ardour. Each night he left the house more disconsolate than before. One particular evening, following a day in which Albert had allowed his imaginings a particularly free rein, neither Albert nor, it would seem, Violet heard the tell-tale creak of the floorboards in the hallway. The door opened and, before either had time to compose themselves, there stood Walter. Following a very difficult interview with Mr Lockwood, during which Albert could hear storms of weeping from the hapless Violet in another room, he found that he had asked for Violet's hand in marriage and been accepted. A date for the wedding celebrations was set for early in the New Year, leaving Albert with several weeks for his passion to cool as the excitement and preparations intensified around him.

PART THREE

1904–1913

Chapter Thirty-Two

Things had indeed changed a great deal at Grange House in her absence, as Ella very quickly discovered. Grace and Mrs Ward were travelling in Europe. This fact, relayed to Ella by Doris, was accompanied by raised eyebrows, which suggested that she didn't believe all was as straightforward as it might seem.

'As for Mr Ward, you'll see for yourself. The poor man seems at a loss.' This was conveyed to Ella within the first hour of her return by Mrs Dawson as she poured her a cup of tea in the kitchen.

'The business has suffered. There was quite a scandal, you know, over Grace and Edgar Broughton. Things were hushed up as best they could but word got out somehow. I'm sure it wasn't from here.' Mrs Dawson stirred her tea thoughtfully. 'I think it was that manservant of the Broughtons'. Anyway, some Lord somebody-or-other, a friend of the Broughtons, cancelled his contract for a house that Mr Ward was to build, and a couple of other people did the same. But memories are short, something else came up to occupy the gossips and it looks as though all is forgotten now. Sending Grace abroad was a good idea, if you ask me. Mr Ward has been busy with projects in Leeds, but it makes for a long day. He won't be back to eat dinner until late.'

Mrs Dawson got to her feet and prepared to clear the cups away. 'I'm pleased to see you, but I'm surprised that you've been asked back, to be honest. Whatever were you thinking of, with that love potion of yours?'

Ella opened her mouth to defend herself then thought better of it. What could she say? It was better that she kept her head down, worked hard and made up for her misdemeanours.

Mrs Sugden said much the same to Ella when she returned from town at the end of the afternoon. After she had welcomed her back with some enthusiasm, she warned her to be on her best behaviour, for she'd not be given another chance. Ella, aware that this was to be an overriding theme, just nodded. She was settling back into her room, unpacking her few things, when word was sent to her at eight in the evening that Mr Ward wished to speak to her.

With some trepidation, and reminded strongly of the unpleasant interview that had taken place there less than a year before, Ella went down into the main house then mounted the stairs to the library. A small table had been set in front of the fire and Mr Ward was eating a lonely supper there. He looked exhausted, white and drawn with dark circles beneath his eyes.

'Ella!' he said as she entered the room. 'I'm pleased to see you back at Grange House. I daresay you have been made aware of events since your departure.' He raised his eyebrows quizzically and Ella, only too aware of her role in these events, blushed furiously.

'Well, first of all, I would like to apologise for my refusal to hear what you had to say. It turns out that it was a very good decision not to involve the constable at the time. Grace did at least have the courage to confess that it was all her doing once she realised that you had been sent away. By the time I tried to make contact with you, you were not to be found at your old address but, thanks to Albert's kind offices, here we are.' Ella felt her colour, which had subsided somewhat, begin to rise again at the unexpected mention of Albert's name.

'So, the situation is as follows. Grace is travelling with her mother in attendance. John has been sent away to school.' Ella, unprepared for his last sentence, couldn't suppress a start and a gasp. Why had no one told her about John? And why hadn't she thought to ask?

'Ah, I see you weren't made aware of this.' Mr Ward pushed his plate away and leant back in his chair, placing his fingertips together. Ella noticed that his food was barely touched.

'I have to confess that this has not been a great success. The school has been in regular contact with me and, while initially they were confident that John would settle, it seems that they have been unable to alleviate his distress at being away from home. They are of the firm opinion he would do better at home for another year or two. Your return, therefore, is timely. With Mrs Ward away, and the demands of my work keeping me from home for the best part of the day, it would otherwise be just as unsettling for John to be here.'

Mr Ward took a sip of wine and seemed to consider. 'I have engaged a governess for John for the time being and then, in a year or two when he is more settled, he can be a day pupil in York. I have a school already in mind. In the meantime, I would like you to return to an arrangement similar to the one you had before, combining household duties with being available to mind John. I have considered your salary in this connection, and feel that, with this additional responsibility, a small increase could be awarded you. Mrs Sugden will explain this to you further.'

Mr Ward, registering the surprise on Ella's face, added 'I think it would be wise to keep the news of this increase from the other servants. I'm not sure they will understand, in view of your previous dismissal from the household. Of course, I am relying on you and trust there will be nothing in your future behaviour to make me regret offering you this chance.'

'I will do my very best at all times, Mr Ward. I am honoured that you would entrust me with some of the care of John –' Here Ella paused as the realisation of what John must have gone through over the past few months dawned on her.

Mr Ward waved her away in dismissal but spoke again as she reached the door. 'Ella, I have every faith in you. I was very taken by your common sense the first time we met, back in Nortonstall. I feel sure I am doing the right thing.'

So it was that Ella had gone to bed that night overwhelmed by the responsibilities and expectations that seemed to have been heaped upon her. She had failed before, acting with naivety. Could she trust herself in the future? Had coming back been the right decision?

Chapter Thirty-Three

Within a couple of days of Ella's return to the house, John was back too. It struck Ella to the core to see how pale and wan he looked and, although his face lit up when he first saw her, just as quickly the shutters came down. At first, he was subdued and wary. After several months during which his world had been turned upside down, he clearly didn't dare to trust his good fortune now that he was home.

Ella decided that the best course was to act as far as possible as though nothing had changed, in the hope that he would settle down and quickly forget his recent trauma. It worked at first, but within a week his newly appointed governess reported to Mr Ward that John was waking in the night with terrible nightmares. She could hear him from her room further along the corridor. As governess, she didn't consider night duty to be part of her role and he was considered too old to have a nursery nurse, so an impasse had been reached.

When word reached Ella, she didn't hesitate. 'Why, he can't be left to himself every night in this state,' she declared. 'If I can be allowed to make up a bed in his room then I am happy to sleep there until this passes. I don't suppose it will be long. Just until he feels secure again.'

It turned out to be many months before John felt secure again and it wasn't until Grace and Mrs Ward returned, both much changed by their sojourn abroad, that Ella was able to return to her own room. John woke several times a night for the first month, then gradually his nightmares receded until they were once or twice a week. Whenever Ella suggested it was time that she moved back to her room, the bad dreams increased in frequency and intensity. She sensed an element of manipulation, but with no female relative at home to take her place at night, it seemed best to let things lie. Edith, his eldest sister, had married, in spite of the initial slur on the family's reputation, and she had now moved down south. Ailsa had taken up residence with her Scottish cousins, no doubt glad to have an escape route from a house where all seemed gloomy and subdued.

John's days, at least, proved to be better than his nights. When not with his governess he didn't like to let Ella far from his sight. Once a few months had passed and he seemed more settled, Ella began to feel that his view of the world was being too restricted as her duties confined her mainly to the house at weekends. It was during a shopping trip to town for Mrs Dawson that she spotted a crowd gathered around a brightly coloured bill posted up in the market. With a sinking heart, Ella realised that once again her deficiency in reading was going to let her down. The poster showed a lion of very noble appearance, an elephant and a host of exotic-looking creatures, not all of which Ella recognised, set in a wild and dramatic landscape. These were all placed around the edge of a central scene featuring what appeared to be the interior of a giant tent filled with people, with caged animals set all around. Ella, turning away in disappointment at her inability to understand anything beyond the pictures, paused, arrested by the conversation next to her.

'Next week, does it say?' The girl next to her was standing on tiptoe and craning her neck to see over the crowd.

'Aye, on Knavesmire for the week,' her companion replied. 'A menagerie and a fairground. Reckon it'll make a good day out. I'll tell Ma and we can take the nippers.' Her friend smiled at Ella as they turned to leave and included her in the general remark. 'About time we had a bit of fun.'

Ella smiled back, delighted to have acquired the information. It turned out to be unnecessary though, for within a day or two the wagons started rolling in and setting up on the great open space opposite the house, much to Mr Ward's disgust.

'We'll have a week of noise and nonsense, that's for sure,' he complained to Mrs Sugden. 'Keep all the doors locked and the windows closed, and be on the watch for any unsavoury characters hanging about.'

Ella's heart sank when Mr Ward's views were reported back by Mrs S. The servants were beside themselves with excitement at the prospect of a fair right on their doorstep, with wild beasts camped on the racecourse. They had arranged their time off in pairs so that they could visit of an evening. Ella had decided to forego an evening visit so that she could take John on the final Saturday afternoon. But would Mr Ward be prepared to give his permission?

Chapter Thirty-Four

Throughout the weekend, more sideshows rumbled in on great carts and wagons. The early spring sunshine glinted on the gilded frontages and a clamour of hammering, shouts and snatches of music drifted towards the house. The maids spent increasing amounts of time cleaning the interior of the windows at the front of the house and taking the curtains down for shaking and washing. 'Spring cleaning,' they said, but it allowed them to report back in great excitement about the developments on site.

Doris had seen other bills posted up around town. 'There's to be waxworks, fire-eaters, swingboats, a shooting gallery. And *ghosts*!' she declared.

A tent had gone up in the centre of the ground, flaunting pennants fluttering in the wind and clearly visible from Grange House. Mr Ward glared out of his library window and declared it to be 'A travesty and an abomination'. He had seen himself as a forward-thinking man, leading the way in building outside the walls of the ancient city, but he hadn't bargained on Knavesmire, which normally provided such a serene outlook, playing host to a fairground on his doorstep.

He turned away from the window. 'I imagine the servants will wish to attend?'

'Yes, Mr Ward. Everyone is very excited.' Mrs Sugden was firm. It might not be to Mr Ward's taste but she was not going to give him the chance to forbid them. She would have a mutiny on her hands.

'And John?' Mr Ward's direct question caught Mrs Sugden off guard.

'Yes... no... that is...' she decided to take the bull by the horns. 'I do believe Ella would like to take him on Saturday if you would give permission. He's talked of nothing else since the first wagon arrived and he's had his nose pressed to the bedroom window at every opportunity.'

'Then he must go. But in the afternoon and for a short time only. They must be home well before dusk, before there is a danger from any bad elements.' Mr Ward looked pensive for a moment then said, 'I'm sure I can rely on Ella to look after him as if he were her own.'

'Indeed, I'm sure she will,' Mrs Sugden said firmly.

In the event, Mr Ward was so irritated by the presence of the fair that he chose to stay over in Leeds until it was gone, so Ella felt able to interpret his wishes a little more liberally. The visits to the fair by other members of the household, and the tales with which they had returned had whetted her appetite, but she was ill-prepared for the size of the crowd drawn there on the Saturday afternoon. The fame of the fair, the break from work and the sunny weather had pulled in people from far and wide.

John shrank back when he saw the crush in front of the menagerie and Ella felt more than a little daunted too but, forewarned by Doris and Rosa, she knew what to do. She gripped John's hand tightly and drew him towards the stalls that lined the edge of the ground.

'Let's have a look here first. The menagerie has timed shows, so once all those people have gone in we should be able to buy tickets for the next one. So I'd say now is a good time to take a look at the side shows.'

And what a lot there was to see! Ella could barely take it all in and John, tempted by everything, couldn't decide how to spend the pennies he had brought with him. First, they stood and watched the people on the swingboats, screaming in delight and fear as they rocked faster and higher.

'Not for us, I think,' said Ella, and steered John onwards towards the shooting range. Again, they stood and watched for a bit, but it was beginning to dawn on Ella that there might not be much here suitable for a small boy to try. It was a relief when John spotted the coconut shy; something for both of them. Although Ella flung the wooden balls as hard as she could they fell uselessly to the ground, having completely missed their target. John had a better aim and did manage to rock a coconut, rather destroying Rosa's theory that they were all glued to their stands.

'Good shot!' Ella said admiringly. 'I think you might have the makings of a cricketer.' She was pleased to see John look genuinely happy at the compliment, despite the lack of a prize. Since the crowd had now moved into the menagerie tent, Ella was able to talk persuasively to the ticket seller and acquire advance tickets for the next performance.

'It's a two-hour wait, though,' Ella warned. 'Let's see how we can fill the time.'

They both felt more at ease amongst the crowds now, and were happy to take their time and look around. Ella marvelled at the way in which the larger shows were decorated. Broad steps led up to the entrances, which were surrounded by gilded pillars supporting the painted façades. The steps acted as a showcase for performers intent on drawing the crowds into parting with their money to gain entrance, and painted panels depicted mythical scenes related in some small way to the performances.

Ella and John stood for some time in front of the Bioscope moving picture house, listening to the barrel organ play through its repertoire. Ella was very curious about the show but was content to admire the enormous amount of decoration outside. Gold curlicues framed the painted panels next to classical statues of ladies in draperies, which would never pass muster in polite society, bearing great bowls overflowing with plaster fruit set on their heads.

They paused before the ghost house, where the paintings and ornamentation were of a much darker hue. Here a man at the top of the steps, beating a huge drum strapped to his chest, winked at Ella and shouted down to her to 'bring the little man inside for a right good fright!' Ella fixed John's hand firmly in hers and pulled him away. His imagination didn't require any further stimulation: it was quite vivid enough already. Luckily, they found the switchback, which promised to be much more suitable. It was situated just behind the ghost house, the music from its central barrel organ threatening to drown out the banging of the drum. Passengers were already streaming down the steps from the cars and Ella and John were too slow to find themselves a seat.

'Don't worry, we can watch this time around and we'll be sure to get a seat for the next ride,' Ella reassured John. As the music started up, the gilded carriages moved off, slowly at first. The passengers laughed and waved at the observers on the ground. Then the speed increased, the hinged sections of the platform beginning to rise and fall as it rotated, faster and faster, until the faces were just a blur as they sped past. Delighted screams from the passengers could be heard above the music but no sooner had it reached full speed then it was slowing down again.

'Get ready!' Ella warned John. The ride came to a halt and the passengers, rather dizzy now, were struggling to their feet as the chain across the steps was drawn back to allow them off. The waiting would-be riders surged forward but Ella was quick off the mark. She darted up the side of the steps, John close behind her, and around the back of the switchback. They hovered politely for a moment or two to allow a rather stout lady and her companion to descend from their carriage. Ella had a proprietorial hand on the carved, curved edge of the carriage, staking her claim. Her heart started to thump hard in her chest as it looked as though there might be competition for the seats but they managed to slide in behind the previous occupants while others circled the perimeter, disappointed, before being turned away to await another chance.

'Hold tight,' Ella advised as the music began again. The operator swung his way from carriage to carriage, collecting their fares as the switchback began its first slow revolution. She got a thrill from watching the envious faces of those awaiting their turn, and soon she began to feel the wind in her hair as the pace picked up. John gripped her hand tightly on the bar in front and soon they were both screaming loudly, and laughing at the same time, along with everyone else on the ride. Now the faces outside were just a blur and it felt as

176

though they were riding the crest of a wave and then plunging to the depths as the switchback lived up to its name. When the ride began to slow Ella wasn't sure whether she was pleased or disappointed but John looked delighted.

'Can we stay on and ride again? Please?'

Ella, trying to stand on what she was surprised to discover were rather shaky legs, shook her head. 'Let's give someone else a turn and try another ride. We can always come back.'

It was a struggle to make their way through the oncoming rush of riders and down the steps on their now rather wobbly legs. Ella was intent on reaching the gallopers, the wonderful painted and carved horses that were rising and falling on the next carousel ride, when John tugged at her arm.

'Someone is calling you,' he said.

'Me?' Ella, surprised, stopped suddenly, causing people behind her to bump into them. 'Sorry,' she apologised to a grumpy man and his wife who went on their way muttering about 'folks who can't watch where they're going.'

'Where, John?' Ella asked, before hearing her name called clearly over the noise of the crowd. Frowning, she turned this way and that to locate the source, until suddenly she was aware of a couple at her elbow.

'I thought it was you! I said as much to Violet.' There stood Albert, unchanged since Ella had last seen him six months ago, with a petite dark-haired woman on his arm. Ella quickly took in her deep burgundy figure-hugging costume and her rather sour expression.

'Albert! Whatever are you doing here?' Ella's heart, only just restored to its normal beat after the heady excitement of the switchback, was pounding furiously again.

'This fair is famous for miles around. Violet had never

been; I had business in York, and so it seemed like the perfect opportunity.'

Albert looked very pleased to see her, Violet less so. 'We were waiting our turn on the switchback and I spotted you going by. I could hardly believe my eyes.' Albert turned towards John and looked questioningly at Ella. 'Won't you introduce us?'

'Oh, of course.' Ella was covered in confusion. 'This is John Ward, the son of my employer. He's in my charge for the afternoon. John, this is Albert Spencer. I've known him since I was about your age. Your father knows him too; they've worked together.'

John and Albert smiled at each other, then there was an awkward pause. Violet needed introducing, to John at least. Albert seemed to collect himself. He addressed himself reluctantly to Ella. 'I believe you two already know each other,' he said, indicating Violet. He turned to John. 'This is my wife, Violet.'

'Pleased to meet you,' John said politely. Ella hoped his words had disguised her involuntary gasp. Albert married! And so soon.

'Congratulations,' she managed to stammer out. 'I had no idea.'

Violet spoke for the first time. 'At the start of the year,' she said, and patted Albert's arm in a proprietorial fashion. 'Now, we mustn't keep you. It's quite clear this young man is eager to be off. And we must go back and await our turn on the switchback.'

Ella, feeling very uncomfortable, was only too keen to be on her way.

'Goodbye. It was lovely to see you... both.' She wondered

whether her pause was as obvious as it had sounded to her ears. Had she meant it to be? She wasn't sure.

She shepherded John towards the gallopers, looking back over her shoulder as she did so. She caught Albert doing the same thing as he headed towards the switchback, Violet purposeful at his side. Ella's eyes locked with Albert's for a moment and the shock of it caused her to look sharply away and swallow hard.

John looked up at her enquiringly but she was quick to point to the crowd in front of the gallopers.

'Are you ready?' she said, hoping there was no give-away tremor in her voice as a result of the encounter with Albert and Violet. 'It looks as though we'll need sharp elbows.' They had to wait out two full rides before they were at the front of the crowd, by which time Ella had been able to marshal her emotions whilst watching the rise and fall of the beauti-fully painted horses on their gilded barley-sugar-twist poles. The jolly music jarred with the mood the encounter had produced. She had hoped never to see Albert again, never to have to imagine where he might be or who he might be with. Married, barely six months since she had last seen him and after less than three months of courtship, if Violet's words were true! It had taken her cruelly by surprise. Sarah hadn't mentioned it once in her letters in all that time.

The surge of would-be riders jolted her out of her reverie. This time John was ahead of her, tugging at her hand. He had his eye on a pair of particularly splendid horses, nostrils flaring and eyes wide, teeth bared as if to whinny, or to smile perhaps. Although others were in competition for the same mounts, Ella was impressed to see John win the day. He made a mock bow and handed her up into the saddle before quickly hopping onto his own galloper as the operator swung around the poles towards them, collecting their fares. As Ella reached into her pocket John quickly said, 'No, my treat,' and counted out the coins into the man's palm.

'Thank you, young sir,' the man said, smiling at Ella. John's actions helped to erase the awkwardness with Albert from her mind and, as the gallopers picked up pace, she gave herself over to the enjoyment of the moment, riding high above the heads of the crowd. This time, she was the one who didn't want the ride to end but as it slowed on its last circuit she saw the crowds starting to stream towards the menagerie and cries of: 'Roll up for the greatest wild beast show on earth!' could be heard, carried on the wind above the jangling music of the barrel organs.

Chapter Thirty-Five

The excitement was already building as the crowd in front of the menagerie listened to the showman promise them, 'Wild beasts such as they had never seen before, right here in front of them in York, if they would only step inside the biggest auditorium the city had ever seen.'

'Look at the paintings, John.' Lions, zebras, tigers, giraffes and elephants adorned the façade, grazing by waterholes in exotic landscapes or, in the case of the lions and tigers, dominated by men clad in red-velvet jackets and white breeches, armed with whips. The menagerie had the grandest gilded pillars to be seen anywhere on site, the biggest plaster curlicues and statues designed to outdo all the rest. The trainers paraded up and down the steps, thrusting out their chests so that their velvet jackets strained the gold frogging, and cracked their whips menacingly to encourage the 'ooohs' and 'aaahs' of the crowd.

As they pushed their way towards the entrance, John suddenly looked doubtful.

'What's inside?' he asked, starting to shrink back.

'I don't know,' Ella said. 'We'll soon find out. But don't

worry, the animals aren't going to be loose. I have a feeling that the show they are putting on outside might be rather more spectacular than anything we see inside.'

Still, it was with a sense of trepidation that they mounted the steps and found themselves entering a great canvas-roofed space. It was dimly lit after the brightness of the sunny afternoon and the powerful odour of sawdust, animals and an overheated crowd made Ella catch her breath. She laughed at John who was making a face and holding his nose.

'You'll get used to it,' she said. 'Let's have a look around.' The auditorium was lined all around the edges with wagons of animals. She could see big cats pacing behind the wooden bars of their cages, but the spectators were prevented from drawing too close and instead had to shuffle their way past wagons of exotic creatures. Monkeys swung from the bars within their cage and seemed to be making faces at those gawping in at them. A bear, hunched in the corner of the wagon next door, glared out at them. He looked perfectly capable of demolishing the bars that secured him with one swipe of his giant paws. Ella shuddered and moved John swiftly on. Brilliantly coloured birds fluttered and squawked in the next wagon, hopping from perch to perch and quarrelling.

'Parakeets and macaws,' John read from the sign. 'And a peacock. That's it, there,' and he pointed at the bird strutting along the floor of the cage, pausing to peck hopefully at the dirt, one leg delicately raised and his magnificent tail trailing behind him.

'Just look at those colours,' marvelled Ella. His iridescent blue-green throat feathers and the black-and-white eyes on his tail fascinated her. She would have liked to watch him for longer, to see whether he would fan his feathers and raise his tail, just like the painting on the top of the wagon, but the press of the crowd forced her on.

Now they were all being marshalled behind a rope barrier to watch the larger animals being paraded before them. First was a huge elephant, with skin that looked too big for him and ears that he flapped irritably. He seemed to fix Ella with his surprisingly small eyes as he shuffled by with his keeper, a chain shackled to his front leg. She felt uneasy. What if he broke free? The camel that lumbered past next was less of a threat. He was large too, but shambling, and he looked quite ridiculous with those strange humps. Ella found herself smiling foolishly at him.

'Are those painted horses?' Ella asked John in wonder as a number of striped horse-like creatures danced past.

He snorted scornfully. 'No, they're zebras. I've seen them in my *A–Z of Animals* book. Look at their manes and tails. They're quite different to horses.'

The main event – the lion taming – was heralded by a great roll of drums. One of the trainers they had seen earlier, taking centre stage on the steps outside, now stepped forward, flicking his whip menacingly. He announced to the now-hushed crowd that he was about to put himself in great danger by entering a cage with the King of the Beasts. Ella noticed that the lion was actually looking rather sulky, backed into the corner of his cage and resting his head with its magnificent mane on his front paws. His eyes were watchful, though, and as his trainer approached, flicking the whip, he lifted his head and roared, displaying a truly exceptional and terrifying set of teeth. The audience gasped and the animals in the other wagons set up an excited chattering, fluttering and stamping at the noise.

John grasped Ella's hand tightly. 'He won't get eaten, will

he?' he whispered fearfully. Ella, who had been worrying about much the same thing, shook her head firmly. 'No, he does this all the time. He knows what he's doing.'

As the trainer stepped forward to open the door of the wagon the lion rose to his full height and snarled menacingly, causing the crowd, as one, to take a few steps back. With a crack of the whip the trainer had the door open and had slipped inside, keeping the beast at bay by flicking his whip close to its nose. The spectators gasped and cried out as the lion was put through his paces, first being made to stand on a painted stool so tiny it looked as though there was scarcely room for all four of his huge paws. His trainer followed this by making him jump through a hoop and then walk a narrow plank balanced across two stools. Through it all the lion snarled and swished his tail angrily. Ella, from a combination of the heat of the crowd and the tension of watching the act, was starting to feel quite dizzy. A final ferocious spate of whip-cracking heralded the grand finale. The lion lay down on the floor and the tamer, victorious, planted his boot firmly on his back. Ella, realising that she had been holding her breath, exhaled slowly as everyone around them applauded and cheered. The trainer nimbly exited the cage and bowed to the crowd while the lion, safely behind bars, stalked to and fro at his back.

'Did you enjoy that?' Ella asked, as they filed back out into the fresh air.

'Yes!' John's eyes shone with excitement. 'I've only seen animals like that in books. Can you imagine, here they all are, sleeping out here at night, just a few yards from our house!'

They both considered that thought in silence, from quite different viewpoints.

Eventually Ella said, 'Well, what would you like to do now? Although I'm not sure we will be able to top that,' she warned.

The sun had sunk towards the horizon while they had been in the menagerie and it would soon be dusk. 'Besides, your father said I had to be sure to get you home before dark.'

'Oh no!' John protested. 'Can't we stay a bit longer? He's not at home: he won't know. Could I have just one more go on the coconut shy?'

Ella looked around her. Lights were beginning to come on around the fairground and she could see that it would look quite magical in the dark. They might never get another chance to witness it. She wavered.

'Just a few minutes then. I don't want them to be getting worried about you back at Grange House.'

John, intent on finding the coconut shy again, was barely listening.

'Back again, young sir?' The stallholder was already gathering the balls to hand over in exchange for John's coin. Then, in a louder voice, 'Make way for this young man. A bowler in the making I'd say. Might be in line for a coconut.'

People drew closer to watch and Ella felt nervous for John. Such was his determination, though, he seemed barely aware of the crowd that had gathered. The first ball went a little wide, the second struck the base of the coconut and wobbled it, to appreciative murmurs all round. John took careful aim with the third ball then let it fly. It hit the middle of the coconut with enough force to rock it but still it wasn't dislodged. The crowd let out a collective, sympathetic sigh and John's head drooped.

'That was the last of my money,' he whispered to Ella. Before she could respond, the stallholder, seeing the crowd beginning to drift away, announced: 'An extra ball for the best contestant of the day.' He handed a single wooden ball to the dumbfounded John.

The crowd regrouped and excited chatter gave way to silence as they registered John's concentration. He took aim and fired straight and hard at the tip of the coconut. It rocked violently once and then toppled over.

The crowd cheered and the widest grin that Ella had ever seen spread across John's face. The stallholder handed over his prize with a cheerful, 'Well done, lad,' then turned his attention to the queue of young men determined to replicate John's success.

John felt the weight of the coconut in his hands then held it to his ear and shook it. 'There's something inside!' he said.

Ella looked doubtfully at the strange nut, with its coarse, fibrous covering. 'However do you eat it? I don't see how you might open it.'

John shook his head happily. 'I don't want to eat it. I want to keep it forever!'

Ella laughed. 'As you wish. It's your prize. But we must go now. I don't want to risk being in trouble for being late.'

Neither of them was in any hurry to part from the bustle of the fairground, though. The mirrors on the sideshows picked up and reflected back the sparkle of the lights and the glimmer of the gilding, which seemed so much brighter in the dark. As they dawdled along, drinking in the atmosphere, Ella was suddenly conscious of how few children there were in the crowd and that the evening visitors were of a different nature to the daytime ones. They were less well dressed and generally younger, but the mood was good natured and faces were flushed and smiling as John and Ella pushed through the crowd, towards the exit. It was there, with a sinking heart, that Ella spotted a grim-faced Mr Stevens.

Chapter Thirty-Six

'There you are!' Mr Stevens sounded angry. 'We were getting worried. Mr Ward expressly said you weren't to stay out after dark.' He paused and looked meaningfully at Ella. 'He telephoned the house earlier to make sure you were back and Mrs Sugden felt she had no option but to say that you were, and that John was ravenous and having his supper but would make a call straight after to tell him all about it. We must make haste.'

Mr Stevens shepherded Ella and John across the expanse of grass towards the house. 'And I can't say that I was very impressed by the nature of the visitors I have seen whilst I was looking for you,' he remarked disapprovingly.

Ella was feeling quite sick with worry. Had she overstepped the mark? Would she lose her place at Grange House once again?

John, meanwhile, broke away to skip alongside Stevens and tell him all about their escapades. His words tumbled out as he described his prowess on the coconut shy, displaying his prize, which elicited an admiring, 'Well I never,' from Stevens. John was in full flow, describing all the animals in the menagerie, as they mounted the stairs to the house.

Mrs Sugden met them in the hallway with a look that froze Ella to the core. She chivvied John straight up the stairs to the library to make a call to his father. Feeling miserable and deflated, with all the wonderful things that she had seen quite erased from her mind with anxiety, Ella went to hang up her outdoor coat and wash her hands before making her way to the kitchen.

Mrs Dawson raised her eyebrows as she entered. 'Was it wise to stay so late? You don't want to give Mr Ward any cause to let you go, you know.'

Ella groaned and buried her head in her hands. 'I realise now how stupid I was but John was having such a good time...'

'I don't doubt it, but you were the adult in charge,' Mrs Dawson said, setting a plate of food down in front of Ella. 'Now, I've kept this warm for you. Let's be hearing what you've been up to.'

Ella, listening out for Mrs Sugden's return, struggled to do justice to both her tales of the afternoon and her supper. She picked at her food until she was spared further misery by the arrival of Mrs S, with John in tow.

'He's going to eat his supper down here tonight. No point in setting a table for him upstairs, all alone. And having heard what he had to say to his father on the telephone, I have no doubt he'll be wanting to tell everyone here, too.'

Mrs Dawson quickly set out some food for John and made a pot of tea for the others. Ella noticed that even Mr Stevens had drifted in to listen. The coconut took pride of place in the centre of the table while John, in between ravenous mouth-fuls of food, described their afternoon. Ella was only called upon to corroborate the finer details, so she could sit back and let her mind wander a little. With the story at an end and the coconut much admired, Ella announced that John needed to go up to bed. Once his face was washed and he was tucked in, with the coconut on his night stand, she set about quietly picking up his discarded clothes and tidying up until his excited chatter died away and he tipped over into slumber. Then, with trepidation, she headed back downstairs.

Mrs S called her into her office before she even reached the kitchen. 'Ella, I had to tell Mr Ward a lie on your behalf this evening. I never want to be put in that position again. Mr Stevens has told me the sort of people that were at the fair this evening and I can only wonder whether you have taken leave of your senses.'

Mrs S paused and looked at Ella, whose heart sank. Was she about to be dismissed?

'If it wasn't for the fact that John has quite clearly had a wonderful time, I would be asking you to pack your bags this evening.' Mrs S paused. 'Mr Ward asked to speak to me after John had described his outing. He wanted me to pass on his warmest thanks to you for giving John such a special day out.' Mrs S allowed herself a small smile. 'But Ella, take care. You simply cannot afford to make another such mistake. You were very lucky this time.'

Hugely relieved and apologetic, Ella slipped from the room and made but a brief appearance in the kitchen, pleading a headache. She made her way up to her bed in John's room, where she lay awake for several hours.

The encounter with Albert had upset her more than she cared to acknowledge. This, coupled with the trouble she had been in this evening at Grange House, made her disposed to making sweeping resolutions. She knew she had had a narrow escape after returning late from the fair, and that she had Mrs Sugden to thank for saving her skin. She had managed to upset Mr Stevens and earn his disapproval, when he had been so kind and helpful to her in the past. Ella reminded herself of the vow she had made when she came back to York: all thoughts of Albert, or indeed of any kind of romance, must now be put firmly out of her mind. From now on, she resolved, her future would be dedicated to working hard and taking care of others.

Chapter Thirty-Seven

So it was that Ella set herself the goal of living an unexceptional life. This was not without its challenges. She was only twenty-two and there were times at night when she stared at the ceiling in the dark and experienced a great wave of self-pity for the life she might have had. But the life in her imaginings involved Alice still being alive, and the family living happily and contentedly in Northwaite. If she examined this further, she could see the flaws in her fantasy. Even if there hadn't been a fire at the mill, and even if Alice hadn't died, the family would still have been faced with the challenges that the part-time shifts at the mill would have caused. Ella's wages would have been halved and Sarah's income would have been affected too: the villagers would have been hard-pressed to afford to consult her for herbal remedies. The secret passion that Albert had harboured for Alice probably wouldn't have been reciprocated and her own life would have followed a very different course – one that wouldn't necessarily have been better. Now she was experiencing what it was like to be part of a large household, in a big city and it was up to her to make the most of it. Even though she sometimes felt at a low ebb she knew that when she awoke the next day her life would go on as usual, with its attendant highs and lows. At times like these, she would remind herself of how lucky she was to be in such a secure position.

Every so often letters came from home, which gave her a boost as well as causing heartache. Beth sent pictures that were a joy; just simple sketches, yet they told Ella so much. Mr Stevens read the captions – which were often unintentionally funny – out loud to her. He read Sarah's letters to her too, clearly finding the process a little uncomfortable although they rarely contained anything private, being concerned mainly with recounting what Thomas, Annie, Beattie and Beth had been up to. Sarah had given up her market stall to concentrate on her herbalism at home but there was so little other information in them that Ella worried yet again about what hardships might be being kept back from her. Yet on her rare visits home all seemed well. Any privations were either long gone or well disguised.

John caught sight of Beth's sketches once, when Ella had left them on the kitchen table. At first, he seemed a little put out that there was someone else in Ella's life, some competition for her heart. He made some unkind comments about Beth's drawing skills and Ella couldn't suppress a sharp retort.

'I daresay that if she'd had the benefit of a drawing master as you do, John, you might find her more your equal.'

He must have taken the reproof to heart for the next day he delivered a drawing into Ella's hands.

'I thought you could send this to Beth,' he said proudly. He had drawn Grange House from the outside with two figures waving from the windows, one being Ella and the other John.

'Why, I'm sure she will love it!' Ella was delighted and so began an occasional picture correspondence between Beth and John that continued over the next few years. No letters were exchanged, just drawings that at first depicted their everyday surroundings, then progressed to people and events, things that had caused them happiness and sadness – little glimpses into each other's lives.

Once Mrs Ward and Grace had returned to the house, John started as a day pupil at school in York, just as Mr Ward had planned. Ella couldn't believe the change this wrought in him, and in such a short time. He seemed to grow in stature as well as in confidence, returning home with tales of friends made and games played. He proved to be a swift runner, delighting in both sprints and cross-country; indeed, anything that took him away from his desk. It was soon apparent, though, that he had little aptitude for schoolwork. Each year his school report suggested that, 'John could be an outstanding pupil if he would only apply himself,' or 'John has the ability to achieve academically, but consistently fails to do more than the bare minimum.' His sporting prowess saved him, along with his easy good manners and charm, which hid a level of anxiety that was still prone to flare up and cause him problems.

The return of Mrs Ward and Grace had given rise to much gossip among the servants. Mrs Sugden generally rose above such things, but even she had commented on how much better Mr Ward seemed with his family back together again. He had lost his tired, drawn appearance and began to make less frequent, and shorter, trips to Leeds. Mrs Ward seemed energised by her lengthy absence and threw herself into re-organising aspects of the house, planning the redecoration of various rooms. Mr and Mrs Ward seemed happy when together; Rosa, whom it was generally felt knew more than she was letting on as Mrs Ward's lady's maid, said rather mysteriously that all was resolved, then refused to be drawn further.

Ella had been rather dreading Grace's homecoming but it proved to be nothing to worry about. Grace returned very much the grown-up young woman. She said she no longer had need of a lady's maid, having looked after herself perfectly adequately over the last year or so, but at the first opportunity she took Ella aside.

'I wanted to apologise to you over what happened. That silly business over the love potion.' Grace looked embarrassed. 'I was horrified when I heard that Father had sent you away. As soon as I realised, I told him exactly what had happened. I was young and foolish. I hope you can forgive me?' Grace paused, as though a thought had only just struck her. 'Did you have a terrible time? Were you without work?'

For a moment Ella considered whether it would achieve anything to tell Grace the truth?

'I helped my mother,' she replied, 'with my siblings. And then Mr Ward was good enough to ask me to return.'

'Your mother must have been pleased to have you back for a short while,' Grace said, looking relieved that it had all worked out so well. 'Now, please don't think I meant anything by refusing to have you as my lady's maid. It's simply that I've managed without one for so long now that I've become used to fending for myself.'

'Of course.' Ella privately doubted that managing during the term or two Grace had spent at finishing school near Lake Geneva whilst travelling with her mother bore any comparison to managing one's wardrobe back home in York, with all the social occasions and visits that this entailed, and so it was to prove. Grace had been back barely a month before Ella found her duties re-organised to accommodate 'assisting Grace', the compromise settled on so that Grace would not feel she had been wrong over the lady's maid issue. She may have grown up, Ella reflected, but she had retained a strong streak of stubbornness.

Before Ella knew it, almost five years had gone by since her return to Grange House. John, now aged fourteen, had gone about his business of growing up while Grace, in her early twenties, busied herself with good works and dodging her mother's attempts to find her a suitor.

'She's too headstrong by half,' Rosa remarked, possibly echoing Mrs Ward's words. 'No man will put up with her. Next we know, she'll be off to London to join those suffragettes.'

Ella kept quiet. She rather admired Grace for spurning the role that society expected of her. She also found the idea of women's rights rather appealing now that her own horizons had started to broaden. Mr Stevens had been helping her learn to read, having diffidently suggested it after some months of reading her mother's correspondence to her. It had turned out to be a long, slow process. She had given up in tears on many occasions, only to be coaxed back by Mr Stevens with promises that it would become easier. He had been right. Gradually, the seemingly incomprehensible jumbles of letters had formed themselves into recognisable words. Once she had taken her first slow, faltering steps along the literary road, she found herself hungry for much more.

Mr Ward's daily paper was always used to light the household fires on the following day. Ella took to skimming through it before it was burnt, tearing out articles that looked interesting. She saved them to read at her own pace, at first following each word with her finger, late into the evening in her own room. She marvelled at the world that was being opened up to her by the ability to read, and wished wholeheartedly that she hadn't allowed it to be such a mystery for so long.

Chapter Thirty-Eight

When Beth had started school back in Northwaite she swiftly realised that she needed to find her place in the rough-and-tumble of the school playground. Her proficiency with letters, encouraged by Annie and Beattie, made her the target for all manner of taunts from the other children. Luckily for her, she worked this out before she was called upon to demonstrate any skill with her fists. Although small in stature, she had a determined character and one of her earliest memories was of Sarah telling her mildly, as she stood glaring at her, fists clenched and bottom lip stuck out, that if the wind changed she was in danger of remaining like this forever. Patricia Hudson, the tallest girl in Beth's class and the youngest of five children (the others all boys), had approached her one day in the playground in what Beth feared was a threatening manner. Beth, absorbed in her favourite summer pastime of sitting alone on the grassy bank making a daisy chain, had looked up to find Patricia standing in front of her, backed up by the regular gang of girls that hung around her.

'I want that,' Patricia demanded, pointing at the daisy chain.

Beth considered. It would cost her very little to hand it over, but if she did so she could already see that she would be laying herself open to potential future problems.

'It's not quite long enough yet,' she said. 'But if you sit and watch me, I can show you how it's done and then it's yours at the end of playtime.'

Patricia sat down heavily beside Beth, her followers ranging themselves at her feet. She watched Beth at work, then had a couple of desultory attempts herself but soon gave up. Her fingers were too stubby and her nails too bitten to be able to pierce the fine stems and thread the flower heads through. Beth, with two or three years of practice behind her, completed the chain without further ado and handed it over. Patricia wore it, unchallenged by any of the teachers, for the rest of the afternoon and the next morning Beth found her services in demand by Patricia's followers. By the end of the week, her fingers were sore and the playground was denuded of daisies but honour had been satisfied amongst Patricia's cronies and Beth had achieved some kind of status. She exploited this throughout her school years, her skill with her pen, her books, her sewing and her art marking her out as different, but in a way that was acceptable and useful to her classmates.

Sarah had high hopes for Beth, convinced that one of these skills would buy her a different sort of future: if pushed, she would have mentioned teaching as her preference for her. It was not to be: in Beth's thirteenth year, the last day of the school term coincided with Ella's arrival for her summer visit. Beth had casual farm work lined up for a few weeks, with no clear idea of what to do after that. Ella shared news of a vacancy for a kitchen-maid at Grange House and within a few startling days, Beth's future was mapped out. On Ella's return to York she sent word to say that Beth was to come for a month's trial. Hugely excited at the prospect of a visit to the big city that she had heard so much about, Beth was packed and ready to go in a flash, barely pausing to consider how Sarah would feel about her absence. It was only as the Bancroft family sat down together to share a meal on Beth's last evening at home that the enormity of what she was about to do finally struck her. Sarah kept remembering things that she thought it was important for Beth to be aware of in her new position in a big city, issuing anxious warnings about speaking to strangers and minding her manners.

'Now, be sure to write at least once a week,' she said. 'If only your mother were here to see you now. She'd be so proud of how you have grown.' With that, Sarah burst into tears.

Beth, who had been rolling her eyes at Sarah's advice, leapt to her feet and rushed to give her a hug. 'She'd be so proud of *you* and what you have done for me,' she said. 'Look how well you have managed, bringing us all up on your own, working to support us. Every time something has gone wrong, you've found a way of making it right. People come from miles around for your remedies: why, you're quite famous!'

Sarah was blushing and smiling through her tears, while Thomas, Annie and Beattie – who had been nodding in agreement with Beth's words – got up to give their mother a hug, too.

'I'll miss you all,' Beth said, 'and Northwaite too. But I'll write and I'll be back to visit whenever I can. And you mustn't worry about me,' this to Sarah. 'I'll be with Ella. I'm quite sure that she will be keeping a very close eye on me!'

That night, in bed, Sarah wept silently into her pillow, reminded of the loss of Alice and of what might have been, while Beth's sleep was disturbed for a different reason. She tossed and turned, waiting for morning to come. There was a big adventure ahead of her and she couldn't wait for it to begin.

Ella almost envied the way in which Beth slotted so easily into the household. She didn't seem to have any of the anxieties that Ella herself had felt when she arrived at Grange House. Of course, having Ella there to turn to gave Beth a sense of security and, because she came to the household on Ella's recommendation, she seemed to bypass any normal probationary period. It probably helped that Ella had talked so frequently of life at Grange House on her visits home. It must have felt like familiar territory to Beth, who could now put faces to names and explore the house that had been described to her on so many occasions.

Was it the confidence of youth or simply her lack of experience that made her so bold in her first days? Ella wondered. She had to chide Beth a couple of times over her lack of deference towards Mr Stevens and Mrs Sugden. They didn't seem to mind, laughing indulgently and saying how nice it was to have someone with a bit of a spark around the place. Seeing Ella's expression, Mr Stevens hastened to add that no offence was intended, but that times had changed since Ella had first joined them and there was no need to be standing on such ceremony in this day and age. Ella reflected wryly that it had taken her several years to be on first-name terms with Elsie Dawson, the cook, and it was something she could never conceive of with regard to Mr Stevens and Mrs Sugden.

'Why, if I had a daughter I'd be delighted if she had such strength of character.' Mr Stevens looked positively wistful and Ella wondered, not for the first time, why he had never had a family. Butlers rarely did, however. The demands of being a key servant in a household, trusted with the day-to-day affairs and organisation above stairs, combined with maintaining one's status below stairs, left little time for any private life. As a butler, you were everybody's property, whilst also being set apart. It was a lonely path to tread and more than once Ella had wondered why Stevens had chosen it, but had never liked to ask.

It appeared that Beth, however, had no such qualms. She and Ella were preparing for bed one night during her second week when Beth suddenly said, 'Did you know Stevens is married?'

'Mr Stevens,' Ella corrected automatically. 'You mean there's a Mrs Stevens! Good heavens, are you sure?' She was startled. 'He's never mentioned her. Where is she?'

'In an asylum.' Beth was quite matter-of-fact but Ella had to sit down suddenly on the bed to digest the news.

'Yes, it's terribly sad. He was teasing me while I was cleaning the silver, telling me he knew exactly how many pieces there were, down to the last teaspoon. I got quite indignant with him, telling him I was totally trustworthy, and he apologised, saying that he hadn't meant anything by it and that if he'd had a daughter he would have liked her to be like me.'

Beth paused, gazing at herself in the mirror as she applied a few more strokes to her hair with the brush. Ella was arrested by how she was growing. Not in stature, for Beth was not only the youngest but also the smallest of the Bancroft girls, but in beauty. Her hair was dark and wavy, whereas Alice and Ella had suffered with their unruly curls, and her dark eyes were swept by long lashes. She was still young, but viewing her reflection in the mirror, Ella could suddenly see how striking she would be before very long.

Beth continued. 'So I asked him whether he was married, and if he had any children. He looked terribly sad all of a sudden and said that he was married but that you would be hard-pressed to call it a marriage as his wife was in an asylum. I didn't know how to respond so there was a long silence, and then he said that she was a distance away and he saw her only rarely and he would thank me for not mentioning it to anyone.'

Beth had the grace to look stricken. 'Oh, and now I've mentioned it to you.' She looked appealingly at Ella. 'But you don't count, do you? You're family and you won't tell anyone.'

Ella shook her head. 'Don't worry, I won't breathe a word to anyone. Poor Mr Stevens! I had no idea. It must be very hard for him. An asylum...' She trailed off and shook her head in wonder. She couldn't imagine what had happened to keep the poor woman there but it must have been for a long time. She had known the butler for over six years and she had never had any inkling of this.

As they settled into bed, Ella thought back over her years of employment at Grange House. She could barely remember Stevens taking any time off to visit family or go on holiday in all that time. He seemed like a permanent fixture in the house. She wondered how old he was. He had seemed a great deal older than she was when she had first arrived there but somehow, now that she was twenty-six, their ages seemed to have evened out despite the ten-year age gap.

Beth's breathing had already steadied into slumber and Ella smiled to herself in the dark. Oh, to be young again, with so few cares in the world and so little to keep you from your sleep!

Chapter Thirty-Nine

'I just can't imagine what he does to get in such a state,' Beth said, exasperated, flinging down a shirt with a three-cornered rip in one sleeve and the stitching coming adrift on the other sleeve's seam. 'I thought this was a running shirt, not a rugby shirt.'

'Perhaps he caught it on some bushes or branches during the cross-country?' ventured Ella.

'Well, I wish he'd be more careful.' Beth hunted crossly through her workbox for some thread.

She'd barely been at Grange House above a month before Mrs S had discovered her prowess with a needle. She'd needed someone to effect an emergency repair on a dress that Grace simply had to wear that evening but had inconveniently ripped straight after putting it on. Beth had volunteered her services and Grace had been delighted with the result, declaring the dress as good as new. Within the week, an old storeroom beyond the kitchen had been converted into a sewing room and Beth found her duties divided between the kitchen and the pile of sewing repairs that the household seemed to create on a regular basis.

At that moment, there was a brief knock and the door to the sewing room swung open. John was framed in the doorway, seeming to fill the space, his head almost grazing the top of the door frame.

'I've come to apologise,' he said cheerfully. 'About the state of my shirt. I wondered why it wasn't back from the laundry yet and Mother told me that you're probably repairing it. To be honest I had no idea that was happening here.'

Beth had blushed scarlet, right up to the roots of her hair. Had John heard what she had been saying? She looked absolutely mortified.

Ella spoke up, as Beth was clearly unable to do so. 'We were just discussing the damage. It looks as though cross-country running is rougher than we thought.'

'It's all those twigs and thorns. We did get a bit lost and go off track. I expect my rugby shirts are worse though. I'll try to be more careful in future.' John shared a rueful smile with both Ella and Beth as he turned to go, then he paused. 'Actually, I really wanted to find out who the fairy fingers belonged to. I've never seen such neat stitching.'

Ella spoke up again as Beth was still dumbstruck. 'John, this is my niece Beth. You two already know each other, in a way. You used to send each other drawings.'

She regretted the words as soon as they were spoken. John had now turned scarlet with embarrassment, while Beth was glaring at her. Their paths hadn't crossed at all in the few weeks since Beth had been there. John was at school, even on Saturdays, and Beth was usually cloistered in her sewing room or helping Elsie with kitchen chores. She'd barely ventured above stairs yet. Their pictorial correspondence didn't seem to have created a common bond; she supposed they must have thought it unlikely that they would ever meet. Now they had, and they both looked as though they wished the ground would swallow them up.

'Well, it's very nice to have met you at last,' John muttered, backing out of the door. He smiled awkwardly and left; his footsteps, practically at running pace, echoed along the corridor into the silence he had left behind.

'I'm sorry, Beth. I've embarrassed you both. I didn't mean to.' Ella was penitent. When John had come into the room, he was acting quite the young master. Ella feared she had deflated him, without meaning to. On top of that she had made John and Beth self-conscious by referring to the drawings. She couldn't help but feel that she'd set them both off on the wrong foot.

As it turned out, there was little chance to remedy the situation. Beth and John continued to see little of each other as time went by, despite occupying the same house. John's last term at school, the summer of 1911, brought the hottest weather ever recorded, with temperatures regularly reaching ninety degrees Fahrenheit. As soon as the term finished, John and Mrs Ward headed for Scotland, to visit relatives but also in the hope of cooler weather. Rosa went with them and Grace, declaring herself unable to stand the heat, soon followed suit. Alas, they found little respite from the unusual and extreme temperatures, even in Scotland, but as Mrs Ward had decided that the house should be cleaned from top to bottom and the rooms redecorated while they were away, they had no option except to remain there.

Mrs S decreed that housework should begin at dawn and cease by midday as the temperatures were so high by the afternoon that any form of exertion risked damage to the servants' health. The shades were kept pulled down throughout the day and windows were only opened first thing in the morning and last thing at night.

Mr Ward, who had stayed in York, was worried about his business. 'The earth's as hard as a rock,' he complained. 'All the men are getting sunstroke and refusing to work unless we can provide some shade. They can't lay bricks; the mortar is drying before they can spread it.' The decorators working their way around the interior of Grange House were equally afflicted, finding the paint drying on their brushes.

'Do you think the world might be coming to an end?' Beth asked Ella one day after lunch as they lay on their beds in their darkened room. Mrs S had declared that naps should be taken in the afternoon, both to escape the daytime heat and to mitigate the effects of sleep-deprivation caused by the hot nights.

Ella could feel the sweat trickling down her temples from her forehead, but hardly dared to move for fear of making herself even hotter. Afternoon sleeps were proving to be disorientating affairs, the heat causing her brain to dance through a series of increasingly preposterous dreams which were hard to shake off when it was time to rise and resume her duties.

'Well we did have a summer a bit like this just four or five years ago. But the heatwave didn't last for such a long time.' Ella, privately, *did* worry that the world might be coming to an end. It seemed as though there was to be no respite from the heat ever again. She feared that at some point the surface of the earth would just burn up.

'I don't remember it being as hot as this. Are you sure?' asked Beth.

'You would still have been at school. Maybe it was a bit

cooler back in Northwaite.' Ella felt a great rush of longing for home as she spoke. How wonderful it would be to be able to escape this terrible heat deep in Tinker's Wood, or to sit with her feet in the icy cold stream that ran past Hobbs' Mill. York felt as though it was exposed on a great dry plain by comparison. She had thought it might be cooler down by the river, but when she had passed that way on her walk back from the market last week it had proved otherwise. The river had shrunk to around a quarter of its normal height and the stench it carried with it cancelled out any small benefit from the possibility of a cooling breeze. Ella had covered her nose and mouth with a handkerchief and hurried past. Now she wondered whether even the stream at home might have dried up. She would ask her mother next time she wrote. She turned her head on her hot and sticky pillow to tell Beth more about the previous heatwave, only to find that she had fallen fast asleep, her hair stuck to her cheeks, which were quite pink and damp with sweat.

Chapter Forty

The return of the Ward family in September brought no immediate change in the weather. The grass on Knavesmire was bleached white and the temperatures were stifling, day and night, despite the imminent arrival of autumn.

'It's like a hell-hole in here,' Elsie complained while she was making the first Sunday roast after the family's return. 'And it isn't even as though anyone has much of an appetite for food when it's so hot outside.' Even the pantry, normally the coolest place in the house, had gradually warmed up over the course of the heatwave. Elsie struggled to keep the milk and meat from going off, and the butter from turning rancid. She was very grateful when Mrs Ward decreed that cooking should be kept to a minimum for the time being, while the heat persisted.

While John had been away, his father had decided that it was high time for him to experience the world of work. Reasoning that it would be better for him to learn to stand on his own two feet rather than start in the family business straight away, he had found him a position with Grey & Partners, a firm of solicitors where John would become their most junior clerk. He had started during his first week back at home and Ella had admired his smart appearance as he set off each morning, perspiring even at that early hour in a starched white shirt and dark suit. At the end of the first week she asked him how it had gone.

John's face fell. 'I can't begin to think how I will get through to the end of next week, let alone see out a full year. I seem to have no aptitude for the work.' Then his face brightened. 'Mr Grey does at least have a tolerably pretty daughter, Marion. She calls by the office most days; it's the only thing that makes it all worthwhile.'

When Ella reported this conversation to Beth she snorted in derision. It troubled Ella that two of the key people in her life seemed to have an antipathy towards each other. They were happy to operate a policy of healthy avoidance, however, and life settled into a new rhythm at Grange House. John was working hard at the solicitors, although Ella suspected this might have more to do with trying to make a good impression on Marion than wanting to impress either her father or his own. John remained closer to Ella, who was fiercely proud of him, than to his own mother and turned to her frequently for guidance when he was troubled. He was struggling to find ways to shine in Marion's eyes outside of work though, and a little less than a year after taking up his position, he confessed to Ella that he was at a loss as to how to go about it.

Marion was two years older than John and about to turn twenty-one, an age when a young lady of her class might generally expect to become engaged and then married within the year. Ella felt John had grown into a fine young man, and that any young lady of social standing in York should be proud to be the object of his affections. Ella wondered why John didn't put himself forward as a suitor.

'It's not that easy,' John said despairingly. He ran his hands through his hair until it was standing up on end and began to pace the floor of the sewing room, where he had found Ella. 'She's made it clear that she feels I am too young and, on top of that, it seems I'm not suitable.'

Ella was puzzled. 'But your father is one of the most well-respected businessmen in York. And one of the wealthiest – just look at this house.' She spread her arms wide to encompass its solid respectability. 'How can that pose a problem?'

'It's because he's seen as having a trade, rather than a profession,' John said ruefully. 'He's a self-made man, whereas Mr Grey is from a legal family, a long line of solicitors, judges and lawyers stretching back I don't know how long. And university educated, too.'

Ella reflected. The strangeness and intricacies of the class system still sometimes eluded her; the boundaries, though invisible, might as well have been high stone walls. From the point of view of appearance, manners and wealth, John should have been perfect. He was tall and good-looking, his skin tanned and his fair hair bleached blond by the sun. He excelled at sport, too; tennis and riding having now replaced his favourite school sports of rugby and running.

'Perhaps, although it feels to you as though Marion is the right one for you, she doesn't feel the same way?' she suggested gently. 'Could it be that if she has any feelings towards you at all, she considers you more like a brother? She seems very close to her father. I wouldn't be at all surprised if she ended up marrying a man rather older than herself.'

Ella's words were to prove prophetic. Within the year,

Marion was engaged to one of the partners in the law firm, a man a good ten years her senior. John was heartbroken and Ella would have given anything to spare him some of the pain. He became pale and thin, the dark circles under his eyes attesting to nights of broken sleep. Ella's heart went out to him: although many years had passed since she had believed there might be something between Albert and herself, she could still remember the hope and then the heartbreak of that time. John struggled on, determined that no one except Ella should have reason to suspect the cause of his distress. As 1913 became 1914, Ella suggested that he should talk to his father about joining the family firm, as much to break the proximity with Marion and her new husband as anything else.

'You've got over two years' business experience behind you now, so you can join your father's business with your head held high and something to offer,' she counselled him. John could see the sense in her suggestion, but a part of him couldn't bear to cut the ties and break all contact with Marion, even though the relationship was futile and a source of more pain than pleasure. So he dithered and hung on at Grey & Partners, indulging in a form of private and exquisite torture for another year until Fate chose to intervene.

In the meantime, as the months passed, the country moved towards involvement in war in Europe with a series of fits and starts, as government assurances that diplomacy had saved the day and that the situation between Austria and Serbia was under control suddenly, and irrevocably, proved to have no foundation. In early August, before Ella and Beth had time to recognise the full importance of what was going on, with a burst of patriotic fervour the country found itself at war.

PART FOUR

1914–1918

Chapter Forty-One

'A letter for you,' Mr Stevens said, as he looked through the late morning's post.

'For me?' Ella was surprised. She'd heard from Sarah only yesterday and hadn't written back to her as yet. Perhaps her mother had forgotten to tell her a piece of news. But when she took the envelope being held out to her, she didn't recognise the writing. The postmark, too, was indistinct.

Mr Stevens smiled at her as she studied the envelope with a frown.

'You can't guess the contents you know. Why don't you open it?' He slid the letter opener to her across the kitchen table.

Ella slit the envelope carefully and drew out a single sheet. Apart from an address in Northwaite, the page held just two lines of script and a signature. She read them, and re-read them, as if hunting for clues.

'It's from an old friend... well, a benefactor I suppose you might say. He's passing through York with his unit and he'd like to visit before they head to France.' She set the letter down. 'Heavens, I haven't seen or heard from him in years.

The last time I saw him was actually here, at the fair on Knavesmire.'

She saw from the change in the butler's expression that he still remembered that night and how he'd had to go looking for Ella and John, when they had stayed out later than expected.

She hastened to move the topic on. 'I wonder what he wants with me now?'

'Well, I expect you'll find out soon enough,' Stevens said briskly. 'Has he suggested a date to meet?'

'Tomorrow. His unit leaves imminently,' Ella said. 'He's asked whether he might come here. He knows Mr Ward, so I'm sure that will be all right. It will be good to see him before he goes away.' Her expression belied her words. She wasn't sure whether she wanted to see Albert Spencer again after all this time. Although she felt sure that the wounds had healed and her heart was impervious to him, or to anyone else for that matter, she had never put it to the test.

When, in fact, had she last seen him? The fair must surely have been eight or nine years ago. She knew that Sarah had seen him occasionally and that he had a son called Walter who would be quite well grown now. His work as a stone-mason took him away from Northwaite for long stretches and Ella had inferred, from one or two remarks that slipped out, that Sarah suspected that his marriage wasn't a happy one, but she hadn't pressed her further on it. Why, though, after all this time, did Albert want to see her?

The next morning Ella found herself awake early, with a vague feeling of something ominous approaching. It was a minute or so before she could work out why this should be, then she remembered with a sinking heart that Albert was

214

due to visit that day. The greying light at the window showed her that dawn was fast approaching so she decided she might as well get up and make a start to her day. She slipped quietly from her bed, taking care not to disturb Beth. There was always plenty to get on with down in the kitchen and around the house and Elsie would be delighted if someone else had stoked up the kitchen range and got the morning routine underway.

As she set about gathering the ash pails and brushes for the upstairs fireplaces, Ella regretted that Albert hadn't given her the opportunity to change his planned visit. She couldn't see where they could easily talk at Grange House. It would be awkward to ask permission to use a room in the main part of the house; the kitchen had no privacy as it was in use all day and Mrs S's office-parlour, which she would doubtless have let her use, felt too intimate. If she had had more warning, she would have suggested meeting in town.

In the event, Albert arrived promptly at 11 a.m., looking almost unrecognisable in his uniform. He said at once that he hoped she would excuse the brevity of his visit, but his unit was now leaving later that same day. He took it upon himself to suggest that they should walk on Knavesmire, since the weather was so perfect for the time of year.

It seemed both strange and appropriate to Ella that this was the last place she had seen Albert, and here they were again, this time in hot September sunshine under a brilliant-blue sky. Only now Albert seemed like a virtual stranger to her. The intervening years had not been kind to him: his hair had greyed, deep lines etched his face and his demeanour had hardened. As they walked along the edge of the great stretch of greenery, Ella wondered whether his apparent coldness and aloofness was an effect created by his uniform.

'The reason I wished to see you,' Albert said, 'was that I wanted to let you know what had happened to Williams.'

Ella stiffened in surprise. This was something for which she wasn't prepared. She hadn't thought of Williams in many years. Alice was often in her thoughts, but her outrage over what had happened, and the part Williams had played in it, had faded with time. It had seemed more important that the family got on with their lives and that Beth was happy and thriving. Ella wasn't sure that she wished to be reminded of Williams and the part he had played in her sister's life and death.

'I tried to find out what had happened to him when I first went back to Northwaite,' Albert continued. 'I wanted to ask him the truth about the fire and why I had been despatched to York so suddenly. I could only discover that within a year of the fire he had gone off to Leeds or Manchester in search of mill work. Then I heard that he was back in the area and was living in Nortonstall.' Albert paused. 'I delayed seeking him out, although I felt it was something I must do. I needed to know the truth. I began to fear that he would leave the area before I'd managed to find him, and I had a few days' leave so I thought I should try. It wasn't difficult in the end. He spent most of his time in the Packhorse Inn by the river. He didn't recognise me at first; I was but a lad when I last saw him. I almost didn't recognise him, either. He'd become fat and slow from the drink and, to be honest, I'm not sure how much he took in of what I had to say to him. I told him what I knew of the events surrounding the mill fire, and how I felt I'd been got out of the way – paid off with my apprenticeship, in effect. I told him I held him personally responsible for Alice's death. He just sneered at me and said, "Prove it. It's your word against mine."

'I was so angry I made to strike him but some of the other drinkers – friends of his no doubt – restrained me and I was thrown out. I went to another inn and drank myself into a stupor, plotting all manner of revenge on him. I never made it home that night. I must have spent it senseless in a ditch by the Northwaite road, for at least that's where I found myself the next morning. It took some time before Violet would speak to me again. But I heard that Williams had been pulled from the river the next morning. Drowned. It's believed he fell from the Packhorse Bridge on his way home. It's likely he slipped off the bridge on his way home. He looked barely fit to stand when I left him.' Albert looked away, avoiding Ella's gaze. 'He won't be greatly missed. I felt you should know, and I wanted you to hear it from me. He's gone, Ella, and I suppose a sort of rough justice has been done.'

Ella was shocked. 'When did it happen?'

'Just a few days ago. It will be in the local papers by now, I expect.'

Ella fell silent again. It was hard to be reminded of the man, then to discover very quickly that he was already gone with no final answers for the family. Sarah had been sure that framing Alice for the fire had been the action of a spurned man, and that Richard's death was accidental. Williams was the only person who knew for sure, and now he was dead. Her musing was interrupted when Albert spoke again.

'I also wanted to tell you how sorry I am. Sorry if I in any way misled you. I'm sure you knew how I felt about Alice. My feelings for you were confused. I may have made mistakes, things I have lived to regret.'

Albert's eyes held hers for a moment, and then he looked at his watch. 'I must go now. I'm not sure if, or when, I will see you again. Goodbye, Ella.'

And with that Albert strode away before she could utter a reply. Ella tried to imprint his last words on her brain. What did he mean by, 'I may have made mistakes?' Did he mean with regard to her? Or Violet? She felt a flash of anger as she wondered whether his visit was to tie up some loose ends to his own satisfaction, before he marched away to war. She wished he hadn't bothered. He had reawakened memories that she felt would have been better left undisturbed, and left her with questions that it seemed unlikely would ever be answered.

She watched him until he was just an indistinct figure in the distance, then she slowly turned and made her way back to Grange House. Clouds were blowing in and the wind had sharpened, shaking leaves from the trees that lined Knavesmire and bringing with it a hint of autumn. Mr Stevens was in the kitchen when she returned, apparently immersed in stowing away the silver, but Ella had a feeling he was waiting for her.

'Your visitor didn't stay long. Is everything all right?' His studied tone hid some anxiety, and Ella felt a sudden rush of warmth for her second family – Mr Stevens, Elsie, Mrs S, Rosa and Doris – people who cared for her, and for Beth, in their own way.

Beth – she hadn't considered what to tell Beth. Ella had told her that the visit was to happen, but what good would it do her to know about Williams? None, Ella thought. She would keep it to herself. Albert's visit could be given some other pretext: to reassure her about Lane End Cottage, for example, before he went to war. She frowned. This hadn't been mentioned and she chided herself for not thinking of it. Would Sarah's tenancy be put at risk if anything happened to Albert?

Would Violet want her to leave? She'd certainly want to increase the rent. Ella sighed, and then she became aware of Stevens waiting expectantly.

'I'm sorry,' she said. 'It was an odd conversation. Rather inconsequential really. I think it had more to do with him joining his unit here in York, and having time on his hands.'

Mr Stevens didn't press her further but Ella had the impression that he didn't entirely believe her. The bustle of getting lunch upstairs and into the dining room saved her from further questions, however, and she forgot all about her concerns regarding the cottage until she received a shocking letter from Sarah.

Chapter Forty-Two

Ella opened Sarah's letter without any inkling that it would contain anything other than the regular news from home. She could barely comprehend what she read. Albert had died, not in some major battle but having volunteered for a night mission into No-Man's Land from the trenches, during which he, as well as two of his fellow soldiers, had been killed. He had been in France barely two months. Albert was the first man from Northwaite to be lost to the war, but Sarah wrote that she feared he wouldn't be the last.

Ella had read the first few lines of the letter, then stolen up to her room to read the rest of it in private, unable to face the questions that would follow when the others saw her give way to tears. She would have to share the news with Beth, but first she needed to absorb it herself. Memories of Albert flooded in: early memories of walks to the mill and back, of meeting him unexpectedly in the market in York, of his visits to Luddenden when she had found her interest in him growing and had felt sure her feelings were returned. It felt like a very long time ago, yet in some ways it was as clear as if it had been yesterday. She remembered her surprise at seeing him unexpectedly in the kitchen after he had returned with Sarah, having come across her in the market. She remembered how it had felt when he had looked her in the eyes, but also how it had felt when he would no longer meet her gaze. She set aside these thoughts, which were too painful, to concentrate instead on how his wife and son must feel, and his parents too. Had they even remotely imagined when he left that it was to head to certain death? It was coming up to December already and the war that many had so cheerfully declared would be over by Christmas seemed a long way from being won.

She turned to the last page of the letter and found a question answered that she had intended to ask Sarah but had forgotten all about. '*Albert came to visit me before he left,*' Sarah wrote. '*He reassured me that if anything were to happen to him my tenancy of the cottage was secure for as long as I wanted it. I'd told him not to be silly, that he would be back before he knew it, and waved him off in full expectation of seeing him again before Christmas. Now I regret so much not saying something more meaningful, not reiterating how thankful I am, indeed we all are, for his kindness to us.*'

Tears started to Ella's eyes and she felt a terrible pang of guilt. When Albert had made a special effort to seek her out before he went to France, ostensibly to tell her about Williams, had it really been to offer her an apology of sorts for what had passed between them? She had chosen to be irritated by what she perceived as him tying up some loose ends. And she hadn't even thought to thank him for the security that his actions in buying Lane End Cottage had offered her family. With a sense of shame at her selfishness she wondered whether Albert had had a very clear idea of the future that lay in store for him in France. Had he perhaps even chosen to put himself in the way of danger on purpose?

Hearing steps on the stairs she hastily hid the letter under her pillow and lay down on the bed. Beth came into the room, concerned as to where she was.

'Could you tell Mrs S that I have a terrible headache, but that I will be down as soon as possible?' Ella felt that the colour of her cheeks, flushed from crying, would add weight to her words.

'Oh, you poor thing. We wondered where you had got to. You must stay here until you feel better.' Beth considerately drew the curtains and then left, while Ella lay for a while in the half-light, her thoughts ranging far and wide. She tried to imagine the day-to-day routine of the war, as Albert must have experienced it, but her imagination failed her. She had seen the grainy newspaper photos of life at the Front, of the columns of soldiers marching through the fields of France, but she struggled to set the Albert that she knew in this terrible place.

After a while, she got up, opened the curtains, splashed her face with a little cold water to cool her hot cheeks and made her way downstairs to resume her duties. She would tell Beth that evening, when they were getting ready for bed. She thought it would be a shock to her, the first time that war had touched anyone they knew, but she didn't think that Beth, being so young at the time, would have been aware of what an important part Albert had played in their lives.

Ella, however, hadn't taken into consideration that most of Beth's childhood had been spent in Northwaite and she had no doubt seen a great deal of Albert. Beth's eyes filled with tears and she had sobbed for quite some time. When she was calm enough to speak she said, 'What a terrible waste of life. His poor wife and son. We must write them a letter of condolence.' And she set about the task at once, making Ella ashamed again for thinking of herself more than others at such a time.

Why had Albert chosen to go to war? she wondered. Was it patriotic fervour, a desire to save his country? Ella wanted to believe this but, the more she thought about it, his mood when he came to say goodbye had not been that of a man heading to war with a belief in a great cause. In fact, he hadn't once mentioned what lay ahead of him; rather, his actions and words were those of a man with a personal mission to fulfil.

Chapter Forty-Three

As the year turned and 1914 became 1915, any New Year celebrations were as muted as they had been at Christmas. Ella felt as though they were all trying hard to hang onto a life that seemed to change daily. Beth took the view that some of the changes were for the better.

'More women are getting the chance to work now that so many men have gone away to war,' she observed. 'And not just as servants. In factories and in other jobs that once would have been thought unsuitable for women. I've heard that you can earn as much as three pounds a week for a night shift in a munitions factory, or thirty shillings for a day shift. Can you imagine?'

They were both silent while they contemplated such riches.

'Well,' Ella said uncertainly, 'that's all well and good but there's lodgings to be paid for out of that. And food and clothes,' she added, warming to her theme. 'We have all that provided here.'

'I know,' said Beth, wistfully, 'but I would like the chance to do something different. It feels as though other people are doing something for the war, but we aren't.'

Ella, with her experience of mill work, felt that, given the choice, she would prefer to see out her days as a servant, rather than working in a factory, but she could understand Beth's restlessness. War seemed to fill everyone's thoughts most of the time: it was in the newspaper and touched on in seemingly every conversation. There was no escape, even at the market. On a trip to buy vegetables from her regular stall recently, she had been puzzled to find that it wasn't where it usually stood. There was simply a gap in the row of stalls. Produce was hard to come by since many young agricultural workers had signed up and gone to war and the stalls had very sparse displays these days compared to pre-war times. But, Ella thought, this must be the first time a stall had simply disappeared. Knowing how much the family that ran the stall relied on the income, she enquired of the neighbouring stall-holders whether someone had fallen ill.

The stallholder to the left simply turned away, her face closed, and said, 'I couldn't say,' then concentrated on serving a customer. The man to the right was more forthcoming.

'It was their name, see,' he said. 'Sounded a bit foreign. There was some here that took exception. Reported them to the market committee. Made up a lot of daft stories from what I could tell. Anyways, the committee took away their licence.'

Ella was aghast. 'Of course they had a foreign-sounding name. They're from Holland originally. This must be put right. Who can I speak to about it?' She looked around as if she might spot an official hiding amongst the cabbages and potatoes.

The man shook his head. 'T'aint no use, miss. You'll do yourself a favour by staying out of it. There's people here who'd have you down as a friend of the Germans if you speak up.' Then he, too, turned away to serve a customer.

Ella shivered in the cold wind that whipped between the stalls and looked around her. Several of the stallholders were looking at her with open curiosity and she realised that tears, of rage as much as anything else, were coursing down her cheeks. She returned to Grange House empty-handed and had to explain herself to Mrs S and Elsie. They were as indignant as she was.

'As if you could be doing anyone any harm, standing in a market selling vegetables!' Elsie exclaimed. 'Why, what did they think they were going to do? Poison us?' The import of her words struck her as she spoke and her hand flew to her mouth.

Ella laughed in spite of herself. 'I think there would be easier ways to cause harm than by lacing the vegetables that you were selling with arsenic.' Then she grew solemn again. 'It seems to me that things are bad enough without everyone becoming suspicious of people around them, people whom they've known for years.'

Spring brought more news from Northwaite, news that filled both Ella and Beth with dread. Sarah wrote to say that Thomas had joined up. Since he had been living with his wife Lilian in Leeds they saw him barely once a year. It seemed he had joined the Pals battalion made up of local men, many of them from the printworks where he was employed. Ella and Beth wondered whether he was going with a glad heart. Although they tried to retain a semblance of patriotic fervour, Albert's death had made them only too aware of the heartbreak and loss of war and they had started to view news of the latest enlistments with something approaching fear.

Mr Stevens overheard them discussing it.

'Well, he'll be training with friends at least,' he said, to comfort them. 'Although how businesses manage when so many of their workers sign up at once, I don't know. Maybe he won't even be needed. Or not in France – not all the troops go to the Front, you know.'

Beth and Ella took it in turns to write to Thomas. His letters were chatty and full of the novelty of being at training camp.

'He's like a child,' Ella said at one point, exasperated, after a letter full of news about the pranks they'd played, the new friends he'd made and the rumours that they might soon be headed to France. 'He's treating it all like a big game.'

'Maybe it's his way of dealing with it?' Beth mused. 'On the other hand, it's probably one of the most exciting things to have happened to him.'

'I hadn't thought of it like that. You might be right.' Ella was thoughtful. Young men who hadn't yet joined up were under increasing pressure to do so. She'd heard John having more than one fierce discussion with his father about it. Once John had discovered that Thomas was now in the army, he asked them frequently whether they had heard from him and what he was up to. As the months passed, he had become more and more keen to enlist, but Mr Ward urged caution.

'He's just thinking about the future of his wretched business,' John stormed one evening, when he had escaped from a row at the dinner table and taken refuge down in the kitchen. 'I'm feeling like a total idiot at the office; I'm young, fit, unmarried. I should have joined up by now. There are rumours that conscription is coming: I don't want to wait until I'm forced to enlist. I'll look like a coward.'

'Your father is worried about you,' Ella tried to soothe him. 'You're his only son. Of course he is concerned about the business – all his hopes for the future are invested in it. But he wants to protect his family too.'

John turned to Beth, hoping for her blessing for his determination. It dawned on Ella that their antipathy towards each other over the past few years had somehow dissipated without her really noticing. She couldn't pinpoint when the change had happened. Was it when John had started work? Had that somehow put them on a more equal footing in Beth's eyes? Or was it that they had both grown and changed from the awkwardness of youth?

She suddenly realised what handsome young adults they had both become, yet contrasting in seemingly every way. John was tall, fair and well mannered; Beth petite, dark and outspoken. Their backgrounds could hardly be more different yet they seemed to have an affinity. Perhaps it was simply their ages – they were both twenty years old. It was an age when they should have been having the time of their lives, but war had got in the way.

She despaired as she thought of how the war was laying waste to so many of the country's young men. The newspapers carried regular reports of the mounting death toll – reports that she could barely bring herself to read. Already names of men that she knew had appeared amongst the lists of the dead, such as Albert, some of John's schoolfellows, neighbour's sons. It seemed as though there was barely a family they knew that hadn't been affected in some way.

In the meantime, while Ella's thoughts had wandered, Beth and John's conversation had turned into a forceful discussion. Beth was holding her own, Ella noted approvingly, and John – far from being put out – was clearly enjoying the debate.

'Time to put all our differences aside,' she said briskly. 'It's getting late and we all have to be up in the morning.' And some of us earlier than others, she thought to herself as she set about making sure that the kitchen was tidy. Beth and John rose to their feet but seemed disinclined to stop their conversation.

'Make sure you turn off the lamps,' she said pointedly as she closed the kitchen door and headed up to bed, smiling to herself. She was fast asleep long before Beth crept into the room sometime later.

Chapter Forty-Four

As the year wore on, first Doris, and then Rosa, left Grange House. Doris went to work at the chocolate factory; with so many of their men gone to war they had started to employ more and more women.

'Is there much call for chocolate these days?' Ella was doubtful. 'Isn't there a danger that the job won't last with the war on?'

Doris shook her head emphatically, making her auburn curls bounce. 'No danger of that. People want sweet treats even more when times are hard. And chocolate is one of the most popular things in the parcels that families send to the troops, so the orders won't dry up anytime soon.'

Beth was envious. 'You'll be surrounded by chocolate all day. What could be nicer?'

Doris laughed. 'It doesn't work like that. The factory is huge and there are separate sections for different things. I won't necessarily be working with chocolate. Maybe almond paste. Or other flavourings. There's a wonderful smell of chocolate, though. It hangs over the whole place.'

Regular reports came back via Rosa for the next few months. 'She gets one of those new electric trams right to work; can you imagine?' and 'She's earning so much that she's even managing to save.' It wasn't long before Rosa announced that she, too, would be leaving.

'Doris has asked me to share a room with her in town,' she told Ella and Beth. 'If I don't leave now I'll be pushed, I reckon. No one needs a lady's maid with things the way they are. All the entertaining, all those visitors we used to have – that life's gone. And it's time I went too.'

Beth thought it seemed like a daring thing to do and she was very taken with the idea but Rosa told her it was no place for her and that some of the women were a rough bunch, smoking and swearing. 'Just like men,' Rosa said.

Even so, Beth felt there was more adventure to be had working in a factory than being stuck in Grange House, helping to run the household on a skeleton staff. At least it would make her feel like she was contributing to the war effort, and give her something in common with John. For John had finally signed up. The tipping point had come when Marion, the lover he could never have and never forsake, died suddenly and unexpectedly of complications related to childbirth. Ella wasn't sure whether it was grief over her death, the need to get away from Grey & Partners or a sense of the futility of his life – or a combination of all three – that finally made John go against his father's wishes. Whatever the cause, within a week of Marion's death, John had paid a visit to the recruiting office in town and been told to pack a bag for camp. He was going to be part of the first wave of fast-tracked officers, due for imminent secondment to an officer cadet camp in Newmarket for training.

In early February 1916, on a bright, sunny day with a bitter wind blowing across Knavesmire, the family assembled to see him off. All the servants were in close attendance, too. Everyone waved, smiled and wished him luck but once he was out of view a more sombre mood descended. Ella observed that Mr Ward looked grim, while Mrs Ward pulled out a handkerchief and dabbed at her eyes before wrapping her coat around her and hurrying indoors. The servants returned to the kitchen.

'I can't believe it,' Elsie sighed. 'I've known him his whole life. Will we ever see him again?' She put her hand up to her mouth, as though she couldn't believe that she had voiced her thoughts, then used the corner of her apron to wipe her eyes.

Ella couldn't trust herself to speak. Memories of John as a young boy came flooding back: of sleeping by his bedside for all those months when he was plagued with nightmares; the feel of his trusting hand in hers at the fair; his confidences about his hatred of work and his love for Marion. Who would be there for him to turn to when he went off to war?

Mr Stevens, seeing how upset Elsie and Ella were, spoke up bracingly. 'He's only left for training camp. It will be a while before they're called on to go anywhere. And who knows, maybe the war will be over before he's needed.'

Beth was silent. Ella suspected that she was thinking of Thomas. His company had been kicking its heels for a while now, eager to be let loose for the job for which they had been trained. They had been sent here and there on exercises and there was regularly talk of them going overseas, but as yet it had amounted to nothing. While she understood the frustration that he expressed in his letters to them, she couldn't help but hope that the situation remained unchanged.

The household now had Mr Stevens, Mrs S, Elsie, Ella and Beth looking after just Mr and Mrs Ward and Grace. However, Mrs Sugden's elderly mother had fallen sick and, with no one else to step in, it fell to Mrs S to return home to care for her until some other arrangements could be made. When the government announced that households should be patriotic and cut their staff to a minimum, releasing their workers to join the war effort, Ella feared that Rosa's words had been prophetic. But Mrs Ward thought differently. She took the unusual step of summoning them to a meeting and addressing them all directly.

'None of you are eligible to be called up. Stevens, I'm afraid you are above the age limit of forty-one.' The butler looked suitably embarrassed. 'However, we are in the fortunate position of being able to help the local community and I propose utilising all our skills to do so. I intend to introduce regular tea parties here for the war widows as a way of reaching out to those in need in the wider community. I'm considering volunteering Beth's skills as a seamstress for any war work required locally, and possibly we can utilise Elsie's experience as a cook in some way. I don't anticipate any of us being idle.'

This plan was to sustain Mrs Ward through the war years and it also helped Ella and Beth to feel as though they were making a valuable contribution. Elsie was prevailed upon to give simple cookery lessons to a small group of local ladies who had lost their husbands, teaching them how to stretch their limited household budgets by cooking economically.

'I sometimes wonder whether their mothers ever taught them anything', she grumbled after a particularly trying session of pastry making. 'I fear they may be destined to spend the rest of their lives eating bread and jam. Bought in a shop, not homemade,' she added with some scorn.

Ella savoured the time she spent with the babies and small children, for Mrs Ward encouraged their mothers to bring them along and set aside a room to be used as a crèche. Even though she spent most of her time on her hands and knees, rooting out the soft balls and toys that had become wedged under the furniture, or separating a couple of toddlers warring over a possession that they both prized, she wouldn't have changed a thing. For the first time, it hit her that she was unlikely to ever have any children of her own. It was some small compensation for this that, whenever she felt like it, she was able to scoop up a small child onto her lap and bury her face in his or her neck, blowing raspberries and giving them a squeeze or a tickle before releasing them.

On days when unusually large numbers of children arrived, usually in the school holidays, Beth would be drafted in to help out but otherwise her role involved a variety of sewing tasks that Mrs Ward found for her. This included creating clothing for the families of the widows, generally making new garments out of old by cutting up their husband's clothes, no longer of any use to them, to make shirts and trousers for sons or pinafores for daughters. She found the task heartbreaking at first, handling the fabric as though it still held traces of its dead owner, but as the weeks passed she became immune to such thoughts. The sewing piled up in her little room so that she said to Ella, despairingly, that it felt as though she was working in a factory, but without the benefits of the camaraderie, or the pay. Mrs Ward had also offered Beth's services to make garments to send to the troops, such as shirts and pyjamas.

'I'm not convinced they ever change into pyjamas in the trenches,' Beth mused as she sewed on yet another set of buttons.

'I think they're probably being sent to the field hospitals,' said Ella, who was helping her out. 'I'm sure they are glad of them there. And anyway, you'll get a break next week. I heard Mrs Ward say that there's a consignment of bandages coming in to be rolled.'

Beth groaned, and rolled her eyes. 'Like I said, just like a factory.'

She had spoken no more about going into the munitions factory, having heard from Rosa who had a friend there that the hours were very long, the conditions frequently dangerous and noisy and, if you were unlucky enough to be chosen to work with one particular explosive, your skin might turn yellow. It no longer seemed like such an attractive prospect.

It was on a hot July day, when Ella was in the kitchen garden looking to see which fruit was the ripest for the evening's dinner, that she heard her name being called by Beth. She was reluctant to leave the peace of the garden, where she had been admiring the brilliant blue sky and enjoying the scent of the roses, made powerful by the heat of the sun, as it wafted across the lawn. It felt almost like a return to happier times, as if the war didn't exist.

Beth's tone sounded urgent so she sighed, set aside her basket and sun hat, and made her way back to the house. Here she found Mr Stevens and Elsie, grim-faced, in the kitchen, while Beth sat sobbing at the kitchen table, a piece of paper before her.

Ella stiffened and scanned their faces. She instantly feared bad news. Names raced through her mind. Was it Sarah? Thomas? John?

'I'm so sorry, Ella.' Stevens stepped forward to support her as she swayed, feeling suddenly faint. He pulled out a chair for her while Elsie hurried to fetch her a glass of water. Finally, Beth raised her head and looked at Ella, her face flushed and tear-stained, her eyes swollen.

'It's Thomas,' she whispered. 'He's dead. In France. Ma has just had word. She sent us a telegram.'

Chapter Forty-Five

The next few hours passed in a blur. When Mr and Mrs Ward heard the news of Thomas's death they insisted that Ella and Beth must return home at once to spend time with Sarah. It was only when Mr Stevens was escorting them to York station that Ella remembered her hat and basket were still in the kitchen garden. How happy she had felt at that moment, only a few hours earlier. Now she couldn't imagine how it would ever be possible to feel that way again.

'Mr Ward would have driven you there himself if the use of a car hadn't been all but prohibited by the war. I hope the journey goes well for you both, without delays.' Mr Stevens looked along the tracks as the train steamed into view. 'You must only return when you are ready.'

But after a day or two at home, both Ella and Beth were at a loss as to how to keep themselves occupied, and longed to return to the bustle of Grange House. Sarah had withdrawn into her grief and, beyond making sure they prepared meals for her, there seemed little they could do. Thomas would be buried in France along with his fallen comrades from the Pals brigade, all but wiped out in the Somme, so with no funeral to prepare for there was nothing to keep them busy and no focus for their grief.

They took long walks around the neighbourhood, through Tinker's Wood and over the moors, talking about Thomas and sharing memories of his childhood. Instead of helping them to grieve it only seemed to exacerbate their disbelief that he had gone. By the third day, when his widow Lilian arrived to spend some time with Sarah, they began to feel that Thomas's memory might best be honoured if they went back to Grange House and took up their war work again.

'You must write to let us know how you are, and if you need anything,' Beth said as they packed their bags again in readiness for departure.

'Annie and Beattie have written to say they will both come when they can,' Ella added. 'With their husbands away in France they'll have to bring the children along too and they didn't want it to be too much for you.'

Sarah, normally only too delighted to see her grandchildren, made a face. 'Tell them not to bother. I can't be doing with a lot of fuss.'

Beth and Ella exchanged worried glances. 'They want to come, Ma,' Ella said firmly. 'Maybe seeing the children will be a distraction for you?'

But Sarah had retreated back into her thoughts, although she hugged them both when they left, thanked them for coming and then she and Lilian waved them on their way.

So, five days after the dreadful news had arrived, they found themselves back in the kitchen at Grange House, catching up on events that had happened while they had been away. The major piece of news was that John was due a few days' leave and would be home in the next day or so.

'He's written to say that he's desperate for some home cooking, so Mrs Ward wants to pull out all the stops.' Elsie was positively beaming at the prospect of cooking something more elaborate than the basic fare the diminished household had become used to. Then she became suddenly sombre as she remembered that Ella and Beth were grieving. 'I'm so sorry. That was tactless of me. It's hardly a time to be thinking about celebrating.'

Ella was quick to respond. 'No, please don't think like that. Beth and I came back because we felt that Thomas would have wanted us to try to get on with life as normal. Well, as normal as it is possible to be in these times. Of course we are terribly sad but having John home will be a good antidote for a few days.'

John's return did indeed give the household a much-needed boost. It took the focus away from all the worthiness of their war efforts and back onto the family, and everyone appeared the better for it. Mr and Mrs Ward seemed rejuvenated at the prospect of the visit, and even more so when John eventually arrived at the front door, full of apologies over hold-ups and late trains, but looking very dashing in his uniform.

He called into the kitchen to see them all that evening and to thank Elsie for a splendid dinner.

'I can't tell you how often I have dreamed of your roast dinners. You have no idea of the type of food that gets served up in the mess – it's worse even than my school dinners. And that's saying something!'

John didn't appear to have lost weight, however; on the contrary, he appeared to have filled out and he was tanned 'from all the drills we have to do outside every day,' he said, laughing, when Elsie commented on how well he was looking.

'Your uniform does you credit, sir,' Mr Stevens said. 'I'm sure we will be seeing an officer's pips before too long.' Ella wondered whether he was envious, wishing himself a few years younger so that he too could have played a part.

John laughed off their admiration. 'I can't tell you how I long to get out of it. It's far too hot for this weather. It'll be mufti for me for the next few days.'

Beth had been silent up until now, but John sought her out with a wry smile as he spoke, then he turned and left with promises to return soon with tales of his time spent in the training camp.

Ella found him deep in conversation with Beth in the garden the next day. She had gone out to see why Beth hadn't come back with the runner beans that Elsie needed and found her sobbing, basket still empty, while John looked on in concern.

'I'm so sorry, Ella. I only found out about your brother this morning. I saw Beth out here and came out at once to tell her how upset I was to hear the news. I didn't mean to cause her more distress.' John ran his hands through his hair and looked despairingly at Ella.

'It's all right; I'll take her back inside. Please don't worry; it's all still rather raw.' Ella ushered Beth back into the house, turning to smile reassuringly at John. As she soothed Beth and fetched her a drink of water when her sobs turned to hiccoughs, she wondered why she couldn't feel like this herself. Her heart felt like a nugget of ice in her chest and her tears seemed to be frozen inside.

John came down to the kitchen again that evening to tell them more about his experiences over the last few months at his training camp near Newmarket. Much of it sounded similar to the tales they had heard from Thomas – pranks in the classroom and a good deal of joshing and ribbing amongst the men. There seemed to be a lot of focus on sport, too. Was it designed to keep them occupied and prevent boredom, or to breed aggression and competitiveness, Ella wondered. One thing was clear: John was enjoying the drills, running and fitness routines, but was less than delighted by the hours spent at a desk.

Chapter Forty-Six

Once John's leave was over and he had returned to training camp, Ella noticed that Beth started to pay more attention to the news filtering through from the Front. Although Mr Stevens cautioned that not everything in the newspapers would be accurate, it was impossible to stop word spreading via those who had returned home injured. The loss of men seemed to be huge and the battle was still dragging on as summer turned to autumn with no end in sight. Names such as St. Quentin and Arras were added to others such as Thiepval and Ypres that British tongues had already become accustomed to threading their way around.

'Is this it?' Beth said to Ella despairingly. 'It feels like stalemate, as though the war will go on forever across a patch of land that isn't even the real problem. So many men lost, and so little gained.'

John's next leave was cancelled and it appeared to be inevitable he would be sent to the Somme too. With so many men dying there each day, Ella and Beth found it hard to believe that this could mean anything other than certain death, but neither of them could voice this to the other. As the weeks passed with no news from John, Mr and Mrs Ward looked increasingly drawn and Ella frequently found Beth weeping over her sewing. Even Elsie's grumbles about the price and scarcity of food did little to distract everyone.

Finally, it looked as though the battle was over, or perhaps it had just petered out. Either way, there was no resounding victory. A letter arrived at the house from John at last to say that although they had finally made it to France there had been no call for his company's services. He was being sent back to Newmarket to complete his training. His tone was very disgruntled, according to Mr Stevens who had been shown the letter, but Mr and Mrs Ward looked noticeably happier and the atmosphere in the house was lighter.

Within the month, John's commission as a second lieutenant was announced in the *London Gazette*. The family was proud but nervous; he had been seconded to a unit that was back out in France. Although the war dragged on, reports that were coming through suggested minor skirmishes only. Any plans for major campaigns were clearly being kept under wraps.

Christmas passed almost without being marked in Grange House; it seemed wrong somehow, with so many lost and so little to celebrate. Ella remembered pre-war Christmases with a sense of wonder. Had it ever been possible to feel safe, happy and affluent; to celebrate with a tree, presents and an abundance of food? John's letter thanking his parents for their Christmas parcel reported a sense of guilt that he had still seen no action, a feeling which had been exacerbated by the spending of Christmas in comparative comfort, way back from enemy lines.

The early part of New Year 1917 saw the focus of the war move away from the land and out onto the seas where German submarines were wreaking havoc on shipping. Beth confessed to feeling relieved that an uneasy stalemate seemed to have been established at the Front. Mr Stevens said rather gloomily that he feared that both sides needed to draw breath and find more troops to bring forward to the front line, an image that silenced Beth and worried Ella.

News in April that the United States was entering the war offered a ray of hope although Beth and Ella were both puzzled as to why a country would choose to involve itself in a war so far distant from its shores. It all made more sense when Stevens pointed out that Germany had been deliberately provocative, sinking American ships and making it almost impossible for the United States to remain neutral.

While the news seemed more hopeful, it offered no imme-diate respite since it would be several weeks before American troops would arrive in Europe. John's letters, however, were full of excitement, according to Mr Stevens. The butler himself thought it inevitable that another big push forward was planned and, although John was circumspect in what he said, to avoid his letters home falling foul of the censor, it seemed clear that they were preparing to be on the move at last.

Elsie found it hard to engage with Beth, Ella and Mr Stevens in the intense discussions that they had on many an evening. 'I'm more worried about where the next meal is coming from,' she complained. Flour was hard to come by and expensive, making a loaf of bread now as much of a treat as cake. Households had turned to potatoes to bulk out their meals, resulting in a widespread shortage.

'It's a good job my cousin has gone to help out on a farm near Knapton,' Elsie said. 'If it wasn't for a bit of bartering I don't know how we would get by.'

Fresh fruit from the kitchen garden was now regularly exchanged for a wild rabbit or two along with a few potatoes. Elsie had suggested that they should turn over more of the garden at Grange House to growing food and Mrs Ward promised to give it serious consideration, with a view to starting the planting in the spring.

Suddenly and unexpectedly, John was home again on leave. He suspected a big push forward in the near future so his guess was that the troops waiting in reserve were being given the chance to return home briefly. Once his leave was over and he was back in France, he thought his company would be working its way forward to the Front, with no chance of further leave for some time.

He had come down to the kitchen after dinner on his first evening, full of praise again for Elsie's cooking. He described the monotony of pretty much everything in camp: the food, the drills, the tasks they had to perform to keep the camp running smoothly.

Beth was puzzled. 'Are you all living in tents?' she asked.

John smiled. 'It's not that sort of camp – at least not for us. We're living in the outbuildings of a farm so we're lucky. It's pretty run-down where we are but I imagine we'll be seeing a lot worse when I get back out there. There are plenty of others living in tents, though.'

He sounded quite cheerful about it and it was clear that he was impatient to return and see some action. Ella found it hard not to be caught up in his boyish enthusiasm as he described their longing to show the Huns a thing or two and to put into practice all that they had learned. He confessed it was tricky being in command of men much older than himself, some of whom had served in the army for years.

'Mostly they try to help me out rather than catch me out,' he observed wryly.

Otherwise, his company was made up of new recruits, men who had never intended to go to war: office clerks and factory workers in the main. Ella was touched by the sense of pride with which he spoke of 'the lads'; as their second lieutenant he clearly saw himself in some sort of protective or paternal role even though he was one of the youngest in the company. He spoke with great enthusiasm of a man who had become something of a hero among them all.

'Imagine, he's only twenty-four and a Lieutenant-Colonel already, with a Military Cross and a Victoria Cross to his name. Some say he'll be a Brigadier-General before long.' He sounded wistful.

Mr Stevens appeared to understand the achievement this represented, while Beth and Ella were simply baffled, although they could see how the meteoric rise of someone of a similar age to John could hold such appeal for him. His eyes shone and his cheeks were flushed as he tried to express how all the men felt about their role in keeping the country safe from invasion and how they all longed to prove themselves. Ella tried to suppress her misgivings about the human cost of war, for now that it had started what was the alternative? She noticed that Beth seemed mesmerised as John was talking and it didn't surprise her that both of them hung back as first Elsie and then Mr Stevens made their excuses and took themselves off to bed.

'Don't stay up too late,' she warned Beth as she headed for

bed herself. The sense that something was afoot kept her from sleep, so that she was still lying wide-awake when Beth crept into the room.

She undressed noiselessly and slipped into bed, lying quietly for a short time before whispering to Ella, 'Are you still awake?'

'Yes,' Ella murmured back.

Beth turned on her side and lay facing Ella, who could dimly make out her features in the darkness of the room.

'John has just told me he could think of no one but me all the time he has been away!' Beth's excitement was clear even in her whispered tones. 'He's asked me to be his sweetheart. And I've said yes!'

Ella was silent.

'Aren't you happy for me?' Now there was a slight edge to Beth's voice, which had risen above a whisper.

'Oh Beth, of course I am. Just very surprised.' Ella paused. 'And wondering how it will be possible. His parents will never agree, you know.'

'It's to be a secret. Just between the two of us. Although of course you know now, so you must swear not to tell a soul. It's because he thinks he is going back to the Front Line. He wants to feel there is someone special thinking of him back home.' Beth laughed. 'That makes him sound very self-centred and he's not. It's more than that, of course. I do care for him, a lot. I was just so surprised that he chose me.'

The more that Ella thought about it, the more she could see that it wasn't such an unlikely situation. John had probably spent more time with Beth than with any other girl of his own age. They were friends now, but whether they could ever be anything more than that she didn't know. Coming from different classes as they did, it would have been virtually impossible before the war, but now so many things had changed. She wasn't sure, in the end, if it would even matter. If John's belief was that his battalion was about to be sent to the Front was true, who knew what the future had in store? She had a sudden memory of Thomas, and an echo of the excitement in his letters when he was sent to the Front. Was the same fate lying in wait for John?

She shivered, despite the warmth of the summer evening. 'Try to get some sleep if you can,' she advised Beth. 'I know you're excited, but if you don't sleep you'll be exhausted tomorrow.'

Beth's breathing steadied into the rhythm of sleep before long, and instead it was Ella who lay wide-awake, finally drifting into troubled sleep just before dawn. She tossed and turned with dreams of Thomas, John and Albert, who had somehow become combined into one person, a person who was walking unheeding into danger while she tried hard to warn them but could not make a sound.

Chapter Forty-Seven

Ella awoke in a sweat, her heart pounding, fearing she was late. The gritty feeling behind her eyes and the heaviness of her limbs told her that she had had very little sleep and it was going to be hard to get through the day. Beth was still sound asleep, so Ella climbed wearily out of bed and dressed before shaking her niece awake.

'Time to get up now. I must get on. We've got tea this afternoon for the war widows. Where Mrs Ward imagines we'll find the wherewithal to make scones for everyone, I don't know. I promised Elsie I would give her a hand. I'll see you downstairs.'

The day was going to be a busy one but Ella was glad of the distraction, resolving for the time being to put the matter of Beth and John's arrangement out of her head. Beth had volunteered to run the crèche today so Ella took her place at the tea party. She had started to find tea with the war widows hard to endure. It reminded her forcefully of the loss of Thomas and today she felt remorse for not having written recently to Lilian, his widow.

Ella was still unable to think a great deal about Thomas's

death. It felt as though there was something terrifying hidden behind a door, a door that she only dared to open a little at a time to catch a glimpse of what lay behind. She hadn't grieved properly yet and she wondered when she would. Perhaps it was because he was buried so far away, in France where he had fallen. The absence of a grave, of a proper burial service at home, seemed to have made his death feel unreal.

It certainly wasn't a topic she could touch on with the war widows. She dispensed tea and scones, along with the last of Elsie's precious strawberry jam, a sympathetic smile on her lips at all times. The atmosphere was a little subdued; whenever one of the ladies laughed she would quickly stifle it, as if mirth was unseemly at such a time. The widows were mostly young; younger than Ella. One or two had brought young babies into the room with them and these provided a common bond for many of the group. Yet Ella saw that others stayed away from the babies, gravitating towards each other and forming their own small group around a table. She guessed they must have been widowed before they had had a chance to start a family. Like her sister-in-law Lilian, they were left with nothing but memories of the husband they had lost.

When Ella at last fell into bed that night, she hoped her weariness would carry her swiftly into a deep sleep, but it was not to be. Beth had stayed downstairs, presumably in the hope of having a few last words with John before he left the next day. Ella found herself lying awake with her thoughts, which she could not prevent from following a loop. Albert, Thomas and now John. Was it possible that anyone could go to the Front and survive? She knew that of course they must, but tiredness dragged her down and muddled her thoughts until it seemed to her that everyone her family loved must be cursed.

Chapter Forty-Eight

Beth, her mouth full of pins, was trying as hard as she could to stop her eyes straying from the task in hand: to pin up the hem of Mrs Ward's dress to a length that would be acceptable to her. To Beth's great alarm, declaring that it would be easier if she was closer to eye level, Mrs Ward had stepped onto a dining chair and from there onto the dining room table.

'If Doris was still here she would be having kittens,' Beth thought, watching Mrs Ward's sensible heels on the table as she rotated slowly so that Beth could do her work. But Doris wasn't here to worry about the polish on the table top. She was long gone, still working in the chocolate factory alongside Rosa.

Beth couldn't stop her eyes sliding over to a photo she had spotted, newly framed and set on the sideboard. Perhaps she could risk a question now that the hem of the dress, created from a serviceable pair of heavy brown curtains that until recently had hung in one of the servant's bedrooms, was all pinned up?

As she handed Mrs Ward down from table to chair, and

then safely to the floor, she said, 'I couldn't help but notice, ma'am, that you've a new photo of John... of Master John,' she added hastily.

Mrs Ward swung round to look at the photograph in its frame. 'Yes, it was taken when he became a second lieutenant. He looks smart, doesn't he?' She turned back to Beth and sighed. 'We had a letter this morning. He's at the Front as we speak, in the trenches. He made light of it but the conditions sound terrible.'

'At the Front, ma'am?' Beth repeated. Her heart was hammering in her chest. She had always known that this moment would come but it wasn't welcome. It seemed that each day brought news that was either good or bad, depending on your perspective. The news was good because the Allies were pushing forward and making gains with each battle, forcing the German army back; yet, if you had family members at the Front then the news was bad, as more and more casualties were reported, and more units had to be drafted in to back up the exhausted troops.

Mrs Ward didn't appear to have registered Beth's question. She had wandered over to pick up another of the photos on display, of a team of rugby players in striped jerseys. Beth had managed to steal a glance at this photo before, her eyes instantly drawn to John standing tall at the back, his half-smile seemingly directed at her, his hair looking fairer than she remembered it on what appeared to be a bright, sunlit day. She followed Mrs Ward over to the sideboard.

'Might I have a look, ma'am?' she ventured boldly. Mrs Ward, surprised, was about to hand over the sporting photo. 'No, I meant the new photograph,' Beth explained.

'Of course.' Mrs Ward had her surprise under control now.

'There's John, just to the right of the captain in the centre.'

Beth was careful not to stare too long at the image, although she was drinking it in hungrily. She couldn't be sure when she would next have a chance to take a look as her duties these days mainly confined her to the kitchen and the sewing room. She conjured dresses for Mrs Ward and Grace out of whatever fabric could be gleaned and endlessly patched and mended the servants' uniforms. Even the household's sheets had worn out, necessitating turning edges to middles in the worn-out flannelette, leaving the servants tossing and turning on the uncomfortable seams created down the centre.

Beth dragged her eyes away from the photograph, suggesting to Mrs Ward that she could change back into her other dress. 'I can finish the hem for you this evening, ma'am,' she said.

'Thank you, Beth. You've done a very good job on this dress. I don't know what Grace and I would do without you. With no material in the shops to speak of, and dresses so hard to come by...' Mrs Ward tailed off. 'I can barely remember what it felt like to have a new frock. I'm quite sure I didn't appreciate it half as much as I do today.'

She sighed. 'And now with Grace heading off to join those Land Girls, why, I don't suppose she'll be needing any more dresses. From what I hear, they wear breeches, overalls and gumboots all day long. Grace seems very excited, I must say, but it wouldn't suit me.'

Beth turned away to hide a smile and gathered up her pin box and tape measure. 'I'll come and fetch the dress from your room in the next half hour, ma'am. I'll need to go and give Cook a hand with dinner now.'

Mrs Ward sighed. 'Dinner. I wonder if Cook has managed to work a miracle on the last of the vegetables?'

Beth forced a smile. 'I think you may be surprised, ma'am. She has found some recipes in a periodical for Seven Ways with Cabbage.'

Mrs Ward looked faintly appalled. 'Thank you, Beth.'

That night Beth relayed her conversation with Mrs Ward to Ella. In her view, it showed that the barriers were coming down between family and servants, and that perhaps there was hope in the future that the family could accept her feelings for John, and his for her.

'I know that times have changed because of the war,' Ella said to Beth while she brushed her hair. 'Men and women have worked side by side on an equal footing for the first time, and women have taken over men's jobs while they are away. But I don't know whether things have changed enough. Mrs Ward may have been down to the kitchen more often, and she may be more familiar with us than she was in the past but I don't think those things have changed forever. I think as soon as the war is over it will be back to business as usual.' Ella paused, then said thoughtfully, 'Although I fear that too many men have died for any sort of return to normality. Who will take their places?'

She registered Beth's stricken face. 'But you mustn't worry about John. I'm sure his regiment will be fine. Why, the war will probably be over before he even reaches the Front,' she added hastily, trying to undo the damage she had already done.

'He's already there,' Beth said gloomily. 'Mrs Ward said they had had a letter this morning.'

John had given his signet ring to Beth before he returned from leave, and she wore it at all times on a chain around her neck, worrying that the outline of it might show through

253

her work dress. No one had commented if it did, and that night she lay awake, turning the ring slowly through her fingers and wishing it could conjure up John, safe and well before her eyes. The memory came back to her of their first kiss – her first-ever kiss – exchanged just before he had given her the ring. She had had no idea that such a simple action could feel the way it did: the gentle pressure and warmth of his lips, the feeling of his skin against hers, his breath on her cheek, his hands in her hair. Nor did she know how she could remember it in such detail because at the time she had been so immersed in the experience that she hadn't wanted the kiss to end.

They hadn't thought beyond the war at all, wishing only for his safe return. Now her thoughts were being pulled this way and that. If he returned safely, it was inconceivable that they could go on hiding their relationship from the family. Yet how could they do otherwise? And if he didn't return... Beth gave a shuddering sigh, turned on her side and pulled the covers up around her ears, as if in this way she could shut out such a possibility.

Chapter Forty-Nine

It was six months before John next came home to Grange House. The change in him was profound. He no longer looked fit and healthy – but the biggest shock was the change in his demeanour. His happy confidence had vanished and he not only appeared thin and pale but jumpy too. He came down to thank Elsie for dinner, as usual, but she knew from Mr Stevens, who had cleared the plates, that he had barely done justice to his food. His eyes sought Beth at every turn of the conversation and Ella, noticing this, racked her brains for a way to enable them to have some private time together. It was Beth who spoke up, having spotted John's jacket hanging over the back of his chair.

'Your button is hanging by a thread. Let me take it and sort it out for you. I'll check the others are secure, too.' She stood up and held out her hand for the jacket.

Instead of handing it over, John rose to his feet. 'I can't let you do that,' he protested. 'We're supposed to look after our own kit. I'm perfectly able to sew on a button if you'll provide me with the thread.'

He managed to produce the ghost of a smile as he spoke

and Ella silently congratulated Beth as she watched them walk away together down the corridor to the sewing room.

Nobody commented on their joint departure; indeed, Elsie and Mr Stevens were intent instead on discussing the change in John.

'Good heavens, what has happened to the boy?' Elsie's face was crumpled with worry.

'If he's been in Flanders I daresay he's seen sights the like of which he'll carry with him for life.' Mr Stevens stared down at his hands as he spoke. He had only recently visited a nephew who was convalescing at home after losing a leg in Flanders. Mr Stevens had been visibly shaken on his return, saying little beyond the fact that he hoped 'never again would men be forced to endure such things.' He told them a little about how the weeks of rain had turned the trenches into morasses of mud and how hard it was to maintain morale under the conditions the soldiers were enduring, let alone fight. He was heard to mutter about 'cannon fodder' and from then on, he had followed the newspaper reports on the fighting with increasing gloom.

Ella hoped that the relative normality of life at Grange House, as well as Beth's presence, might go some way to soothing John's ills. He returned from the sewing room shortly after and wished them goodnight with a slightly brighter countenance. Beth did not reappear and Ella guessed she had arranged to meet John again in secret once he had spent a little more time with his family upstairs.

The small group duly said their goodnights, Ella telling the others that Beth had some sewing that she needed to finish, and they each made their way up to their rooms. Ella must have dozed off, for the grey tinge to the light coming from outside told her that dawn was not far off when she heard Beth trying to slip unobserved into their room.

'Beth! Wherever have you been? It must be early morning, for goodness sake.' A rush of anxiety made Ella's tone sharper than she had intended.

'We've just been talking. John is in a terrible state. The things he has seen... I know he hasn't told me the half of it. He's carrying it around inside like a great weight. It's to do with his men. So many of them lost and he holds himself account-able. And many of those that weren't lost have been terribly injured. Can you imagine what it must be like trying to drag injured men away while the bullets are still flying, while you are out in the open with nowhere to hide except amongst the bodies? And these people are your friends, your family over the last few weeks, the people who have kept you sane, who have watched over you while you slept.'

Beth's words spilled out in a rush and then she fell silent. Ella couldn't decide whether she should feel angry with John for sharing such details with Beth, or proud that Beth was clearly the person he trusted most and felt best able to confide in. They had talked a long time; she wondered how much more he had revealed.

As if reading her mind, Beth said, 'He wouldn't tell me anything else. He said he regretted telling me as much as he had, but he felt that if he didn't tell someone he would go mad. We were sitting in my sewing room – we'd arranged that he would come back after you had all gone to bed. After we'd talked a bit he just put his head on my lap and fell asleep. He looked so exhausted that I didn't like to wake him, so I just sat there.' Beth paused. 'I tried to doze but he kept starting half-awake and I stroked his hair to soothe him back to sleep.

Then he started twitching and talking in his sleep. I doubt he had any rest even though his eyes were closed. Finally, he woke up properly and he admitted that he rarely had more than two or three hours' sleep at a time these days. It's no wonder he looks so worn and ill. He went back to his room; he didn't want me getting into trouble on his account.'

Beth sounded so despairing that for a moment Ella found herself wishing that John hadn't chosen to make her his sweetheart. She could have been spared all this grief and upset. It was all the fault of the war, as were so many of the things in their lives that they couldn't control.

She became aware that Beth was speaking. 'I'm sorry,' Ella said. 'What did you say? I was miles away, thinking of something else.'

'I was saying that I wished I had a good-luck charm to give him,' Beth said. 'To keep him safe and remind him of me while he's away. But I've nothing of any worth.'

'It doesn't have to be something of worth,' Ella said robustly. 'Or at any rate, the worth lies in the emotion invested in it. It needs to be something to remind him of you, and of home.'

Both of them fell silent again, thinking.

'What about a drawing?' Ella said eventually. 'He can keep it folded in his pocket and carry it with him at all times. Or a lock of hair?'

'I like the idea of a drawing!' Beth was enthusiastic. 'But of what?'

'You don't need to come up with anything right now,' Ella said, only too aware of how soon their day would start. 'Try to get an hour or two's sleep. You'll have time to think of something tomorrow, before he has to go back.'

That evening, when John came down to the kitchen to bid

them all farewell before his early start the following morning, Beth handed him a folded piece of paper.

'Don't open it,' she admonished him, as he made to do so in front of the assembled company. 'I've made you a drawing as a good luck charm. Take it with you and keep it close.'

The smile that John gave her as he tucked the paper, still folded, into his top pocket was closer to his old self than anything they had seen over the last couple of days.

'What a good idea!' Elsie exclaimed after John had left to spend the rest of the evening with the family. 'I remember how you two used to give each other drawings when you were small. It will be nice for him to have something from home to remember us by. Something that will last longer than the bit of food I've been able to send back with him,' she added ruefully.

Ella thought she noticed Stevens give Beth a sharp look, but her expression was demure. She had been clever to hand over her drawing in full view of everyone; she must have guessed that there would be no further opportunity to talk privately with John before he left.

And so it proved. By the time they all rose to start their day the following morning, John had already gone. They weren't to see him again for many long months.

Chapter Fifty

Beth set down her sewing then picked it up again. She looked at the clock. Was it possible that barely five minutes had passed since she had last looked? If it hadn't been for the second hand ticking inexorably around the face she would have sworn the thing was broken. She exhaled slowly, trying to still the nervous fluttering of her heart.

The door opened and Beth half started to her feet, her hand rising to her mouth, her sewing falling to the floor.

'Did I startle you?' Ella stepped forward and picked up the sewing. 'Oh, Beth, you look all at sixes and sevens. Why don't I fetch you a cup of tea or something?' She looked critically at the sewing she had picked up. 'I think you'd be better finding something else to occupy you. It looks as though you'll have to unpick all of this.'

She smiled at Beth and took her hands. 'Don't worry. He'll be here in no time, I'm sure. Mr and Mrs Ward will want to spend time with him but I know he will ask for you as soon as he can.'

Beth could only manage a tremulous smile. It was October 1918, nearly a year since she had last seen John. Nearly a year in which she had fretted endlessly, trying to keep track of his whereabouts and wellbeing with whatever news the servants could glean from the family. She had poured her heart out in her letters to John. At first, it had been odd writing to someone who wouldn't be able to reply. John wrote regularly to his family and they replied just as frequently, but Beth and John had never been able to work out how he might get letters to her. He couldn't write to anyone else in the household – one of the servants for example – without it coming to the attention of Mrs Ward. And members of the household were the only people in York that Beth knew and trusted. So, after getting over her initial feeling that it was pointless – embarrassing even – to write to someone who couldn't reply, Beth had come to find it liberating.

She wrote to him as if she were writing in her diary or, as she often felt, as if he were standing in the room next to her, where she could see him but he was trapped behind a glass wall, unable to speak or respond but simply to listen, mute. She didn't need to worry about anything in his replies, his tone, his possible reaction to something she had said, or his state of mind.

She took care to remain positive in everything she wrote. She didn't want him to worry about any of the privations that his family might be facing when he himself had far greater things to endure. She filled her letters for the most part with trivia, the day-to-day doings of the household, who had visited, what she had done. She took care not to mention the visitors who came and wept because they had lost sons somewhere on an unknown French field, fallen in the line of duty in a hail of gunfire, or picked off as they attempted night manoeuvres. Nor did she mention the son of their nearest neighbour who had returned injured, and whose cries could sometimes be heard through open bedroom windows at dead of night, or even in the daytime as he was wheeled around the garden next door.

She mentioned her sewing, the weather and, with increasing boldness, how much she missed him. At first, she had written to him more as a friend, unsure of her position with regard to anything beyond that. But, of an evening as she curled up on the bed in the room that she and Ella shared at the top of the house, her mind would turn to the thoughts that had occupied her as she sewed during the day: her longing for John and his physical presence; his easy smile as he had stuck his head around the door of her sewing room in the past, proffering a shirt with missing buttons or riding breeches with a ripped seam requiring her skilled needle.

Now here she was, waiting to see what a mess the war had made of him. She knew that his left hand had suffered injury and his neck was scarred. This much had filtered through to the servants when news first reached Grange House that John had been injured. Very few details were available at this point and Mr and Mrs Ward were greatly worried. Mrs Ward was frequently seen around the house with red eyes that attested to weeping, and Mr Stevens reported that Mr Ward spent most evenings pacing the library floor until long gone midnight.

More news finally came in the form of a letter from John, occasioning much relief. He was in the military hospital in Rouen and would be returning home as soon as he was able. By some strange quirk of fortune, he had been adjusting his collar – easing its chafing against his neck – at the very moment that he was hit by a sniper, his left hand taking the impact of a bullet that would otherwise have entered his neck and probably killed him. Beth felt the colour drain from her face whenever she thought of it.

It had been two long weeks before word came that he was on his way home. Details of the time and method of his arrival were somewhat vague, but by late afternoon a military ambulance turned into the drive and an orderly helped John down from the back. Mr Stevens reported that his hand was heavily bandaged, his arm in a sling, his neck in a collar and he appeared thin and pale.

Chapter Fifty-One

Years later, if anyone asked John about his army experiences, his face would close up and he would turn away. On the rare occasions that he answered, he would say that his memories of that time were very different to what was portrayed in the history books. If he had been present at any of the battles neatly parcelled up as Passchendaele, Ypres, Cambrai or Canal du Midi he could only give you a very narrow focus. His memories were muddled, consisting of periods spent trudging through mud, snow and freezing rain worrying about where and how his men would be billeted; of the terrible noise of shell explosions, of bullets, of tanks; of plans changed; of friends lost and companies almost wiped out; of life having to go on in what seemed like an unending hell while he tried to keep his men motivated; of the ghastly stench of the trenches; of exhaustion, hunger and anger; of land gained and just as quickly lost.

Ella's memories of the same period didn't really match the history books either. She remembered that they all seemed to be constantly hungry as more and more foods became scarce, then rationed, while cups of tea often seemed to be their main form of sustenance. Her abiding memory was of a sense of drabness everywhere, of a life lived in monochrome. Colour seemed to have leached out of life, out of people's worn and patched clothes, out of the dusty streets, out of the food on the plate, out of people's careworn faces. Occasionally there would be a period of almost hysterical joy, an antidote to the prevailing mood, when a soldier returned home safely on leave. It soon subsided and everyone lapsed back into their strange new world. The streets held only women, young children and older men; all the men of an age to fight having been swallowed up by the army. She was sure that the sun must have carried on shining, the flowers blooming and the birds singing, but somehow these things featured only rarely in her memories of that time.

PART V

1918–23

Chapter Fifty-Two

The months that had elapsed since John's return home had seen momentous events. The war had been declared over in November, and while that caused rejoicing for so many people for so many reasons all over the country, Ella felt sure that she was not the only one to be thankful for one reason alone – that it meant an injured loved one had no need to return to the front line. For while the injury to John's hand had healed relatively quickly, it had proved more difficult to find an easy cure for his state of mind. He did his best to appear to be the same man who had gone to the Front with high expectations of victory, but whatever he had witnessed there had 'consumed his wits', according to Mr Ward. The night terrors of his childhood had returned to haunt him, but this time the shadowy unknown figures of dreams from the past were made real and terrifying by what he had experienced. The same horrors stalked him by day and it seemed he could find no peace. He took to walking out from the house at all hours, although mainly at night so that he could avoid any entanglement with the demons that awaited him once he closed his eyes in sleep.

The family had looked forward to celebrating a peacetime Christmas that, although it would still be austere, should have reflected a sense of optimism about better times ahead. Instead, it was marred by anxiety over John's increasingly fragile state of mind. The household had been kept awake by his pacing the house and muttering throughout the night of Christmas Eve, and his lack of sleep made him erratic and confused company on Christmas Day. As soon as possible after Christmas, Mr Ward called out the doctor to examine John, and spent a good hour in consultation with him behind the locked door of the library once the examination was over.

The convalescent home that the doctor recommended proved to be less than successful. It was full of young men with worse physical injuries than John, as well as a good many with similar mental disturbances, but this only seemed to serve as a reminder of what he was so desperately trying to escape. He returned after a month with better sleep patterns established, thanks to nightly sedation, but still with the deeply haunted look that appeared likely to become a permanent fixture on his features. Less erratic in his behaviour, he had become withdrawn instead.

Beth was quite beside herself with worry and distress. She had very little opportunity to spend any time with John, and in any few snatched moments together she found him too unsettled to take any pleasure in her company.

'It's no good,' she said despairingly to Ella one evening. 'Whatever we had is lost. I feel sure that if it were only possible to spend a stretch of time together, I could take away some of the pain and help him to be calmer. But I have no idea how that can ever be possible. I think all connection between us has gone for ever.' She spoke so sadly that Ella, deeply upset herself by John's situation, resolved to find a way to help.

In the end, it was Mr and Mrs Ward's growing impatience with John's lack of improvement in health that played into her hands. Their delight in John's safe return had given way to irritation at his inability to recover quickly, something they saw as a sign of weakness. Mr Ward had suggested more than once that John just needed to 'pull himself together and show a bit of backbone.'

After the failure of the convalescent home to provide a lasting solution, the doctor had suggested that they might like to follow a new line of thinking on recovering from mental exhaustion, which involved a good deal of fresh air and exercise. He was suggesting a period spent in the Alps, with ten-mile walks every day that would, when combined with the fresh air, guarantee a healthy night's sleep and a subsequent return to normality of the brain. Although Mr Ward had been initially enthusiastic, Stevens had reported that, on reflection, he now felt it wouldn't be safe to send John to the Alps alone, and he was at a loss as to who might be employed to accompany him.

Ella had pondered the situation for a day, without consulting Beth for fear of raising her hopes, then asked to speak to Mr Ward. She had thought her plan through carefully, trying to ensure that she was prepared for every possible objection that Mr Ward might raise. Then she had proposed to him that John could just as easily benefit from a stay in the peace of the Yorkshire countryside, with a great many miles of moorland to roam at will, yet close enough to York for his parents to be able to visit him regularly to check on his progress. Ella and Beth, who knew the area well, could be his walking companions whilst staying close by in Northwaite with Ella's mother, and would be on hand should any problems arise.

To Ella's astonishment, after a short period of deliberation, Mr Ward had agreed. Indeed, he had commended her for her thoughtfulness and set about arranging the trip within the week. It dawned on Ella that he was perhaps glad for the problem to be removed from his sight; whatever the reason, the plan also worked some sort of magic on John. His general demeanour was much improved before they even left York, while Beth was beside herself with excitement and had a hard job hiding it from the others.

'You are so clever, Ella,' she exclaimed, on an almost daily basis. 'However did you get Mr Ward to agree? I just know that we can make John better. Why, already he seems calmer and he has told me how much he is looking forward to discovering the countryside where we were brought up, and to meeting Sarah. Stevens said to me that it's the first time he has seen John show any enthusiasm for anything in weeks!'

Chapter Fifty-Three

The Wards came to visit John during his first week away, as he had known they would.

'They'll check up on me,' he said, 'to make sure everything is proper. And then they will leave me alone.'

John was staying, as arranged, at The Royde Inn in Nortonstall, which he had described to his parents as tolerably comfortable. He made a wry face when telling Ella and Beth about it and, when pressed, he confessed that he found it hard to sleep, his rooms being above the bar, which was noisy until late in the evening. The food, still subject to rationing, was less than good, despite the possibilities that the countryside offered in the way of wild and foraged food.

'Then you must come and stay with us,' Beth declared. 'There's no sense in you being billeted all the way down the hill, staying somewhere that you don't like, when we are supposed to be looking after you and we have plenty of room here.'

At the time, they were sitting in the parlour of Sarah's cottage, beside a fire specially lit for the occasion to drive away the chilly March breeze. When they had first arrived there, Ella and Beth had been taken aback by the state of Lane End Cottage.

'What need do I have for this house now, with you all gone?' Sarah had demanded. Beth and Ella looked at each other. This querulous tone wasn't something that they had heard from Sarah before.

'My bedroom and the kitchen suit my purposes,' Sarah went on. 'I've shut up the other rooms.'

This meant that the rest of the house felt damp, dusty and very much unloved. During the first week of their visit, when they weren't keeping John company, Beth and Ella spent as much time as possible restoring order at home. Sarah had grumbled at the unnecessary use of fuel to light a fire and this turned out to be but a symptom of the wider economies that she had been making in their absence. They found very little in the way of food in the house, not even any of the preserves that she had been in the habit of making every autumn for as long as Ella could remember. The furnishings were grubby and Sarah's clothes were becoming threadbare.

'It would serve no purpose,' she said, when they asked her why she hadn't replaced the worn-out towels, or bought a new coat instead of wearing the one that had seen service since well before the war.

'What need do I have of new things? There's no one to see them, and no one comes to visit. I'll soon be gone, anyway.'

It was said in a matter-of-fact way, with no rancour or accusation directed at them. Nonetheless, Ella and Beth felt cut to the core by what they perceived as their neglect of Sarah and set about putting things to rights as best they could.

It was relatively easy to banish dust and dirt, replacing it with the scent of beeswax polish and freshly laundered linen.

Windows that were cleaned until they sparkled and let in the spring light exposed cobwebs lurking in the dimmest corners, which were quickly whisked away. Primroses picked from the hedge bottoms brought a touch of freshness to every room. Yet Sarah's spirits remained low. It seemed as though she had decided that sixty-two years was to be her allotted lifespan.

'Do you think she is actually ill?' Beth asked Ella anxiously, as she perched on the end of her bed.

'I don't think so,' Ella replied. 'She's been poorly in the past but there's no physical illness that I can see now. She's a bit slower getting around than she used to be, I grant you, but I don't think it's that.' She turned back the covers and prepared to climb into bed.

'I think she's lonely and has probably been so for a while. She's given up on enjoying life, and that attitude has become a habit. She has isolated herself on purpose: she even seems to have given up supplying remedies, too. We'll have to see what we can do to change this while we're here.'

Privately, Ella had resolved that Sarah couldn't be left like this and that it was her duty to return and care for her. With Beattie and Annie both married and living in Leeds with their young families to bring up, Thomas gone and Beth with her whole life ahead of her, she could see no other option. She would return to Grange House at the end of their time here and hand in her notice.

A little reassured, Beth settled down to sleep, leaving her thoughts free to roam down the valley to Nortonstall, to climb the stairs to John's room in The Royde Inn and to slip into his room to watch over him while he slept, to keep the night-mares at bay.

In the end, it was John who provided a solution to their

problem. Ella had been alarmed at Beth's suggestion that John should come to stay. Not only was she aware of the potential impropriety of the situation, but John was used to the space and luxurious surroundings of Grange House and would undoubtedly find the simplicity of Lane End Cottage not to his taste. She feared an invitation to stay would be an embarrassment to John and an imposition on Sarah.

'Nonsense!' Beth stoutly counteracted all her arguments. 'John can come as a boarder. That should silence any village gossip if it worries you. As for luxury, well I hardly think The Royde Inn provides that, do you?'

So within the week John was installed in the room that had once belonged to Thomas and seemed to find the simplicity of his surroundings very much to his liking. Above all, it was the peace that he found most appealing. By day, the only disturbances were the passage of the occasional farm vehicle or a barking dog. At night, the hoot of the owl was the only sound to pierce the velvety blackness until the sky lifted to grey streaked with orange and the dawn chorus heralded the arrival of another morning.

At first Sarah was reserved around John, keeping her distance and seemingly a little in awe of his social class and status. She started to take an interest in cooking again, though, and when John thanked her enthusiastically for the rabbit stew that she dished up early in his stay, Ella noticed her colour faintly with pleasure.

By the end of his third week, John had written home to let his family know that he felt the stay in the country was doing him good and to beg leave to keep Ella and Beth with him for a further two weeks. When Ella learnt that he had also notified them of his change of temporary address she felt sure that the Wards would summon Beth, or both of them, back to York. However, John's letter must have been very persuasive, for an answer came back by return, giving them all permission to stay on.

John and Sarah took to staying up late together, in companionable silence in front of the dying embers of the fire. Beth and Ella would exchange looks, then bid the pair of them goodnight and head for the stairs. When they were safely in their room, preparing for bed, Ella would hear the murmur of voices start up from the room below. She could distinguish nothing of what was said, but the tone of the voices seemed to imply that Sarah was asking questions and John was responding, sometimes at length.

After the third such evening, while they were preparing breakfast, Ella plucked up courage to casually ask Sarah what their late-night chats were about.

'Oh, just the war.' Sarah was brief.

'The war?' Ella was startled.

'Yes, his experiences at the Front.' Sarah hesitated. 'I thought it might help me understand. About Thomas,' she added when Ella looked at her questioningly. Then, as if to discourage further discussion she bustled about, setting dishes on the table and calling up to the younger folk that breakfast was ready. Beth was going to find it hard to reacquaint herself with the routine and rigours of the Grange House day when she returned, Ella reflected ruefully.

She shared the information about the chats with Beth later, when they walked out to see whether they could spy John returning from one of his lengthy solitary walks.

'I think I feel even worse about it now,' Ella confessed. 'It should have been obvious to me how Ma would grieve over

Thomas. And we left her here all alone, until her grief hardened in her heart. That's why she could see no point in going on.'

Both women walked on in silence, each deep in thought. Ella was reflecting that, for her mother, the death of her only son, Thomas, after the loss of Alice, her first-born, must have been a hard cross to bear. She bitterly regretted not going back to spend more time with her mother after Thomas's death. It now seemed to Ella that her own grief had somehow been blunted by the sheer number of casualties and bereavements, both amongst people connected with the Ward family and nationwide. Those times had been so strange. For Sarah, up here in Northwaite, it must have been overwhelmingly difficult, shutting herself away, alone with her grief. Ella could see it all so much more clearly now. When she was in York, Northwaite had seemed like a distant dream; now she was here this was reversed and it was York that seemed unreal.

Beth's reflections were more pragmatic in nature. If John's presence was useful to Sarah, was there a way of prolonging this? It tied in with something she had been thinking about, and hardly dared to dream but really, was it such an outlandish idea? Could she and John live here permanently, close to her mother?

Chapter Fifty-Four

When the wind tore at John's scarf, threatening to rip it from his neck, it made him laugh out loud. It had a kind of primeval force, something beyond his control. The long, weary weeks in the trenches, trying to outfox the enemy under a seemingly relentless barrage of noise and bullets, interspersed with days of jumpy boredom, had made him appreciate a force that was purely of nature, that couldn't be tamed by man. Each day, whatever the weather, he took delight in striding out and was often gone for hours. He came back exhausted, often soaked through, but exhilarated. Fearing for his health, both mental and physical, Ella and Beth begged him to take more care, but he shrugged off their concerns. After a week or so, when it became apparent that he was suffering no ill effects and was, if anything, fitter in mind and body than before, they relaxed their watchfulness.

Their stay at Lane End Cottage passed quickly, with evenings spent by the fire discussing topics that ranged far and wide but never once touched on John's experiences of war. That discussion was saved for late at night, when he was alone with Sarah. The door was firmly shut on the topic of war as far as his everyday relationship with Ella and Beth was concerned. John now wanted only to look forward, his head filled with wild schemes that, as the weeks passed, increasingly involved Beth.

Hanging back from the pair of them when they all walked out together, Ella saw the delight they took in each other, how Beth couldn't stop herself from reaching out to touch his hand or arm to direct his attention to something in the landscape, or how John held her gaze whenever he spoke to her. Ella witnessed the bond between them growing and saw how their distance from the day-to-day life of the York household seemed to make anything possible. It was a delicious freedom.

John hadn't shared the real reason for their extended leave of absence from Grange House with Ella and Beth. Spanish influenza had struck the city of York, part of a worldwide epidemic that seemed set to pile on the agony of the ravages of war. It targeted the able-bodied young rather than the sickly and the elderly, making Mr Ward keen for John to stay in the fresh air of the sparsely populated countryside, where they were all less likely to be at risk. He had sent Mrs Ward and Grace to Scotland to stay with Edith and, alone at home, had no need of Ella and Beth's services in the house. Cook and Stevens were doing a perfectly fine job, he said.

So John had put all thought of York, and the forthcoming pressures of picking up the reins of the family business, out of his mind. He knew that his father harboured ambitions for his only son to step into his shoes in the family firm, and it seemed to make perfect sense. But the construction industry held no attraction for him, nor did running a business. Freed temporarily from any expectations, he concentrated instead on the enjoyment he was getting from spending so much time outdoors and from the tranquillity of his room in Lane End Cottage. It was almost spartan after his room in Grange House and it suited him perfectly.

Luxury was anathema to him after his experiences in the trenches. He had longed to be home to escape from its privations and yet, when he had returned at last, he found himself prey to many confusing emotions, the most persistent of which was guilt. Guilt for being alive when so many of his company hadn't survived; guilt for not being able to share his experiences with his family (partly from a wish to protect them and partly because he couldn't bear to relive the horror); guilt for not being a stronger and better man. He felt he was failing everyone on all counts. He was home again, not unscathed but comparatively unharmed, and yet he couldn't seem to settle, to appreciate his luck, to move on. His thoughts drew him back to the battlefield, over and over again.

While in Northwaite he'd found that it helped to discuss things with Sarah. She was seeking to understand what Thomas had experienced, knowing that she would never be able to ask her son. Perhaps because she wasn't family, he felt more able to open up to her. Not knowing the circumstances of Thomas's death, he was careful to protect her sensibilities, but he found their late-night conversations unaccountably soothing. He shared random thoughts and memories with her and felt able to relay some of the things that troubled him, so that when he went up to bed he slept better than he had in weeks.

His dreams were no longer filled with the smell of mud, of damp wool, of fire and fear, and the sounds of gunfire and mortar shells; the awful silence after a blast which was invariably followed by terrible screams and cries for help or, even worse, of low, desperate moans. He hoped he hadn't simply handed his nightmares on to Sarah but she also seemed to benefit from having someone to talk to about Thomas, someone to share a mother's worry as to how his life might have ended, thoughts which she had kept to herself until now and brooded over at length.

In the strange aftermath of the war they were adjusting to their lives being changed in ways that would have previously been unimaginable. As spring started to work its magic on the land, so John and Sarah started to climb slowly out of the depths of their despair, taking comfort from a companionship that would never have been open to them before.

Chapter Fifty-Five

By May 1919, Mr Ward considered that any danger from the influenza epidemic had faded and so, with great reluctance, the three companions started to prepare to return to York. Ella, having seen a great improvement in Sarah's spirits and wellbeing, was concerned that she would go into a decline once they had all left.

'You mustn't worry,' Sarah instructed her. 'I've the garden to see to, and the brighter weather always lifts the spirits.'

Ella was not convinced by her positive demeanour. During the last few weeks they had all become used to spending time together. The house would feel very empty without them, she felt quite sure. Could she return to spend time with Sarah, giving up her position in Grange House? It was already being run with fewer servants after the frugality of the war years. The problem was, she was one of the remaining trusted servants. How would the Ward family react if she left? Would it affect Beth? And would she be able to find any work in the Northwaite area?

Beth wasn't looking forward to their imminent return, either. She had so enjoyed the time spent in Northwaite; it had been blissful to have no demands on their time other than those of their own creation. John had slotted into her family with ease, so that he felt like one of them, while their fondness for each other had deepened into love, a love that had been expressed quietly in snatched moments and shared glances, in caring for each other's thoughts and feelings. How could this be sustained in the Ward household, where she would be John's servant once again? Her thoughts were like rats in a trap, racing hither and thither to try to find a way out. She felt sure that the return to York was going to be beyond what she could bear.

John, too, was plunged into a new despair at the thought of what lay ahead. Although his health had improved while he was away, he sensed it was but a fragile recovery. He was worried that the return to a noisy, bustling city would quickly undo much of the good work. His father would see the improvement in his general health and encourage him to take up the reins of the business. He would undoubtedly see it as being essential to occupy his mind, to prevent him dwelling on his war experiences.

On their last evening in Northwaite, with all bags packed, a nervous air descended on the house. Sarah shooed them all out for a walk while she prepared dinner.

'You've been under my feet all day,' she said. 'I know it's been raining but it's cleared up now. Off you go and take a turn around the village. The fresh air will do you all good.'

She waved away all offers of help, declaring that she was looking forward to having the kitchen to herself – and so Ella, Beth and John set off into the village at a slow pace, enjoying the early evening light as the sun dipped towards the horizon. The birds sang from every roof and tree top, sounding joyful in the cool, fresh evening air after the dampness of the day.

'Let's walk around the churchyard for one last look at the view over Nortonstall,' suggested Beth. They wandered to the furthest reaches of the churchyard and stood in a row behind the low, grey-stone wall in silent contemplation of the view down into the valley with the town spread out below them. Lights were beginning to twinkle in the streets as dusk crept on, and wood smoke from the chimneys hung in the still, damp air, creating a faint mist over the town. Ella observed John reach a hand out to Beth to entwine her fingers with his.

'I'm going to say goodbye to Alice,' she said, making a tactful withdrawal. 'Why don't you two enjoy the view for a little longer, then come and join me?'

Once she had reached Alice's grave, she risked a look back, to see Beth and John silhouetted in an embrace, her head on his shoulder while he appeared to be murmuring softly to her. She looked swiftly away, tears pricking her eyes, aware yet again how difficult their return to York was going to be. She turned to the gravestone, put her hands on the cool stone and closed her eyes, trying to conjure up Alice's face.

'Alice, if you can hear me, help me,' she whispered. 'Help me find a way to bring some lasting happiness for your daughter.'

A few minutes later John and Beth had joined her. Beth stood silently, her head bowed, and John put a protective arm around her shoulders. He knew the story of Beth's mother and had accepted the tragedy with little remark, other than a slow nod of the head. When he had asked who her father was and had been told that he was unknown, he'd said, 'I see,' but not in a censorious way. It had gone unremarked ever since.

'We'd best be getting back,' Ella said. 'I fear more rain is on the way and we're ill-prepared.'

They hurried from the churchyard through the side gate

into Church Lane, John pausing for a moment to cast a last glance back along the row of cottages beside the church.

'Do you know,' he said. 'I've always thought you'd be hard-pressed to better this row of houses for beauty in the whole of Yorkshire.'

The cottages did indeed look inviting in the evening light, their gardens bursting with life, and lamplight sparkling in the downstairs windows.

'I heard there's one for rent,' Ella remarked, as the first slow drops of rain began to fall.

'Really?' John asked. 'Do you know which one?'

'Ask Ma,' Ella said. 'She's the one who told me. But we'd better make haste now or we'll all get wet.'

They made the return journey to Lane End Cottage at a fast pace, breaking into a run as they drew closer and the rain quickened.

They burst through the door laughing, dishevelled and only a little damp, with spirits lifted by the exercise, to be greeted by the delicious aroma of roasting lamb, a special dish in honour of their last evening together. Time passed quickly, filled with much good humour and reminiscence and although John stayed behind to talk to Sarah after Ella and Beth had climbed the stairs to bed, their discussion was much briefer than usual.

The next day dawned bright, but breakfast was a sombre affair. Sarah endeavoured to be cheerful but there were, inevitably, tears when it came to parting company. Mr Ward himself came to collect them in his motorcar. He was insistent on meeting Sarah and thanking her for the great kindness shown to his son. He was generous in his praise for the aspect of her house and its delightful garden, and paused at the gate to examine the carved-stone gateposts.

'Why, these are quite magnificent,' he exclaimed.

'They're Albert Spencer's work, sir. He was a friend of the family,' Ella explained.

'Ah, Albert,' Mr Ward looked saddened. 'The loss of yet another good man.'

The party returning to York was less cheerful than Mr Ward might have hoped. Ella and Beth, mindful of their employer's generosity in allowing them such a long stay in Northwaite, kept up their end of the conversation as best they could. Mr Ward, however, soon became aware of John's morose expression, which seemed to grow gloomier the further they drove from Northwaite.

They all lapsed into silence, which continued for several miles until Mr Ward ventured a comment on John's wellbeing.

'I must say, you are looking a great deal better than when you left York. You seemed to have filled out a bit. It must be due to Mrs Bancroft's home cooking. Ella and Beth have described to me the long walks that you have been in the habit of taking, which I am sure must have been very restorative. I hope, once you have settled back home, that we can talk about you joining me in the office.'

Mr Ward risked an enquiring, sideways glance at his son who was now staring straight ahead, stony-faced.

'I'm not sure that I will ever be able to do that,' John said, in a low voice.

Ella and Beth exchanged nervous glances in the back. Mr Ward swerved slightly, then seemed to take a firmer grip on the steering wheel.

'It's early days yet,' he said, placatingly. 'Let's review the situation in a week or so, shall we?'

Chapter Fifty-Six

'Thank heavens', Elsie exclaimed, the minute Beth and Ella walked into the kitchen on their return to Grange House. 'I was at my wit's end, what with Grace and Mrs Ward just back from Scotland and no one to help me but Stevens and the girl.' It seemed as though Enid, introduced to the house shortly after the war, was doomed to remain forever 'the girl' in Elsie's eyes. She hadn't warmed to her, finding fault with whatever she did at least five times a day, but she was aware that if Enid left they would be lucky to replace her. Girls didn't view being in service in the same way as they had before the war, mostly seeing it as a stop-gap rather than a career choice.

'Not that Stevens is much help at the moment, either.' Elsie bustled about, putting the kettle on and lifting down the cake tin. The bell from the house summoned them before Ella could ask her what she meant.

Elsie started to swiftly lay up a tray. 'They'll be wanting tea now that they're all back.'

'I'll take it up,' Ella said. She realised as she said it that she felt strangely resentful. Serving Mr Ward was one thing, but John had been living as one of them, in their family home,

288

for the last few weeks. In the event, when Ella carried the tray into the sitting room, only Mr and Mrs Ward and Grace were present.

'Thank you, Ella,' Grace said, moving swiftly to hold the door for her. 'You can leave the tray and I'll pour. I've heard a little about your time in the country. It all sounds rather marvellous – very *Wuthering Heights*.'

Grace smiled expectantly at Ella, who looked blank. Whatever was she talking about? And where was John?

'We won't have need of the extra cup and plate. John is resting after the journey,' Grace continued. 'He looks well, though. It's clear that country air and exercise was just what he needed.' She looked wistful. 'It's so lovely in that area. I remember it well from last year, when I visited a few sheep farms nearby.'

Ella smiled, dipped her head and withdrew from the room. As she did so, she considered Grace's situation. She and Grace were of similar ages, both in their late thirties, both unmarried. The war years had suited Grace in some ways. A tall, striking woman, she seemed to lack the interest in fashion exhibited by her mother and sisters, and had a general impatience with the pursuits considered seemly for a young woman of her generation. After her girlish infatuation with Edgar Broughton, she hadn't exhibited any interest in another man as far as Ella knew.

When John had joined up she had become restless. The lack of opportunity for involvement in a practical way in the war effort had bothered her. She had done what she could in the way of fund-raising for the troops, working alongside her mother, but when an opportunity had arisen to join the York-area organising committee of the Land Girls, she had leapt at it. After that, she was barely at home. She learnt to drive very quickly and took off around the countryside to visit farmers in need of agricultural help. With the young labourers gone to war, Land Girls were often billeted with farms to help out and it was Grace's duty to check that they were being well looked after. She stepped in herself to help out at key times such as harvest. As the country made the transition from war to peace, she was still employed by the committee. With so many men lost in the war there was still a need for women to work the land, but the situation had settled down and before they left for Northwaite, Ella had heard her say that she wouldn't be needed for much longer.

What would the future hold for both of them? It looked as though marriage wouldn't now play a part in their lives. The war meant that there were barely enough eligible men for the younger girls of marriageable age. It seemed unlikely that two spinsters of their age would find suitors now. Ella didn't mind for herself. She had long ago put all thoughts of marriage from her mind, burying them along with her dream that Albert Spencer had any kind of interest in her. She wondered whether Grace cared about her own situation, though.

As Ella settled back into the kitchen with a cup of tea and a slice of Elsie's Victoria sponge cake, she was listening with only half an ear to Elsie describe what had been happening while they had been away. She was content for Beth to pay attention and ask any questions; she knew that she could always get her to recount anything that mattered later that evening in their room. Her thoughts were, instead, occupied with a worry that their stay in Northwaite had somehow made her unfit for service. She seemed to have returned to York with a different attitude towards her employment, and to the people for whom she worked. If she could not overcome this, she could see that she might well have to leave, bringing to the fore once again the question: what else could she do?

That evening, as the pair unpacked in their room, Ella opened the window to let in the cool air of a spring evening. Birdsong drifted across the gardens, the melodious notes of the blackbird singing his heart out as he tried to hold back the encroaching dusk.

'Poor Stevens,' Beth mused as she shook out the dresses and hung them up.

Ella turned from the window. 'Stevens? Why? What happened?'

'Weren't you listening?' Beth laughed. 'I thought you looked a bit preoccupied. Elsie looked very put out by your lack of reaction to her tale.'

She turned away to fold blouses and undergarments and stack them neatly into drawers.

'Well?' Ella demanded impatiently.

'He's on leave at the moment. His wife died in the asylum. He'd tried to keep it from everyone, as you know, that he even had a wife. But it all had to come out in the end. She was caught up in the influenza outbreak; it swept through the asylum. He's gone to organise the funeral.'

Ella turned back to look out of the window. This was sad news indeed. She wished that she had been there when Stevens had heard it. He must have felt very alone. She wondered what would happen now. He had lived a strange kind of half-life for many years, married in name only yet with a great responsibility to bear. She supposed the lifting of the responsibility would bring a kind of relief, but she hoped that it wouldn't usher in guilt to fill its place.

'We must make a fuss of him when he comes back,' Ella said, half to herself. That night, as she lay in bed, her thoughts whirled and churned and kept her awake. She had a sense of great change in the offing, and didn't know whether she welcomed or feared it, nor what this feeling was founded upon. It seemed, though, that their stay in the country might have set the wheels of change in motion.

Chapter Fifty-Seven

By the time they had been back from Northwaite for two weeks, however, Ella had started to readjust to her situation. She was still worried about Sarah and how she would be coping without them, but she'd decided that one of the main reasons she was so unsettled was that she'd barely had longer than a few days' holiday at a time over the last eighteen years. Taking several weeks away had given her a different outlook on her life. She wondered whether she was feeling more at ease because John had been at the office all day for the past few days and therefore out of the house. When he came home he was exhausted and took dinner in his room. After their easy companionship while they were in Northwaite she had found it difficult to return to their former relationship, even though it wasn't a traditional one of son-of-the-household and servant. Luckily, she wasn't called upon to serve him; Stevens was back and took care of that. He'd returned to Grange House a week after them and Ella immediately felt happier. The house had felt odd without his presence. She had to restrain herself from offering him an over-enthusiastic welcome; it wouldn't be seemly for someone in mourning.

'I was so sorry to hear your news,' Ella said, then immediately felt awkward. It sounded a bit impersonal. 'I mean, about your wife.' Then she realised he had never mentioned his wife to her. 'Beth mentioned her to me. I hope you don't mind. It must be very hard for you.'

Stevens looked downcast, then smiled at Ella. 'It was hard. But it was harder many years ago when I lost her to her illness. She had no life to speak of, really. I suppose it was better this way; her prospects were bleak. But it will take some getting used to.'

After that, no more was said and Stevens took up his duties in his old manner. The household felt steadier somehow, and Ella relaxed.

Then John suffered his breakdown.

'It's no good!'

Ella glanced nervously around as John spoke. The words had almost come out as a shout and, although they were well away from the house, in the kitchen garden where she had often taken him as a child, she worried that they would be overheard. In any case, it could surely be only a matter of time before one of them was missed in the house.

'Sssh. You've only tried it for a short time,' she ventured, soothingly. 'It's bound to feel strange. Having to get used to sitting at a desk, dealing with phone calls and paperwork...' Ella tailed off. Her imagination of what might be involved in office work was limited and she could visualise nothing further.

John was sobbing now and Beth, crouched by his side, was clutching his hands desperately. She looked up at Ella with anguished eyes. John had returned unexpectedly to the house just after lunch, refusing all offers of food from a flustered Elsie who hadn't expected any of the family to be in until the evening. He had vanished, to his room they all presumed. It was Beth, coming out into the garden to pick rhubarb to add to a pie, who had found him huddled in a recently raked vegetable bed in the farthest corner of the garden, his back to the wall and his head buried in his hands.

Noticing that Beth hadn't returned from the garden, and with Elsie's pastry chilling in the larder, ready to be rolled out, Ella had come looking for her.

It was clear that the introduction to the family firm wasn't going well. John was finding it stressful dealing with people, paperwork and noise. Even getting to the office, based in the centre of York, jangled his nerves. The honking of car horns startled him and he found it difficult to negotiate the traffic on the streets: a mix of horse-drawn buses, carts and bicycles, as well as an increasing number of motorcars. In the office, the staccato clatter of typewriters penetrated the walls of his room and brought back nightmarish reminders of gunfire on the front line. He felt a little calmer on his visits to the firm's construction sites, but the shouts of the workers and the quantity of mud raised other unpleasant memories. At night, increasingly, he had flashbacks, waking with a thumping heart, never sure whether or not he had screamed out loud. As a result of all the sleep disruption, each day became a greater challenge, a bigger mountain to climb.

Ella assessed the situation and came to a quick decision. She seized the knife that Beth had dropped to the ground and quickly hacked a few stalks of rhubarb.

'I'll take this to the house and come back with some –' she hesitated, at a loss. 'Tea?' she ventured. Then she flew up the path and into the kitchen, startling Elsie, who was rolling out the pastry, and Stevens who was leaning against the dresser as he chatted to her.

'Whatever is the matter?' Elsie laid down her rolling pin.

'It's John.' Ella was flustered. 'He's – unwell. Beth found him in the kitchen garden. He needs help. I thought I'd take him water. Or tea, perhaps.'

Distracted, Ella looked around as though she might find the solution to her anguish in the kitchen.

'Leave this to me.' Stevens opened the dresser and took out a bottle, lifting a small glass from the shelf.

'May I?' he said to Elsie, but without waiting for a reply he took the brandy and headed off down the garden path.

'Should I go too?' Ella was unsure.

'No, leave it to him. There are some situations men are better at dealing with. Not many, mind.' Elsie chuckled to herself, pulling herself up when she registered Ella's distraught expression. 'Look, why don't you help me? Can you give that rhubarb a wash and chop it for the pie? We'll poach it a little first.' Elsie busied herself fetching a chopping board and knife and so Ella settled to her task, her eyes trained on the back door. With the rhubarb in the pan, Elsie instructed her to add water, ginger and sugar, then to set it to simmer. Gradually Ella relaxed a little to concentrate fully on the task in hand.

At last Beth reappeared in the kitchen from the door into the house, rather than from the garden. She looked very pale and shaken.

'How is he?' Elsie and Ella demanded, with one voice.

Beth shook her head. 'Not good. He calmed down a little after the shot of brandy and we were able to persuade him to stand up and start walking to the house. Then that infernally noisy machine that they use to cut the grass started up next door and John just crumpled onto the path and covered his head. It was awful.'

She closed her eyes briefly at the memory. 'We tried to shout over the wall to get them to turn it off but they couldn't hear us. Stevens had to drag John into the house. He was a little better once he was inside, so Stevens took him up to his room. I think he's called the doctor and Mr Ward.'

Beth sat at the table and briefly put her head down, amongst the mess of flour and pastry trimmings.

'What's to be done?' she asked despairingly. 'However is he going to fit back into his life?'

The three women contemplated the situation in silence, each with their own set of worries. Elsie sighed and set about clearing and cleaning the table.

'I don't know what Mr Ward will make of it. He had his heart set on John following him into the business.' Elsie shook her head. 'That wretched war. It's taken away lives in more ways than one.'

She was prevented from further comment by the reappearance of Stevens in the kitchen.

'How is he?' Ella asked.

'The doctor is with him now. He's giving him something to help him sleep. He'd like to wait to speak to Mr Ward. He's on his way over from the office now.'

'Should I make some tea?' Elsie ventured.

Stevens smiled. 'I think the doctor would prefer a whisky. You all look as pale as ghosts, though. I'll bring the brandy back. Looks as though you could all do with a drop. Don't worry now,' he added, turning to address Ella and Beth. 'I'm sure it's not as bad as it looks.'

He turned and went to offer refreshment to the doctor, and shortly after, they heard the sound of the front door banging shut and Mr Ward's feet heavy on the stairs.

'Brandy!' Elsie sniffed, disappointing Ella who had thought a nip might be just the thing. 'I'd like to see me getting tonight's dinner on the table if I took to the bottle.'

Chapter Fifty-Eight

Confirmation that John had indeed suffered a breakdown came when Ella, returning a dress that Beth had altered, found Grace at her writing desk in her room.

'It looks as though he must be sent away somewhere to recover fully,' Grace replied when Ella enquired after John's health. 'The doctor was talking about a hospital he knows of. Somewhere they can give the proper kind of care for people with his sort of health problems.' Grace hesitated. 'Problems of the mind.'

'You mean an asylum?' Ella was deeply shocked.

'I suppose so. He didn't refer to it as such. But yes, I think that's what he meant.'

Ella hung up the dress in silence. She hardly knew how to respond, or what to make of such news.

'It's awful, isn't it? Father is very upset. Mother has taken to her room. And John is sedated. It's so dreadful being downstairs I decided I would rather be up here.'

Grace sat back in her chair and Ella reflected on the lack of warmth between her and John, something that had been in evidence ever since she had known the family.

'The awful thing is,' Grace continued, 'I think I can see an opportunity for myself.' She seemed to be testing the water with an idea that she found almost too daring to contemplate privately. 'If John is too ill to learn the business, then I'm going to suggest to Father that he takes me on. I don't have the schooling that John has had, but what use is Latin and Greek in the construction industry? I learnt so much when I worked on the organising committee for the Land Army about people and how to get the best out of them, settle their grievances and such. I can handle money as well as any man. I think I would be good at it. And, more importantly, I'd like to do it!'

Ella wondered whether Grace was talking to herself and whether she should just slip away but Grace suddenly swung round to face her.

'What do you think, Ella?'

Ella was caught unawares. 'Well, I really couldn't say. It's unusual for a woman to go into business, isn't it?' Then she paused to consider. 'But I think you are right. I do think you would be good. And why shouldn't women work in the same way as men? We've shown them that we can over the last few years.' She felt her cheeks grow quite hot as she warmed to her theme.

'However, I do think your father will need some persuading.'

Grace sighed. 'You're right, I know. But that doesn't mean I shouldn't try.'

When Ella got back to the kitchen it was clear that news of the severity of John's illness had already reached them. Beth was sobbing while Elsie did her best to comfort her and Stevens looked on helplessly.

'I'll take her up to our room if you can manage without us for a while?' Ella asked.

'You go ahead,' Elsie said. 'It doesn't look as though there'll be much required in the way of dinner upstairs tonight.' She sighed as she contemplated the food that she had already prepared.

Ella led Beth up the stairs to their room, where her sobs soon calmed.

'You've heard the news?' she asked Ella. 'The doctor is talking about an asylum for John.'

'I know.' Ella tried hard to look for the positive. 'Perhaps he thinks it's for the best. That he can have treatments there that will cure him.'

'That's nonsense!' Beth was suddenly fierce. 'You saw how well he was when he was with us. It all went wrong when he came back here. He needs peace and quiet, but that doesn't mean he needs to be locked away. He needs fresh air, the countryside, simple food. He doesn't need that wretched job of his father's, and the pressure of stupid, social dinners.'

She was starting to sob again, this time more out of rage than sorrow.

'The trouble is, Beth, he needs to work. He's a man. It's expected of him.' Ella paused, her recent conversation with Grace fresh in her memory.

'Well, times have changed,' Beth declared. 'Anyway, I don't think his family even care for him. It's all about status for his father. And his mother went away and left him when he was quite small. As for Grace, well she's just cold...'

'They behave differently to us. You can't judge them by the same standards.' Ella tried to soothe Beth. 'And don't judge Grace too harshly. She could be John's saviour in all of this.'

Ella refused to be drawn any further on what she meant, other than telling Beth that Grace had a plan.

'Well, I have a plan too,' Beth declared stoutly. 'I'm not going to stand by and let this happen. And you must help me.'

Ella could only nod, whilst wondering what scheme Beth was hatching and where this would all lead.

Chapter Fifty-Nine

Mr Ward stayed home from the office the next day, following his wife's entreaties to do something about the terrible situation they were in. By the end of the morning he had cause to question whether this had been a wise decision.

His day had begun with a visit from Grace who had followed him up to the library straight after breakfast. Had anyone been standing outside the panelled door, they would have heard Mr Ward's voice rise in disbelief shortly after the interview began. Then Grace could be heard speaking again, her voice adopting a forceful tone, which cut right through any interventions that Mr Ward attempted to make. There were some moments of silence before a debate continued between the pair, conducted in more moderate tones. After twenty minutes Grace could be seen leaving the library, looking a little flushed but with what appeared to be a triumphant glint in her eye.

Mid-morning found Beth making her way up the stairs, bearing a tray containing a coffee pot and cup and saucer. A discreet observer would have noted the pallor of her complexion, the trembling hand that she raised to knock at the door and the way in which she took a deep breath and drew herself up to her full height on being instructed to enter.

The murmur of Mr Ward's initial thanks was followed by the delivery of a speech by Beth, in low, impassioned tones. There was a lengthy silence when it came to an end, then a succession of apparent queries uttered by Mr Ward, which were answered in a firm voice by Beth. After twenty minutes, the door opened and Mr Ward ushered Beth out. He could be heard promising to think it over before he stood for a minute in the doorway, watching her gain the top of the stairs before he shook his head and withdrew into the room, closing the door firmly.

Beth managed to get halfway down the stairs before stopping and clutching the banister for support. After a minute or two she pulled herself together, took a handkerchief from her pocket and blew her nose, looked hastily around and then continued down to the kitchen.

Shortly afterwards, a third visitor could be seen making her way to the library. Entering without knocking, Mrs Ward closed the door behind her and began to speak the moment she did so. Mr Ward heard her out for several minutes before interrupting her. He spoke at some length before it was her turn to interrupt him with what appeared to be a barrage of questions. They were both silent for some time and so it was that the doctor found them when he was shown to the library by Stevens, shortly before lunch and directly following a morning visit to check on his patient.

Mr Ward remained shut up in the library for the rest of the day, Stevens bringing his lunch up on a tray while Mrs Ward departed to take lunch with the doctor downstairs. Throughout the afternoon the library door remained firmly closed but the rumble of one-sided speech from the other side of it suggested that Mr Ward had spent much of the time on the telephone.

It was not until the evening that Ella came to realise what Beth had meant by her resolution of the previous day: that she would not stand by and let this happen. After Beth had begged to be allowed to take up Mr Ward's morning coffee she had kept her head down and been uncharacteristically quiet. She had got on with her duties but asked to be excused serving lunch to Mrs Ward and the doctor.

'I'll help clear up afterwards,' she promised, leaving it to Ella and Stevens to take care of the dining room.

Whenever Ella had tried to take her to one side to ask her what was happening she had professed an urgent errand or duty to attend to, promising, 'Later,' with an apologetic smile.

So Ella was unprepared when Stevens said that Mr Ward wished to see her in the library after dinner. She quickly removed her apron, smoothed her hair under her cap and, filled with a mixture of anticipation and dread, mounted the stairs.

She knocked, entered and found Mr Ward gazing pensively into the empty fireplace.

'Please sit down, Ella,' he said, gesturing to the empty chair opposite his. Ella, who would have been happier to stand, sat down on the edge of the seat as if poised for flight.

'Where to begin...' Mr Ward appeared to be musing out loud as he marshalled his thoughts.

'Ella, it has been a day of surprising news. It seems that my son is engaged to be married.' Mr Ward paused and lifted an eyebrow as Ella raised a hand to her mouth in a belated attempt to stifle a gasp of surprise.

'Ah, I see you did not know. Or perhaps you knew and you are surprised that the news has come out? Hmmm?'

Once again, Mr Ward appeared at a loss.

'Well, as I say, surprising news. Yes, your sister—'

'Niece,' Ella murmured.

'Would have me believe that she and John are engaged. Did you know anything of this?'

'Indeed, I didn't, sir.' Ella's thoughts were racing. Was this true? If so, when had it happened?

'I challenged her on this notion, thinking perhaps she intended to take advantage of John's current incapacity to press some preposterous cause.' As Mr Ward paused, Ella tried hard to swallow her indignation.

'However, Beth produced a ring which she said served as their engagement ring. It was a signet ring, one we had presumed lost when John was in hospital in France.'

'Beth tells me that in fact John never wore the ring to war. Instead, she has been wearing it on a chain around her neck for close to two years now, ever since she and John first became engaged. Of course, none of the family knew of this and it would appear that you didn't, either.'

Ella shook her head, mute.

'Well, in the normal course of things Beth could not expect this engagement to be honoured.' Mr Ward looked positively pained. 'I daresay some youthful infatuation developed between the pair of them. It's inconceivable that they imagined they might have a future together.'

Mr Ward paused again. He was clearly finding the conversation, one-sided though it was, very difficult.

'However, Beth is quite... *determined* in her plans for their future. She made it very plain to me that she felt the doctor's

306

advice with regard to John's condition was wrong. Instead, she has proposed that they be married at once and return to your village.'

Mr Ward looked grim. 'I must say, had I the least inkling of this very improper situation I would never have agreed to your staying there in the first place.'

Ella shut her eyes briefly. She had started to feel quite sick. She had no idea where this conversation was leading, but instant dismissal for herself and Beth looked like a very strong possibility.

'Your sister – niece – is very persuasive,' Mr Ward continued. 'She pointed out to me how much John's health had improved while he was away, and how quickly he has been unsettled by his return to York. She has convinced herself that a return to Northwaite is the best, if not only, solution to John's ills.'

Mr Ward paused again. He seemed to be feeling his way through the situation as he spoke.

'I have to confess that I have no liking for placing John in the asylum. It grieves me deeply to think of John in such a place. The effect on the family will be immeasurable. My hope was that John would one day marry, live close by and take over the family business.'

There was a long pause during which Ella shifted uncomfortably. She wasn't sure what was expected of her and, indeed, why Mr Ward had wished to speak to her.

'I've had to very quickly learn that I must adjust my expectations. I must be content that John was spared by the war and we must adapt to the consequences. Grace has also surprised me today, with a plan that until a day or so ago I would have found equally preposterous. I will not speak further of it now but you know as well as I do how convincing Grace can be.'

Mr Ward gave Ella a wry glance.

'So, having sought further opinion, I'm disposed to look favourably on some elements of this outlandish plan. Rather than move John to an asylum I am proposing that he should be transferred to the care of your mother, with Beth in attendance to provide additional nursing help. This is unorthodox and it has earned me the displeasure of John's doctor, but Mrs Ward is in full agreement. If there is not significant improvement in John's health within three months then we will need to reconsider. If there is, then I am resigned to the fact that John will need a quieter life than he can reasonably expect in York and I will be prepared to look favourably on a formal engagement taking place between my son and Beth.'

Mr Ward sat back, exhausted by the events of the day and by the radical change to his thinking that had been forced upon him.

Ella sat quite still, stunned. If she understood Mr Ward correctly, he was prepared to countenance a marriage between Beth and John, provided that she could work some sort of miracle in restoring him to health. An immediate cause of joy for Ella was that she could cease to worry about Sarah; Beth would be there with her, and John too, hopefully quickly on the mend. A cynic might have deduced that the shame of his only son marrying beneath him was as nothing to Mr Ward compared to having him incarcerated in a lunatic asylum, but if it suited Mr and Mrs Ward to have John hidden away in the countryside then it suited Ella very well, too.

'You must be wondering why I called you here?' Mr Ward summoned some more strength in order to draw their interview to a conclusion. 'I have to confess that simply speaking to you has helped me to clarify my thoughts. However, in addition to ascertaining what you knew of the apparent engagement, I wanted to be sure that you wouldn't consider this too great an imposition on your mother?'

As Ella emphatically shook her head he hastened to add, 'We will of course settle on a regular sum to ensure she has everything that she needs to take care of John in her home. I also wanted to have your thoughts on the situation. In many ways, Ella, you have been more of a mother to John than his own kin.' Mr Ward waved away her protests. 'No, I know that to be true. And you know Beth better than probably any other person alive. If John were in –' Mr Ward hesitated and Ella sensed that he had been about to say, 'his right mind' but checked himself '– in better health, would you consider this a good match? Is it one to which you would give your blessing?'

Ella's eyes were brimming with tears and she could only nod, speechless, at first.

'I would, sir. I can't think of a couple better suited,' she said simply.

For the first time in an hour Mr Ward's face relaxed a little.

'I had hoped to hear that. These are strange days indeed but we may yet come to see this as a blessing. Thank you, Ella. I feel somehow more hopeful than I did at this time yesterday evening.'

Mr Ward subsided into his chair and Ella made her way slowly up to her room. She couldn't face the kitchen and the enquiring faces just yet. While she needed to think through the implications of what she had just heard, John lay in a darkened room on another floor of the house, sedated and unaware of the far-reaching decisions being made on his behalf.

Chapter Sixty

Beth came upstairs a little later, to find Ella sitting in their room in the deepening dusk.

'What did he say to you?' she asked Ella, hesitantly.

Ella summarised.

'You mean he's going to agree?' Beth was incredulous.

'Yes, it looks like it.'

Beth was silent for a moment or two, absorbing the information.

'You know we're not really engaged. I made that bit up. Well, not entirely. Look.' Beth undid her top button and pulled free the chain holding the signet ring.

'John gave it to me on that visit home, when he asked me for a keepsake. But when we were in Northwaite, just before we came back to York, he did say to me how much he wished we could be married.'

'Oh, Beth. And he probably said how impossible it was, too?'

'Well...' Beth looked uncomfortable.

'So, unless I'm mistaken, John is going to wake up to discover that he is not only going to be sent back to Northwaite but that he is apparently engaged. What happens if he denies all knowledge of this?' Ella was deeply troubled.

'We'll have to get word to him somehow.' Beth, having got this far with her plan, wasn't about to give up. 'I'll talk to Stevens. He's able to visit John's room. If I take him into my confidence, I'm sure he'll help us.'

Beth got to her feet and Ella was quick to follow.

'I'm going to come with you. You may need some help in persuading him.'

Ella was worried about how all this might appear, but they found a willing ally in Stevens. Like Mr Ward, he had no wish to see John incarcerated in an asylum, whether or not it was considered to be for his own good. After all, unlike anyone else in Grange House, he had first-hand knowledge of life in such a place.

'It's no place for a young man like John,' he declared, when they explained the situation to him. 'I saw how much better he was when he came back from Northwaite. Peace and quiet is the best medicine. And I've been aware for a long time of the feelings between the two of you.' Here he smiled warmly at Beth, who blushed. 'Leave it with me. I'll make sure that when he comes round from sedation, the nurse calls me first before the family so I can apprise him of what's going on. Mind you, I suspect the drugs will have made him so groggy that he won't be making much sense anyway.'

And so it proved. John remained under light sedation for a few days, the time it took to make the arrangements and organise his transfer back to Northwaite. Mr Ward insisted on driving once more and when he returned to York that evening he looked less drawn than he had for several days.

Stevens reported that Mr Ward had said that John appeared

calmer and happier the closer they drew to Northwaite. He'd left him sitting in the garden with Beth, and Sarah had promised to write regular bulletins on his health.

Within the month, John was adding his own missives to his father and, at the end of three months, during which time Mr and Mrs Ward had made monthly visits to their son, Mr Ward declared himself ready to consider John and Beth formally engaged. Moreover, he had taken a cottage for them in Church Lane, and was prepared to countenance a more-or-less immediate marriage, provided it was a quiet ceremony.

'A cottage in Church Lane!' Ella looked wistful when Stevens relayed what he had gleaned. 'That's the loveliest street in the village. They're very lucky.'

Beth had written occasionally, describing John's progress.

'You'll find him much changed,' Beth wrote. 'And changed for the better. He's feeling so well that he's talking about finding some employment locally. Perhaps tutoring or something similar that will not be too arduous.'

When word reached Ella that the marriage had been agreed and the date set, she felt quite bereft. Although she was delighted that everything had worked out so well, it felt as though she no longer had a role to play. She missed her family: Sarah and Beth and now John, who felt very much a part of them all. And, if she was honest with herself, she felt jealous of their closeness while they were all in Northwaite together. So when Mrs Ward told her she was to have a week's leave, with most of it to be taken in Northwaite in the week prior to the wedding, she couldn't have been more delighted.

Yet when she arrived at home she was upset to find that she felt uncomfortable at first. Sarah, Beth and John were so at ease in each other's company that she felt like an outsider

– even an intruder at times. Beth was quick to disabuse her of the notion when she expressed it.

'Oh, Ella, we've been so looking forward to your arrival. It's true, we are all happy here. I don't think I can believe how lucky I am. I have to pinch myself every morning! And it will do us all good to have you here. We are in danger of becoming very dull otherwise: abed by nine o'clock every evening.' Then she looked solemn. 'John still has a long way to go before he is fully well, you know. I hear him cry out often in the night. And although Ma has been wonderful, I think she may be glad when we have a place of our own.'

Chapter Sixty-One

Beth bent her head over Sarah's sewing machine. She felt as though this was the most important dress she was ever likely to make and, although she wanted to take it slowly and get it right, she couldn't help herself. She pressed the treadle and soon she was stitching as quickly and confidently as though she were stitching the seam on a sheet.

At the end of the seam she paused, sat back and looked at Ella. 'So, tell me again. What did I do when you said you were coming back to York?'

Ella laughed and shook her head. She had told Beth the story many times over, yet she seemingly never tired of hearing it.

'You cried and said you were coming too. That you didn't see why I should leave you to look after this boy John and anyway, why couldn't you look after both of us? And then on the day I left you were nowhere to be found. I searched high and low for you and it was only when we were about to set off in the cart for Nortonstall station that I heard a sneeze from the back. I turned around and lifted one of the empty flour sacks and there you were, hiding. You were all dusted over with the flour, which had got up your nose.'

Beth was as enchanted with the retelling as she had been the first time she had heard it.

'And what was I trying to do?'

Ella played her role in the story, as usual. 'You were planning to come with me to York. You didn't realise that the cart was only taking me a couple of miles, to the station. You were only little – you had no idea about distances and the length of journeys.'

Beth looked thoughtful. 'I remember how sad I was after you had gone. I cried for what felt like days. It seemed like everyone left me. Alice – my real mother, that is – and then you.'

Ella looked stricken as Beth paused. 'But then Albert said I ought to be at school and he was right. It made a big difference. Suddenly I had friends to play with in the village. I still wondered why you preferred John to me, though.'

'It wasn't like that.' Ella protested, as she did every time.

'I know that now,' laughed Beth. 'But when you are only seven years old the world is – I don't know – very black and white. It must have been hard for you, too.'

After a succession of sunny days, the family held their breath, fearing that the good weather couldn't last. Luck was on their side, though, and the day of the wedding dawned fine yet again. Beth's dress was quite beautiful, Ella decided. She'd modelled it on something she had seen in a magazine, creating a simple column of cream satin: full-length, which somehow made her look taller. The neckline at the front was demure, while a 'V' at the back was edged with lace and hidden for the most part by her hair, which was drawn back from her face to hang in soft curls down her back. Ella wondered whether Mrs Ward had had a hand in providing the fabric: it looked and felt expensive.

Sarah had made her a simple bouquet from whatever she had found in flower in the garden. John wore a suit that he had owned since before he went to war. It was painful to see how it hung from his frame, testament to the weight loss caused by his illness.

Mr and Mrs Ward arrived on the morning of the simple ceremony. 'We've left Grace in charge of the office,' Mr Ward said, looking both alarmed and surprised that he had done such a thing. Mrs Ward was wearing a lilac costume and a very chic hat, quite outdoing the rest of the wedding party. At first, there was a little awkwardness between them all as they made their way into the church. The Wards seemed determined to put a good face on things though, and to smooth over the social differences between the two families; it was clear that John was very happy and there could be no doubt that everyone wished the couple well.

The church was simply decorated with flowers, again by Sarah, and the sun streamed through the windows, bathing them all in such a brilliant light that Ella felt almost dizzy.

Mr Ward visibly winced during the signing of the register, when he saw that in the space for the bride's father's name there was but a dash. However, he made no comment and they passed once more out through the great doorway of the church and into the sunshine. A sudden breeze rustled through the dry leaves of the elm trees edging the churchyard with a sound that surprised Ella into thinking there must be running water close by. As the party passed along the church path a small girl stepped forward, propelled by her mother's hand in the small of her back. She took a handful of rose petals from her basket and threw them. The breeze lifted them, dropping them to swirl around Beth and John. Beth beamed and laughed, throwing her head back to watch the petals float down around her. They caught in her hair and the folds of her dress, splashes of pale pink that were dislodged as she moved and floated to the ground. Crouching beside the little girl, she took a handful of petals from her basket, burying her nose in them to inhale the sweet muskiness. Then she stood up and scattered them in return over the little girl, who clapped her hands in glee. John had been having a few quiet words with the mother, whom Ella recognised. He had been helping her with letters to claim her invalid husband's war pension.

'I told her that when she gets married here I will come and return the favour and shower her with rose petals,' Beth said, hugging the little girl. Suddenly solemn, Beth turned to the wedding party. 'I wonder if we might pay a visit to one person who can't be with us today, but would have so loved it?' She bent again, whispering into the girl's ear, and took another handful of petals.

Looking a little apprehensive, Mr and Mrs Ward followed Beth and John's lead and fell into step behind them, leaving Ella and Sarah to offer their thanks and say farewell to Mrs Holmes and her daughter. They caught up with the others at Alice's grave.

'This is my mother,' Beth explained to Mr and Mrs Ward, indicating the gravestone. 'My real mother, although of course I have always regarded Sarah as my mother.'

She smiled affectionately at Sarah, then bent her head, and the rest of the Bancroft family followed suit, each offering up their own silent prayers. Then Beth flung the rose petals into the air, where the breeze lifted and swirled them back over her and John, much to their delight and surprise. Arm in arm, Beth and John followed Mr and Mrs Ward out of the church gate to head back to Lane End Cottage for the wedding breakfast. They had gone but a few steps along Church Lane, however, when Mr Ward pulled a large key from his pocket, declaring he had a surprise for them. He set the key into a blue-painted front door and opened it with a flourish.

In bundled the whole party, in great excitement. Ella had a sudden flashback to their move to Luddenden all those years ago, and how thrilled they all had been to have a house with space enough for them all, and a garden. The Church Lane cottage was small but it was quite lovely, Ella decided at once. A great stone fireplace dominated the living room, which opened into a kitchen containing a black-leaded range set into another stone fireplace. The kitchen led in turn into the garden, which was flagged and had flower borders running down each side, still sporting the last bright remnants of summer blooms. A gate at the back opened onto a path leading down towards Tinker's Wood and the valley beyond. One corner of the garden was shaded by a small rowan tree and, stepping through the door, they startled a flurry of birds that had been feasting on the brilliant-orange early berries that festooned its branches.

A few pieces of furniture had been placed in the cottage: upstairs a metal-framed bed and side tables; a table and chairs for the kitchen; a couple of easy chairs by the fire in the parlour and various ornaments and pictures, all gifts provided by the Wards.

Beth and John turned and hugged each other, then Beth turned to Mr Ward.

'Thank you,' she said. 'I never thought it possible I could be this happy.'

It was Mrs Ward who spoke up. 'My dear,' she said, 'we can never thank you enough for helping to restore John to health. We couldn't have imagined that we would ever see him so well.' Seeing tears well in Beth's eyes she turned hastily to Sarah and Ella. 'And our thanks to both of you, too. You have all played an important part.'

Mr Ward had slipped away into the kitchen and returned bearing glasses and a bottle of champagne, which had been hidden away in a kitchen cupboard while it cooled in a bucket of cold water. The group finally relaxed in each other's company, the mood aided by the effervescence of the alcohol. Ella reflected that Mr and Mrs Ward also deserved to be commended for the efforts they were making. It couldn't be easy for them to see their son living in what they must perceive as much-reduced circumstances. Everywhere they looked, at the house, at the village, at Sarah's cottage, they must have seen a lifestyle very far removed from the one with which they were familiar. Yet, they had managed to look beyond this and see that it was the right thing for John. Perhaps Mr Ward, who had always prided himself on being a forward-thinking man, could foresee that this was just the start of great changes that were on their way; changes that would affect the way people worked and lived and their relationships with each other as the country strove to heal the scars left by the war.

Chapter Sixty-Two

Mr Ward had originally wanted them all to dine in Nortonstall, but John had been so horrified when this was suggested that it was quickly vetoed. Instead, an informal gathering at Lane End Cottage had been agreed upon. After they had all walked back from Church Lane, Sarah and Ella set up a table in the shade of the apple tree and laid out the wedding breakfast. Ella was glad that the weather was so perfect. If it had rained, they would all have had to remain in the parlour and she feared it would have dampened the mood. Out in the garden, everything felt much easier and freer. Ella found herself having what was probably her first proper conversation with Mrs Ward since John had returned from the war, and Mr Ward seemed to enjoy Sarah's company just as much as his son did. Ella, taking plates back to the kitchen, came across them deep in conversation about the benefits of herbal remedies.

The mood was very relaxed when the time came for Mr and Mrs Ward to take their leave.

'John, now we can see what drew you to Northwaite.' Mr Ward swept his arm in an arc, taking in the garden and encompassing the countryside visible across the fields as he did so. 'We wish you and Beth every happiness here.' Mr Ward turned to address Sarah. 'And it has been a delight and a privilege to spend time with you, Mrs Bancroft. Words cannot express our thanks for the way you have helped John in his recovery. Ella, we look forward to seeing you back in York at the end of your stay, with more news of the happy couple.'

With a flurry of kisses and handshakes, John's parents were on their way. After they had left, John subsided with a sigh onto the blanket spread out on the grass.

Beth, conscious of the dark smudges beneath his eyes, said, 'An afternoon nap for you, I think,' and tried to pull him to his feet. He retaliated by pulling her towards him, catching her off balance so that she flopped down beside him with a shriek. He wrapped his arms around her and pulled her in close so that they lay together on the blanket, his nose nuzzling into her neck. Within a minute or two, and with a deep sigh, he was asleep.

Ella, a little light-headed from the champagne, helped Sarah to clear the glasses and plates into the kitchen. They washed up in silence, glancing every now and then through the window to where Beth and John dozed, looking for all the world as though they had fallen to earth from the sky.

Ella searched her consciousness for any shadow of doubt or concern, but could find none. It had been a wonderful, happy day and she had no doubt that a truly happy future was in store for this pair. She experienced a pang of sadness: this was surely something she would never have herself. As if sensing her subtle change in mood, Sarah laid down the drying-up cloth. 'I'm going to make some tea. And then it will be time to wake up those two lovebirds and walk them back so they can spend the first night in their new home.'

Chapter Sixty-Three

A few days after the wedding, Ella returned once more to Grange House. She felt bereft, as though her whole world was fragmenting, a feeling that was exacerbated by on-going changes in the York household.

Mrs S had elected to remain in the country, saying that her elderly mother was still too ill to be on her own, which left Stevens, Elsie and Ella running the house. They had worked together for so long that it was very much second nature to them, and they had long since relaxed into relative informality around each other. Ella missed Beth and John terribly, although she took comfort from the fact that they would be company for Sarah. She found herself longing for the countryside and the fresh air too, now that the household duties stretched her to such an extent that she rarely found time to even step outside. In contrast, Stevens seemed to be finding his duties much reduced and he was restless.

'They really have no need of a butler,' he declared one evening as the three of them sat in the kitchen. 'And I would say they have no need of this house now. I wouldn't be surprised if they were to leave it.'

'What would they do? Where would they go?' Ella felt a dawning sense of anxiety. If Stevens's words were prophetic, she could face the prospect of having to look for a new job very soon.

'Perhaps they might move into something smaller in York?' Stevens was musing. 'Or maybe even move up to Scotland. They've grandchildren there that they've barely seen over the years. Grace seems to have the business under control. Mr Ward could easily come down by train once a week if he's needed.'

Elsie and Ella looked at each other, startled by this unexpected view of the future. Their thoughts began to follow similar anxious paths but, when nothing untoward happened over the next few weeks, they gradually forgot their concerns.

Stevens's lack of duties meant that he was frequently to be found in the kitchen during the day. He always leapt to his feet to offer Ella a hand when she came struggling in with the pail of ashes after cleaning the upstairs fireplaces, and he proved just as able as Elsie and Ella at peeling the vegetables. At first, they were perturbed by his involvement.

'You shouldn't be doing this,' Ella or Elsie would say, attempting to seize the vegetable knife from him, or trying to prevent him dirtying his clothes with the ashes.

'And why not?' he would ask, carrying on as though nothing had happened. 'I've nothing better to do and I'm perfectly capable, you know.'

Gradually it came out that he had been the eldest son in a fatherless household headed by a mother too sick to work. Before he was old enough to work himself, he had been responsible for cooking and caring for his younger sisters as well as his mother, for organising the cleaning of the house and obtaining parish relief. When his mother died, he continued to take financial responsibility for the family until he was sure that all the girls were settled.

Then, at a loss as to what work he could do, he had entered service and over a period of five years found himself rapidly promoted. Suddenly, on a whim and perhaps as an antidote to the overwhelmingly female environment that had been his life up until then, he enlisted and found himself fighting against the Boers in South Africa.

This last revelation came as they all sat around the kitchen table in the lowering light at the end of the day. Stevens's interest in the war they had just endured now made more sense to Ella. It was now clear that he had some prior knowledge of the war machine and how it worked; of how battles were won and lost. She noted that he didn't dwell on his war experiences but moved quickly on and talked instead of how, when he returned and sought work once more, he was extraordinarily lucky to come across Mr Ward. He had known him previously as a visitor to the house where he had been employed prior to the war. Their meeting was fortuitous: Grange House had just been built and Mr Ward was looking for a butler to head his staff.

'So you must have been quite new to the house when I arrived here. Yet you seemed so settled and confident and everything was running so smoothly, it never occurred to me that you hadn't been with the family for years,' Ella marvelled.

Stevens laughed. 'I'm glad it seemed that way to you. Most of the staff had come from the old house in Micklegate, so I felt very much the new boy for some time. Mrs Sugden and Elsie here were my saviours at the time. I was barely thirty; really very young to be a butler.'

Ella, who had worked with Stevens for nearly twenty years, was now beginning to wonder whether she actually knew him at all. He had seemed such a remote figure when she first joined Grange House and, although their relationship had shifted onto an easier footing with time, she had never known much about his background. It had taken Beth's artless curiosity to discover that he had a wife. In fact, she realised that Stevens had left any mention of his wife out of his account.

'When did you marry?' she found herself asking before she could stop herself.

Elsie raised her eyebrows, but Stevens smiled. 'You were right to ask. I seem to have managed to leave that bit out. I married young: much too young, when I was barely eighteen. It wasn't long after my mother died and I can only think that I was looking for a helpmate, someone who would be a support to me while I took care of my sisters.'

Stevens paused, then exhaled slowly. 'I misjudged things rather badly. Clara, my wife, had a very sensitive nature, something that I initially found appealing. With time, I realised she actually had a great many nervous problems and when she fell pregnant these seemed to be exacerbated.'

Ella was startled. Stevens had never mentioned a child: was there to be another surprising revelation?

He continued. 'Alas, when she miscarried, she collapsed mentally as well as physically, blaming herself for being unfit to carry a child, along with all manner of other ravings. Gradually, I was able to unravel something of her history: it seemed that she had been cruelly abused by a family member while barely out of childhood. The strain placed upon her by keeping this quiet for so long had caused her deep-seated distress. She saw the loss of our baby as retribution from God for her wickedness. I was unable to convince her that God would not be so harsh in His judgements and, despite my best efforts and those of some of the medical profession, she was confined to an asylum at the age of just twenty-one. She never left it until the day she died.'

Stevens paused for so long, deep in thought, that Ella wondered whether their conversation was now over. She couldn't begin to imagine how devastating this tragedy must have been, nor what it must have cost him to keep it buried. Dusk had long since descended but neither she nor Elsie felt they could break the spell by getting up to light the lamps.

It was Stevens who rose to his feet eventually and said briskly, 'Good heavens, why are we all sitting here in the dark?' In an instant, he'd closed the door on his past and his reflective mood was gone. As soon as the lamps were lit, his memories were banished to the shadows once more.

Chapter Sixty-Four

As the new decade dawned, Mr and Mrs Ward finally announced that they had decided that Grange House was too big for them now that John and Grace had both left home. Grace had taken a house in town, saying that she wanted to be within walking distance of the office and her friends, despite her mother's disapproval of an unmarried woman living alone.

'I think you'll find I'm classed as a spinster, Mother,' Grace had laughed. 'It's perfectly acceptable for a woman of my great age to live alone.'

So the Wards were to spend a few months in Scotland, while they decided whether they would settle in Edinburgh, leaving Stevens, Ella and Elsie trying to work out what to do next. Elsie had been with the family nearly thirty years; Stevens and Ella had both seen near enough twenty years' service each. Stevens was the only one who seemed to be excited once the news was relayed to them. He retained his composure, however, and listened gravely while Mr Ward broke the news of the family's planned departure, laying out the terms of the servants' notice period. As soon as the trio were back in the kitchen, Stevens became jubilant.

'Finally!' he exclaimed. 'I knew it was coming. Now I can get on with planning the rest of my life.'

Ella and Elsie were despondent. 'I wish I felt the same way,' Elsie said. 'I suppose I'd best go and stay with my sister in Leeds once we're done here. I'll look for another position from there.' She didn't sound too happy at the prospect.

Ella stared into the cup of tea that Elsie had made, biting her bottom lip. She would go back to Northwaite, of course. It would be lovely to see Beth and John and, with Beth expecting her first child, perhaps she could be of some use to them all. Sarah might be glad of her company, too, but as for seeking alternative employment, well, she wasn't sure where to start. The way people lived had changed greatly since the war and servants weren't much in demand these days, except in the largest houses. Probably the best she could hope for would be a position as a live-in companion to an elderly lady.

The last month of service passed mercifully swiftly. The house had to be cleaned from top to bottom and possessions cleared out or packed away in boxes. Mrs Ward came upon Ella as she sorted through the toy cupboard in the nursery.

'You must take whatever you like, to give to John and Beth for the new baby.' Mrs Ward paused. 'In fact, please make up a box, Ella, and I will speak to Mr Ward about driving over to see them both before we leave for Scotland.'

Ella nodded, only too well aware that during the six months that had elapsed since the wedding the Wards hadn't once visited the newly-weds. She wondered whether John minded not seeing his parents.

Would the new baby be a boy or a girl? Ella wondered, as she sorted through the old toys. They were all John's, those belonging to his older sisters having been discarded a long time ago, but it hardly mattered. She was sure that John would be delighted to rediscover them, even if it would be some while before a spinning top or a wooden hoop would be suitable for the baby whose birth was still over three months away. She picked up the *A–Z of Animals*, John's favourite book as a child, and flicked through it, smiling when she reached the Puffin page. She rested the open book on her lap as she knelt on the floor, surrounded by the pile of toys, and gazed unseeing into the distance. It seemed such a long time since John had shown her this picture in the kitchen, well before she was able to read, and so many things had happened in that time. Shaking off the melancholy that was in danger of descending, she devoted herself instead to the task before her. By the end of the afternoon, the nursery was clear apart from one large wooden trunk awaiting its new home.

Although Ella had been dreading her last day at Grange House, by the time it dawned she was glad to go. With all the rooms packed up and much of the furniture sold or sent to storage, it no longer felt like the place she had called home for so many years. The Wards had said their farewells a day earlier, before they headed first to Northwaite and then on to Scotland. They had been fulsome in their praise and their thanks for everyone's hard work and loyalty over the years. Shaking their hands, Mr Ward had pressed an envelope on each of them, wishing them the very best for their future.

'It's just a small bonus, for long service and to help you in some small way as you step into your future,' he said. Ella, surprised, felt tears start to her eyes. Mrs Ward said, rather awkwardly, that she felt sure they would see Ella again in Northwaite when they came to visit their new grandchild. Ella, wondering privately how likely this was, smiled, nodded in agreement and waved them off, Elsie and Stevens at her side.

'Well,' Stevens said, as they stood at a loss, not quite sure what to do next. 'I think we should drink a toast to our future. I saved a bottle of Mr Ward's champagne: I rather think we deserve it.'

Later that evening, as Ella made her way up to her room – head spinning a little, since it transpired that Stevens had saved a rather nice bottle of wine, too – she reflected that tomorrow evening she would be home once more in Northwaite. It was an exciting thought, one that brought a smile to her lips. In the next instant, a wave of sadness threatened to overwhelm her. Stevens and Elsie were also her family now. How would she manage without seeing them every day, after all these years?

Telling herself firmly not to be silly, that it was the start of a new chapter in her life, she sat down on the bed and looked at her bag, packed and ready to go. It stood against the wall, her travelling dress and coat hanging above it. The house seemed very quiet with just the three of them left. She wondered whether Stevens and Elsie were prey to the same mix of emotions; they had all been very jolly that evening, reminiscing over times past, and they had drunk more than one toast to the future in a spirit of great optimism. Ella, sensing all that positivity starting to ebb away, resolutely turned off the lamp and climbed into bed. She closed her eyes tightly and waited for sleep to claim her, telling herself that everything would seem brighter once more when morning came.

Chapter Sixty-Five

The first inkling that Ella had of how her life was set to change came after she had been settled for some weeks back in Northwaite. Beth had sent word to Lane End Cottage via her neighbour's son, Joe, that Ella was to come at once to their house in Church Lane.

Ella, suddenly anxious and in a hurry to leave, struggled with trembling fingers to do up the buttons on her coat.

'Do you think the baby has come?' she asked her mother. 'But then why didn't she ask for the both of us?' The neighbour's boy had been unforthcoming with information, simply saying that there was a visitor.

'Do you think the visitor is the doctor? If so, why didn't he say so?'

Sarah laughed and opened the door to usher her out. 'You'll know what it's all about soon enough. Now, make haste. And don't forget to come back soon and tell me all about it. I'm as mystified as you are.'

Ella was quite out of breath by the time she arrived at Beth and John's cottage. When it was Beth who opened the back door to her impatient knocking she was quite taken aback.

'Oh, I had expected to find you abed and with the midwife in attendance. I was worried.'

Beth patted her swollen belly ruefully. 'Nothing happening as yet. Although I didn't feel able to make the walk over to you, which is why I sent Joe from next door over with a message. Now, come and see our visitor. He's with John in the parlour.'

Ella followed Beth into the kitchen and through into the tiny front parlour. A man stood at the window, his back to the room as he looked out towards the church. He was just a silhouette and Ella could make out nothing of his features but she was instantly transported back through the years to when Albert had turned up so unexpectedly in Luddenden. Her heart lurched and she almost said his name out loud, but at that moment the figure turned towards her.

'Mr Stevens?' she said uncertainly. 'Why, whatever are you doing here? Is something wrong?' Her mind raced but, with Grange House and everything associated with it now gone, she couldn't come up with a reason for his presence.

Stevens smiled broadly and ignored her question. 'It's been lovely catching up with Beth's news,' he said. 'And it's wonderful to see John looking so well. He's promised to show me one of his favourite walks later, before I have to take the train back to York. But I have to confess that it's you I came to see. I have a proposal to make.'

'A proposal?' Ella echoed, feeling suddenly faint. Whatever could he mean?

John stepped forward and offered Ella a chair. 'Here, sit down. Beth and I will go and make some tea. We've heard a little about it already. We think you'll be pleased.'

'I hope you didn't mind me sharing the news with them

first,' Stevens said apologetically after John and Beth had left the room. 'It seemed rude to turn up on their doorstep out of the blue without some sort of explanation.'

Ella sat down suddenly. 'How did you...?' She broke off.

'Find you?' Stevens finished her sentence. 'Oh, that wasn't difficult. Mr Ward wrote here quite frequently. I remembered the address from the envelopes. Now, as to my proposal. But first of all, I must insist that you call me George from now on. We're no longer in service, after all.'

'George,' Ella murmured obediently, wondering when he was going to get to the point.

Before he could continue, the door opened and Beth came in with the teapot, followed by John bearing a tray of cups and saucers.

Beth took in Ella's expression. 'Has he asked you yet?' she demanded.

Mutely, Ella shook her head, starting to feel panic-stricken. Whatever could this be about?

'I was wondering whether I could persuade you to join me in Scarborough?' Registering Ella's look of bewilderment, Stevens hastened to add, 'In a business venture, of course.'

'Scarborough?' Ella was bemused. Her most recent memory of the town was of the damage it had suffered so early in the war, when it had been shelled from the sea. The atrocity had forced the whole country into the realisation that, despite being an island, Britain was just as vulnerable to invasion by Germany as Belgium and France. Prior to the war, Scarborough had been a fashionable holiday resort, but Ella had never been there. York was the furthest she had travelled. She had never even seen the sea.

'Yes, Scarborough.' Stevens, or George as she was going to

have to become accustomed to calling him, pressed on. 'I've come into a legacy, enough to buy a small guest house there. We can take holidaymakers in the summer months and boarders in the winter. And Elsie has agreed to come as cook.'

'Elsie?' Ella felt she could do nothing but parrot his words back to him. This looked set to be a day of surprises.

And so it was to prove. No sooner had Ella digested George's proposal, and started to view it with some enthusiasm, having gathered her wits enough to question him further, than Beth suddenly gasped and looked stricken.

'What is it?' John looked concerned.

Beth tried to stand. 'I think the baby might be on the way!'

Everyone leapt up at once and the small sitting room was suddenly full of anxious people, all getting in each other's way. Ella and John helped Beth upstairs and Joe-from-next-door was dispatched once again, this time to fetch the midwife. Ella suddenly remembered that Sarah needed to be told what was happening.

'I can go and fetch her,' George said firmly. 'You're needed here and John is in too much of a state. Just tell me where to go.'

He was back within the half hour with Sarah, no longer so spry on her feet, on his arm. He tried to slip away then, but this time John was firm.

'Don't abandon me. I need some male company at a time like this,' he said, in mock despair. So George stayed and paced the floor with him, taking him out on short excursions around the village when John could no longer stand the sound of Beth's cries from the room above. By the end of the afternoon, an exhausted Beth and an ecstatic John were the proud parents of baby Christopher, who seemed disposed to be wide-awake when he wasn't being noisy.

'I'm away now to catch my train,' said George at last, after he had been thanked by John for all his support and made to promise that he would return in due course to be Christopher's godfather. He turned to Ella. 'I'll send word when I have found a suitable place in Scarborough. It should allow you plenty of time to spend with your nephew first.'

Ella, quite overcome with all the emotion of the day, seized his hands. 'Thank you! I'm very much looking forward to it. I can't quite believe how lucky I am.'

'I think the luck's all mine,' George murmured, smiling to himself as he closed the front door behind him. Much noise and laughter, punctuated by faint cries, came from the open bedroom window above as he strode along Church Lane and onwards through the village, before heading down towards the station at Nortonstall.

Chapter Sixty-Six

Scarborough delighted Ella from the moment she arrived there. The view out over the sea entranced her and she made sure that all her excursions took her on routes that looked out across the bay. She loved the steep climb up to the ruins of the castle, the Italian Gardens so beautifully laid out on South Cliff, Peasholm Park and the Valley Gardens; she even enjoyed crossing Valley Bridge with its breath-taking drop below.

Her new life in the town proved to be a joy in more ways than one. It had been hard work at first: she and Elsie ran the guest house more or less single-handedly for the first few months, with George coming in every day from his tiny flat nearby to man the front desk and help out wherever he was needed. Over a period of a couple of years, as seaside holidays increased in popularity after the war years, and Scarborough became a fashionable resort once more, they had been able to add to their staff and their burdens eased a little. In her free time, Ella had taken up painting again. She joined a local art class, concentrating on painting flowers and local land-scapes with such astonishing results that George had insisted hers should be the only paintings to be hung around the hotel. Ella wondered whether she had been the only one to be amazed when, a year after they had started to run what looked set to be a very successful small hotel, George asked her to marry him. She had surprised herself by saying 'Yes,' without hesitation. She had come to see him as her best friend in the world, someone from whom she never wanted to be parted, so it seemed but a small step from that to becoming man and wife. Freed from her role as servant, Ella had blossomed, enjoying the relative freedom she had as both a mature woman and a co-proprietor of a business. Sometimes, in quieter moments, she looked back over the years and shook her head in disbelief: who would have thought that she would be married after all, just before she reached her fortieth birthday, to the steadiest, kindest man you could ever hope to meet. A man whose love for Ella, it turned out, had been nurtured quietly and secretly over many years without her ever suspecting. She accused George of being devious in the way in which he had persuaded her to join him in Scarborough.

'There I was, thinking you were in need of a housekeeper and all along it was a wife you were after,' Ella teased.

George just smiled and refused to be drawn but Ella's heart was full. For the first time in her adult life she had discovered how it felt to have someone care for her, and to put her needs above their own.

When the peak summer season was over and it was safe to leave the hotel in the hands of their experienced manager, Ella and George would drive over to visit Beth and John, still living a quiet, but contented, life in Northwaite and now with a new addition, baby Eileen, to join young Christopher.

'As if they weren't spoilt enough by their doting Granny

Sarah!' exclaimed Beth when Ella and George arrived bearing a huge teddy bear for the new arrival and a shiny red toy fire engine for Christopher. Alas, Christopher wasn't pleased by the amount of attention that his new baby sister was receiving, and in a fit of bad temper and jealousy was caught trying to tear the ears off the new toy bear.

When all efforts at distraction had failed and Christopher's wails showed no sign of abating, Ella whispered something to George who obligingly vanished out into the garden. After a few minutes she reached out her hand and said, 'Come on Christopher, shall we go and see where Uncle George has got to?'

Trustingly, he put his small, damp palm in hers and she squeezed it gently, transported in an instant back over the years to when Beth, and then John, had done just the same thing. Clasping baby Eileen tightly to her shoulder she led Christopher into the garden, where George was loitering casually by the rowan tree.

'Do you want to come and see what I've found?' he asked Christopher, who broke free from Ella's grip and toddled towards him very fast. George bent down to catch him, then swung him up to shoulder level and pointed into the branches of the tree.

'You know, I do believe this is a fairy tree,' he said. 'And I think the fairies have left a gift for you.'

'Where? Where?' Christopher's eyes shone with excitement.

'I have a feeling that you might only be able to see it if you promise to be a good brother to your baby sister.' George said. 'I believe the fairies are very particular about that sort of thing.'

'Promise...' muttered Christopher, clearly finding it a struggle.

George grasped Christopher around the middle and held him up before him. 'Look a bit higher. Do you see anything now?'

With a squeal of excitement, Christopher reached into the branches and pulled out a shiny, foil-wrapped bar of chocolate, which had been wedged into a fork of the main trunk. His eyes were like saucers as George lowered him carefully to the ground, and he cast one or two glances upwards as if to check whether he might have missed anything else.

'Fairies,' Christopher breathed. 'Fairies have been.' And with that he took off into the house, desperate to show his mother the amazing find.

Ella and George exchanged broad smiles, trying not to laugh. Eileen stirred on Ella's shoulder and turned her head, opening her eyes sleepily to regard George with a piercing blue gaze. Ella felt a sudden throb of worry. She and George could never have this sort of family life together. Would this be a problem for him? For herself, she was resigned to the fact and deeply grateful that she could at least enjoy Beth and John's family. She was already looking forward to the time, hopefully not too far in the future, when they could come to the seaside in the summer, spending hours on the sand just like other families. Perhaps Beth and John would even leave the children with her and she could find out, for a week or two, what it felt like to have a family of her own.

'Aren't we lucky?' George said cheerfully, reaching out to take Eileen from Ella. 'We get all the advantages of being parents when we want to, without any of the worry or the sleepless nights.' And he gave her a big, reassuring smile and put his arm around her waist as they moved back into the house.

As Ella followed George down the narrow hallway she brushed against a picture frame, knocking it askew. Her eyes skimmed over the contents as she straightened it. It held a much-folded piece of paper, grubby along all its creases and somewhat ragged around the edges, which had been flattened out behind the glass. Frowning, she peered at it, wondering why it was considered worthy of framing. It was a sketch of a cottage, with two people standing side-by-side on the front door step.

It reminded her of something, and it took her a moment or two to work it out. Suddenly it dawned on her: it was similar to the drawings that Beth and John had exchanged when they were children. This must be the token that Beth had given John when he came home on leave during the war. She had sketched her hope for their future together and it had turned out to be remarkably prescient. He must have carried it around and kept it safe all the time he was away.

She paused on the threshold of the room: George was on his hands and knees alongside Christopher, showing him how to raise the ladder on the fire engine; Beth was sitting in a chair by the fire, cradling a sleepy Eileen; and John was surveying the scene with such an expression of pride that she didn't know whether to laugh or cry.

'Is everything all right?' he asked her, puzzled by her look.

'It is indeed,' she said. 'It is indeed.'

Postscript

In a tall Georgian house in York, much neglected after the death of its owner James Weatherall, dust swirled gently in the shafts of sunlight creeping through the shuttered windows, then gathered on the surfaces not already shrouded in dust sheets, while his one remaining family member, Esther, tried to decide what to do with the place. Before the war Esther had made a life for herself far away from home in a rented room in a crumbling palazzo in Venice, unable to bear her father's disappointment that she had never married and provided him with the grandchildren he craved. She had exchanged the sadness that had engulfed her father since the death of his son Richard for the more exquisite sadness of a life where she could pass unnoticed along narrow streets, immersed in a language only half understood, reinventing herself as a woman with a mysterious romantic past. She had chosen her surroundings to be as unlike the landscape of her youth as it was possible for her to find; the still dark canals bore no resemblance to the rushing streams that tumbled from the moors past Northwaite and onwards to Nortonstall, while the grand Venetian architecture carried only the faintest echoes of the solid practicality of the buildings of York.

She was reluctant to return and make the decision as to what to do with her life. While there was no doubt that the money from the sale of the house would be useful to her in the future, she was worried that during the time needed to effect the sale she might be drawn back to make a life in the city and never feel able to return to Venice. Her friend, Grace, had written and urged her to come back before the house fell to wrack and ruin. Grace had advised her that she would find York a lively place to live, much recovered from the war years and with a great many diversions to please and occupy a single lady of some standing. Esther reflected that if only her brother Richard had survived, he and his wife would undoubtedly have produced an heir and she would not be faced with this decision. Months passed while she prevaricated.

Meanwhile, in a locked cupboard in one of the shuttered rooms, the one used by James Weatherall as a study until his death, a bundle of documents bound with cord sat on one of the shelves. Untouched for many years, they were the private papers of his son, Richard Weatherall, deceased. In amongst the documents was a sealed, unmarked envelope. Within it, a single folded sheet of paper: a birth certificate dated January 1895. The child's name was Elisabeth Weatherall; the father Richard Weatherall; the mother Alice Bancroft.

What would have happened if James Weatherall had noticed the envelope and opened it? Could he have brought himself to love Beth, the granddaughter that he knew nothing about? And would it have made any difference to her marriage, her happiness and her children if he had?

Can Alice save her family?

Lynne Francis

Alice's Secret

A gripping story of love, loss and hope

Sarah is trying to start over,
but can you ever escape your past?

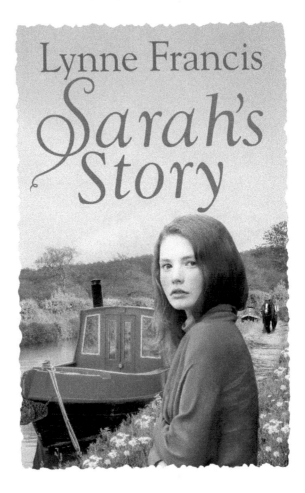

Lynne Francis

Sarah's Story

A heartwarming tale of family, romance and triumph
in the face of adversity